BEAUTIFUL
DEATH

BOOKS BY JOHN DEAL

CJ O'Hara Crime Thrillers

All the Natural Beauties

Under a Blood Moon

Beautiful Death

BEAUTIFUL
DEATH

JOHN DEAL

DARK LAKE
PRESS

DARK LAKE
PRESS

BEAUTIFUL DEATH
ISBN-13: 978-1-7375382-4-0 (paperback)
ISBN-13: 978-1-7375382-5-7 (eBook)

This book is a work of fiction. The names, characters, places, and incidents are either
the product of the author's imagination or used fictionally. Any resemblance to actual
persons, living or dead, businesses, companies, events, or locales is entirely coincidental
and unintentional.

Dedicated to the wonderful people of the Lowcountry, a place with beaches, marshes, lots of water, a diverse culture, a long history, and the two littlest men in my life.

She loathed men. Their bumpy, coarse, hairy bodies repulsed her. They were only valuable to her for two things—riches and breeding.

But men loved her. She was the woman every man wanted, and their lustful eyes stayed glued to her wherever she went. She was charming, flirtatious, and sexy. All she needed to do was pick the perfect target.

On rare occasions, she enjoyed having a man's arms around her, his warm breath on her neck, hands exploring, and the longing throbbing in his veins. This evening, her mood was somewhere in the middle between repulsion and excitement. Was it seeing him, or what she intended to do?

She bent closer to the glass and passed the lipstick across her lips. It was his favorite color, cherry red. A slow, deep breath escaped her as she stared into the full-length mirror at her slender, fit, and well-proportioned naked body.

As she gazed, the corners of her mouth curved with malicious pleasure. His eyes would flare when she dropped her dress and exposed the white lace she would wear underneath—a perfect combination of classy and sexy, with a touch of slutty.

The crimson minidress she had purchased was exquisite. It picked up the wine tint of her hair, dyed brunette, enhancing the color of the strands. She was gorgeous and bewitching. The hem hit her at the exact spot on her upper thighs to reveal just enough skin, and the tiny tie in the back allowed a swift exit when the moment arrived. She always gave her dates a bit of a show that included a gradual buildup before she unveiled the pleasure awaiting them.

At 9:00 p.m., she stepped into the heels that matched her dress and peered in the mirror one last time. She always planned her arrival so she would be late. She delighted in making men wait, creating suspense and giving her the upper hand. She performed a quick inspection of her bag and made for the door.

Her alpine-white BMW 325Ci convertible slid into a dimly lit parking spot, and a twist of the key stilled the engine. Before she stepped out of the vehicle, she checked her makeup. Her look was impeccable, especially with the eye pencil used to give her that smoky look. The end of her finger added a dab of her unique scent behind each ear. Her eyes twinkled, and she giggled.

Men are such simpletons!

From a young age, she had learned to manipulate and make them do whatever she wanted. She had invariably got her way every time. She assured herself tonight's rendezvous would be like all her dates, but this was a lie.

As usual, the night would start with an envelope filled with cash, a little wine, and dirty talk before progressing into long, passionate kisses, followed by energetic sex until he was worn out. But this night, she had a special surprise for him. One she had plotted when she found out she was pregnant. It would be the ultimate shock of his life.

Would she be sad when he was no longer present? No. Not at all.

———

The door groaned as it closed behind his date for the evening. His moments with her had flown by, but he couldn't endure much more. He released a long, deep breath as he lowered himself onto the bed. A shower was in order, but he was too exhausted. The bedding was baby-duck soft, and he couldn't muster the effort to extract himself. Instead, he let the darkness envelop him as he switched off the light.

Minutes later, his trembling fingers flipped on the bedside lamp. Numbness gripped him, and his breaths came slow and shallow while his heart raced. He fumbled around with the sheet, panting rapidly, attempting to gain control.

His world was blurry, and people in outrageous attire were everywhere. Their lips were moving, but there was no sound. His muscles refused to move; he was incapable of getting up from the bed. Hot vomit spilled from his mouth as his reality blurred out of focus. Then he slipped away forever.

PART ONE

A ROOM WITH NO VIEW

ONE

Ten Years Later
Saturday, April 16
The Boroughs, Charleston, South Carolina

What a shitty way to end my Saturday night.

Detective CJ O'Hara steered onto Duncan Street, and the sign marking her destination appeared. Only moments ago, before the text had called her to a crime scene, she'd been wrapped in Ben's arms with his lips pressed to hers. She hated how her job consumed her personal life. It would only get worse with her promotion to lieutenant. Plus, now she'd be required to manage others.

A tightness gripped her chest as she thought of Paul Grimes, her former boss, and how he'd lost his life during her last case. The troubled young man, Elias Lewis, had murdered him and two others before she stopped him. It was Paul's role she'd now fill, which dampened the promotion.

While everyone told her it was wrong, she'd added his death to her guilt over her parents' and older sister's deaths. If she had caught the perp sooner, Paul would still be alive. If she hadn't cried to come home from a sleepover, causing her parents and older sister to be on the road that night, a drunk driver wouldn't have killed them.

Life is damn cruel and unfair.

She squeezed her black Ford Explorer in behind a cruiser adorned with flashing red lights. She sucked in a deep breath and pulled her shoulder-length auburn hair into a ponytail. "Stop whining and do your damn job," she mumbled to herself.

She grabbed her notebook, dragged herself out of the vehicle, and approached the twenty-something-year-old officer standing at the end of the walkway of the Duncan House, a bed-and-breakfast in The Boroughs district.

"Hello, Detective. Officer Jones asked us to call you. He said something's fishy about this scene." The officer turned and pointed behind him. "He's in a room in the back. Go down the alley and you'll find the suite. You'll see the name on the doorplate, The Ashley."

She nodded as she strode past him into the darkness, reminding her of the Palancar caves she'd entered during a scuba diving trip in Cozumel. She wasn't a fan of dark spaces, so she focused on the soft light from the open doorway twenty feet away. A second officer stood guarding the door.

As she slipped on booties and surgical gloves, he told her Officer Jones was in the bedroom past the sitting room. They had one dead male.

"Johnny!" CJ called out as she entered the first room, decorated with black cherry furniture and gold fabrics contrasting with the light oak parquet floor. Two empty wine bottles sat on a glass coffee table, but only one glass.

"Back here."

The familiar face of Officer Johnny Jones met her as she stuck her head in the bedroom. Johnny was Black, five years younger than her thirty-three, stood over six feet tall, and had chestnut-brown eyes and close-cropped, jet-black hair. Since working together on her last major case, chasing down a killer who murdered his victims using a perverse style of hoodoo, he had become one of her favorite officers.

"Hey. Whatcha got?"

"The owner called us and said one of their frequent guests has had a heart attack. I'm not sure if that's right," he said.

She squinted. "Who's the owner, and how did they find him?"

"The guy's name is Lawrence Simpson, known as Larry. He said he saw the man last night, but he didn't come to breakfast or check out as planned, so Larry came to check. He mentioned he knocked multiple times but didn't receive an answer, so he entered. Found him here, dead on the bed."

"Does our dead man have a name?" she asked.

Johnny eyed his notes. "Charles Ralston, from here in Charleston."

"A local." She leaned in closer to the nude man, who looked to be in his early fifties. "What's he doing staying in a bed-and-breakfast?"

"I'm not sure," he said, shrugging. "Maybe a staycation. The owner was tight-lipped, possibly because he was freaked out by having a dead man in his place."

CJ nodded as she scanned the bedroom. The room was spacious, with a king-sized bed and matching nightstands on each side, a seven-drawer dresser complete with a mirror, and a love seat. Like the sitting room, the furniture was black cherry. The thick white bedspread was thrown off the foot of the bed. The white sheets were tangled, and stains were visible near the body; one near the man's head, the other near his waist.

"So, you don't think it's a heart attack?" she asked.

"No, not really," he said, shaking his head. "I can't explain it, but it doesn't feel right." He moved closer to the body. "It appears the guy puked—and recently had sex." He pointed to the open bathroom door. "There are damp towels on the floor. Someone showered, but our boy here doesn't look like he's had one." He paused before he said, "He has dried semen on his ..."

CJ entered the bathroom and stared at a pile of light gray towels in the corner. Without turning back, she said, "It's possible he showered before he had sex. There are two empty wine bottles, but only one glass. He may have showered, had too much to drink, had sex, puked, and then keeled over. I guess we won't know until the coroner examines the body. Have you called them?"

"Not yet," Johnny said. "I wanted you to look first."

She nodded. "Fair enough. Let's get the coroner and forensics over here. I'd rather be safe than sorry if the death's not from natural causes. In the meantime, let's chat with the owner again. Find out what else he can give us."

Moving closer to the bed, CJ motioned to the indentation in the down pillow beside the dead man as she bent down. "Hard to tell, but it looks like two people were in bed at some point." Carefully, she picked up the pillow and held it out to him. "Do you smell perfume? A sort of minty vanilla?"

Leaning down, he sniffed. "Yeah, it has that aroma."

She placed the pillow back. "Let's make sure forensics scours the bed. Hopefully, we can find fluids or something we can use to identify who else was here."

While Johnny called the coroner and Crime Scene Unit, CJ continued investigating. She dropped to a knee and searched under the bed using her Maglite. "Nothing under here," she whispered.

Johnny ended his call and stood watching her. "Funny thing. The room is too clean."

"Yeah, that's what I was thinking," she said. "It's almost like someone wiped things down. The techs will have to see what they can find, but I didn't notice visible fingerprints on the nightstand or dresser." She stood and went back into the bathroom. "The bathroom counter seems like it was wiped down too."

CJ scanned the suite. "Something else is interesting about this room. The sitting room doesn't have a window, and the one in the bedroom is small and overgrown with vines outside. Plus, it faces a brick wall only a few feet away, so there's no view."

He glanced around. "You're right. You'd think the owner would at least trim the vines back. It's almost like—"

"He wants to keep it private for his guests," she said, finishing his thought. "Okay. Well, how 'bout you grab the owner?"

"I'm on it," he said, heading for the door.

While she waited, CJ made a list of the clothes thrown across a side chair and hanging in the closet. Charcoal suit pants and jacket, a white dress shirt, a maroon tie, and a pair of boxers and socks covered the chair. Black dress shoes with a matching belt sat underneath. A pair of tan khakis, a yellow polo, a dark brown belt, and Docksides were in the closet. A small bag holding another pair of boxers and socks sat on the shelf alongside a brown leather Dopp Kit.

She went outside and motioned to the officer guarding the door to come over. "Where's our dead guy's vehicle?" she asked. "I'm assuming he didn't walk or take a cab."

He shrugged. "We're not sure. A vehicle's not in the parking lot."

She twisted her head from side to side, hoping to relieve the knot in her neck. "Okay. We need to locate it." She scanned the exterior of the building with her Maglite. "You find any cameras?"

"Nope," he said. "I overheard the owner say ain't none on the property or this portion of Duncan Street."

Dammit!

Johnny returned with the owner, introduced everyone, and the three remained outside under an overhang.

CJ glanced up and pointed. "Mr. Simpson, why are these two lights not working?"

He fidgeted. "Uh—I'm not sure."

Johnny reached up. "The bulb's loose." He tightened it, and the light returned. The same quick fix restored the second light. "Someone loosened these on purpose."

"Wasn't me," Simpson blurted out.

CJ began questioning the fifty-five-year-old owner as Johnny stood silent. Simpson was short and stocky, with graying black hair retreating to the back of his head. His deep brown eyes stayed fixed on the stone walkway, and his arms were crossed. He shifted his weight from one foot to the other.

"Okay, Mr. Simpson. You said the man was named Charles Ralston and lived in the area, correct?"

"Umm … yeah," he said, shifting his weight again.

"Do you have his home address?"

Rubbing the back of his neck, Simpson mumbled, "Maybe … well, I should."

She kept her gaze fixed on him as he squirmed. "I'd appreciate it if you'd provide it. In fact, if you'd volunteer to let me examine your records, we'll skip a warrant."

"Uh … I guess that'd be okay."

"Thank you. What's Mr. Ralston's wife's name? I'll need to contact her as soon as I leave here."

"Sorry. I don't know her name." The blood left his face. "I mean … I'm not sure if Mr. Ralston is married. I take the privacy of—"

"Okay." CJ leaned in close. "It's easy to see a wedding band has been on his finger." The soon-to-be bald man stared at the ground without blinking. "By the way, who was the guest who visited?"

He froze. "I ... I don't know what you're talking about. Mr. Ralston was alone."

Liar. "Based on our search, I believe a woman was with him. Is it normal for your guests to have visitors?"

"I don't appreciate being grilled," Simpson snarled. "I better talk to my lawyer." He bobbed his head. "Yes. Yes. That's what I should do."

"That's your right," she said. "I'm not sure why you need a lawyer, since all I'm trying to do is determine what happened here. I haven't accused you of anything."

Simpson remained quiet with his head down as he chewed his lip.

"Okay. You call your lawyer." CJ paused and let him squirm before she said, "Can I still review your records?"

Simpson rubbed his chin. "I guess ... but no more questions without my lawyer. Come with me." He turned and headed down the walkway to the main building, and she followed.

As she sat at an antique oak table thumbing through the guest log, Johnny entered and told her the coroner and CSU had arrived. He left, and twenty minutes later, she found him on the walkway near the door of the suite.

"You find anything, CJ?" Johnny asked.

"Getting answers from Simpson was more challenging than pulling teeth." She chuckled. "His records showed the dead man's home address and vehicle information, and he's stayed here ten times since Simpson bought the place two years ago. Ralston lived in Dunes West in Mount Pleasant and drove a charcoal Range Rover."

Johnny frowned. "Why stay here if you live so close?"

"Exactly. Unless you're having marital trouble or hiding something. Speaking of that, our Mr. Simpson is hiding something too."

TWO

Sunday, April 17
The Boroughs

It was nearing two o'clock in the morning as CJ sat in her truck, reviewing her notes. A soft drizzle clouding her windshield had joined the shadows. The coroner and CSU had been processing the scene for almost two hours, and she hoped they'd finish and brief her soon. She pinched the bridge of her nose and squeezed her eyes shut.

Rattling snapped her back to attention as a gurney emerged on the walkway. Johnny motioned to her. She slipped on her rain jacket and climbed out of her truck.

As she walked up, the face of the Tyvek-clad Medical Examiner Thomas Whitehall lit up. Nearing sixty, he had become more than a colleague. He was a genuine friend, and she dreaded how her life would change once he retired at the end of the year. She'd miss this slim, silver-haired man and his kind, bluish-gray eyes. She hoped whoever replaced him as ME would be half as competent.

"Good morning, Thomas."

He glanced at his silver Tag Heuer watch. "Yes. I guess good morning is in order. I lost track of time and didn't realize we were this far past midnight. We'll brief you as soon as Eddie finishes up, and we can all go home to bed."

"Works for me." She stretched her arms. "I could use some sleep."

"I enjoyed yesterday's party and am proud of your promotion to lieutenant." He patted her arm. "When is the official ceremony? I want to attend."

CJ shrugged. "I'm not sure. I assume sometime this week. The chief told me the mayor wants to attend."

"Yeah, she wouldn't miss a chance for a photo opportunity." He laughed. "You were Charleston's first female detective, a helluva achievement, and now you've been promoted. Knowing the mayor, she'll take credit for clearing the two major cases you solved." His face turned serious, and in a low voice, he said, "I'm so pleased with how you're taking care of yourself. That mess when Paul was killed scared us all."

She sniffed and wiped her nose as Eddie approached and greeted her.

Eddie Rodriquez was a lead CSI who was exceptional at his job, like Thomas. But he was only thirty-one, so he'd be around for a while. Eddie was Hispanic and five eight with an athletic build. No matter the situation, he was upbeat. His short, curly brown hair stood out from all angles as he pushed his hood back. "I have my prelim if you're ready."

"Sounds good to me. Let's move over under the awning for better lighting."

Once everyone was ready, Eddie opened his notebook and cleared his throat. "First, this is one of the cleanest scenes I've ever worked on. Much of the suite was pristine, almost as if by design. We collected the two empty wine bottles and glass in the sitting room. One bottle and the glass had fingerprints. I'll need to confirm, but the prints appear identical and are probably from our victim, based on their size. The other bottle was clean, as was the rest of the room.

"Moving to the bedroom, we didn't find any prints. We collected the sheets and pillows and will analyze the stain near the man's head and under his thighs. It appears he vomited at some point."

She stared at her notes. "It looked like just liquid to me. Do you think it's the wine?"

The CSI nodded. "Yeah, most likely. The wine bottles are labeled as Cabernet, and the stain's dark. It had a rich, sweet odor, but we'll analyze it to be sure."

"Did you detect a scent on one of the pillows?" she asked.

"I did. It's hard to describe exactly … vanilla and … mint. Possibly a perfume."

CJ and Johnny glanced at each other.

Eddie held up a list so she could read it. "We bagged the clothes the man wore. We found nothing unusual except a long hair stuck to the shirt. I'll examine it under the microscope, but it appears dark brown. Our guy has short, black hair with specks of gray, so it's not his."

Her pulse picked up. "Can we obtain DNA?"

"Doubtful. It's only a strand, there's no follicle."

"Damn," she said. "Is it fair to say the perfume, hair, and signs of sex point to a second person in the room?"

"Yes," Eddie said. "We'll see what we find in the lab, but my guess is a woman was in the room with our vic."

"Of course, it may mean nothing if Ralston died of natural causes." CJ's eyes cut to Thomas.

The silver-haired man smiled. "Can't wait for my turn, can you? Well, I'll need to do an autopsy, but I'd put the man in his early to mid-fifties, one hundred eighty pounds, and in good shape. He takes care of himself and hits the gym, so a heart attack is less likely. I can't say yet based on my field eval. I'll need to open him up. He's been dead about twelve hours based on the state of rigor."

He paused as he ran his finger down his notes. "His pupils were dilated, and he had a rash covering the upper part of his back. The pupils could be from the man's sleep pattern, medicine, or trauma. I'm not sure about the rash yet."

"Would a brain injury cause the pupils to dilate?" she asked.

"Hmm, it's possible." Thomas nodded. "I didn't find any visible signs of an injury to his head. The autopsy should help determine the cause."

As she jotted more notes, she asked, "What about drugs?"

"I'll check that out as well."

She looked back at Eddie. "What else?"

"Thomas can jump in, but nothing else unusual about the body except the dried fluids on his crotch. We collected samples and will run them for DNA."

"We can determine DNA from semen or vaginal fluids, correct?" she asked.

"Yes. Assuming, of course, there's no contamination."

"DNA from the second person would be a great help," she noted.

"Yep," Eddie agreed. "If we can match it to someone in the system."

Thomas spoke up. "The only other thing I found on the body were some faint scratches on the man's back. When I do the autopsy, I'll look at these under the microscope."

"What kind of scratches?" she asked.

"I'm not sure, but it appears they came from fingernails. They didn't break the skin, but they're visible." Thomas called a tech over. "Can you show the detective the photos of the victim's back, please?"

The tech scrolled through his camera and held it up to CJ. "Maybe the woman ran her fingernails across his back during sex," she said, her eyes within inches of the screen. "The scratches are more pronounced in the middle and fade as they go out."

Thomas leaned in. "Makes sense. I'll tell you what. I'll do the autopsy tomorrow after church and provide you with the cause of death, but I'll examine these marks tonight once we arrive at the morgue. I don't want to risk losing them."

CJ grimaced. "Do you normally work on Sundays?"

"Only for you," Thomas said, winking. "In all seriousness, we need to know ASAP if we have a death by natural causes or something sinister. Besides, I bet you work tomorrow also … I mean, today."

"I'll take the fifth." Flipping through the pages in her notebook, she asked, "Eddie, did you find a wallet, keys, or a cell phone?"

"Nope. We didn't find any personal items."

"How 'bout a wedding ring? A white line shows where one had been on his finger."

"Nope."

The distraction of a man climbing out of a silver Mercedes over Thomas's shoulder caused CJ to pause. As she stared at him, the man opened a black golf umbrella and marched straight at the group. He was in his late fifties, with a nose reminding her of a carrot on a snowman. He wore an expensive black suit, pressed to perfection, and a bright red power tie.

"Excuse me. Who's in charge here?" he asked.

"That would be me," she said, offering her hand. "I'm Detective O'Hara."

Well over six feet tall, the man straightened himself to his full height and peered down at her without making an effort to take her hand. "Well, Officer, I'm Percy Winston Ricardson III, and I'm here to represent my client, Lawrence Simpson." He handed her his card.

CJ pursed her lips as her blood pressure bumped up. "I didn't realize your client did anything wrong. I'll happily arrest him if he's committed a crime."

His eyes narrowed. "Don't get smart with me, young lady. My client informed me you were accusing and harassing him."

She forced a laugh. "That's bullshit. I was simply asking basic questions to discover why he has a dead man in one of his rooms."

Ricardson twisted his lips and snorted. "From this point forward, you will discuss everything with me first, and I'll decide if my client answers. So we're clear, I'm in charge."

CJ frowned and nodded tightly. "If you think so. By the way, in the future, please use my proper title. I'm Detective Cassandra Jane O'Hara, of the Boston O'Haras, with the Charleston Police Department's Central Investigations Division. I'm sure you're familiar with the CID." She dug into her pocket and pulled out a thin black leather card holder. "Here. Take this in case you forget. Since we're buds now, how 'bout I call you PW and I'll be CJ?"

He snatched the card from her and glared at it before heading toward the main building.

After he walked off, the laugh Johnny had been struggling to contain escaped. "What an asshole. Way to stand your ground."

"That guy's been here in Charleston a long time," Thomas offered. "You're right. He's a first-rate asshole. He's friends with people in high places and is part of the good ole boys club, so be cautious of him."

She sighed heavily. "Okay, so where were we? Do you guys have anything else?"

Thomas shook his head.

Eddie flipped through his notes and frowned. "I have one last item. The bathroom was clean like the rest of the place, but we found one print on the bottom corner of the mirror. It appears to be the same size as the ones on the wine bottle.

"Funny thing though ... we collected three bath towels, three hand towels, and two washcloths. The owner told me he had four of each in the suite. We looked everywhere, but some are missing."

"Maybe housekeeping screwed up," Johnny said.

"No." Eddie shook his head. "The owner told me he always cleaned The Ashley himself. He cleaned it at six o'clock on Friday evening before Ralston checked in around seven thirty."

CJ's eyes narrowed. "Someone took them. I wonder why."

THREE

Sunday, April 17
Downtown Charleston

Scarlett removed the pink scrunchie, tipped her head back, and ran her fingers through her shoulder-length brunette hair. She splashed a bit of water on her face, and her hazel eyes stared into the mirror in the changing room. Scarlett seldom decorated herself for work, choosing a plainer look to avoid attention. She was adept at turning it on and off.

The digital clock on the wall read 2:15 a.m. Her twelve-hour shift had ended—it was time to go home and crawl under her blanket. But based on what she'd overheard on the police scanner at the nurses' station, she needed to make one quick stop and see for herself. Being in the know with what was happening with her crime was the primary reason Scarlett had volunteered to work on a Saturday night. Usually, this time was for her dates.

She pulled off her scrubs and pushed them into a green duffel bag. Her heart-shaped face went bright pink when another nurse entered and caught her admiring her nearly nude body. "Uh, it's been a long night," Scarlett said. "I'm ready to change and head home."

The young Black nurse chuckled and said, "Lucky you. I still have four hours left."

As Scarlett zipped up her faded blue jeans, the other nurse grabbed a brown paper bag from a locker and exited. "I'm headed to the break room to eat a bite. I'll catch you later."

After she buttoned her long-sleeve navy shirt, Scarlett put her hair back into a ponytail and topped her head with a Charleston RiverDogs baseball hat. She grabbed her bag and hustled out the door and down the hall before disappearing into the stairwell.

Downtown Charleston was winding down. Scarlett drove her alpine-white BMW 328i along Calhoun Street with plenty of cover as the people left the crowded bars. At Coming Street, she took a left and pulled her car into a small parking lot catty-corner to the Mace Brown Museum of Natural History.

For a few minutes, she sat and gazed at vehicles passing before grabbing a red umbrella, hopping out of her car, and walking across the sidewalk down Duncan Street. She stayed on the side of the street closest to the museum and across from the Duncan House. As she strolled, she met a college-aged man who stood staring at the flashing red lights.

"Oh, no. Is someone getting arrested?" Scarlett asked in her best shaky voice.

"No. A person died." He pointed to the van as it emerged from the Duncan Street entrance. "That's the coroner."

Her hand flew to her mouth. "That's awful. What happened?"

The sickly thin young man with a severe case of acne shrugged. "I'm not sure. A guy told me they found some old dude who died in one of the rooms. Sucks, eh?"

"Yes. That's just terrible," Scarlett said, giving him her sad face while his eyes locked on hers.

"Listen, it's kinda late for a pretty lady to be out alone—"

"I was grabbing a little fresh air after a long day working on an exhibit in the museum." She knew where he was going and wanted to cut it off.

"Oh. Okay." He swallowed hard. "Well, where are you headed? I'm happy to walk—"

"Thank you, but I parked my car over there," she said as she pointed back from where she came. "I appreciate you asking." Before he tried again, she added, "I need to go home to my husband, anyway."

He slowly nodded with love-struck eyes and she decided to throw the poor fool a bone with a little thrill. She held out her umbrella. "Can you hold this for a second?" He took it and she hugged him, pressing her body against him. Her laugh stayed buried as he moaned.

FOUR

Sunday, April 17
Mount Pleasant, South Carolina

Telling someone they'd lost a loved one was the second-worst part of CJ's job. The absolute worst was watching a person say goodbye to a critical piece of their life lying on the cold steel table of the morgue.

The sky continued to spit at CJ as she steered her Ford Explorer onto the ramp leading her to Highway 17 and the two-and-a-half-mile Arthur Ravenel Jr. Bridge. The moisture created halos around the bridge's lights positioned to illuminate only the suspension cables and roadway to protect migratory birds. They'd soon turn off the lights after dark for the upcoming loggerhead turtle nesting season. At 3:00 a.m., traffic was sparse.

As she reached the bridge's peak some five hundred and seventy-five feet above the Cooper River, the lights of Mount Pleasant twinkled at her against the black water. Within minutes, she made a left onto Highway 41, which would take her to the Dunes West community and the home of Charles Ralston. She had an emptiness in her stomach, and her mouth was as dry as the sand on the beach in July.

Slowing, she took the right turn onto Dunes West Boulevard toward the gated portion of the community. A bleary-eyed guard waved her on after she provided her destination and flashed her badge.

The Ralston home was in the Marsh Landing subsection, where houses backed to a tidal creek. A massive, two-story structure sat on the back of a spacious lot, barely visible against the dark sky. Her truck crawled along the driveway that split the perfectly manicured grass. She didn't know what a home like this sold for, but it was more than she could afford.

CJ put her truck into park and stopped the engine. A wave of coldness crept over her, and her stomach went from empty to churning. A sudden burst of light blinded her as she approached the black double-entry doors. Whoever was home knew she was coming. CJ collected herself, took the six steps onto the porch, and knocked.

"Who is it?" a female's unsteady voice asked from behind the door.

"Hello, this is Detective CJ O'Hara with the Charleston Police Department. I want to speak to Mrs. Ralston about her husband."

"Charlie's not here. He went to a meeting in Greenville."

"Actually, I'd like to talk with his wife," she said. "It's late, but it's important."

"Do you have any identification?"

CJ slipped her gold badge from her belt and held it to the narrow, vertical sidelight. She also held up the identification on a chain around her neck. "Here you go." Since she was wearing jeans, a long-sleeve white shirt, and boots, she added, "As a detective, I don't wear a uniform."

"Hold on."

The door lock clicked, and a woman appeared who had obviously been asleep. Her brown hair was tangled, and her eyes were puffy. CJ guessed the woman was in her mid-thirties and only five foot four. The woman remained standing in the cracked doorway, staring at her.

"Thank you," CJ said as she feebly smiled. "I'm sorry for bothering you in the middle of the night."

"Like I said, Charlie's not home."

"Are you his wife?"

"Yes. I'm Ava."

"Ava, would it be okay if I came in so we could talk?"

The woman sighed and motioned her through the door into an adjacent den larger than CJ's two-bedroom apartment. She pointed to a mahogany leather chair. "Please have a seat." She sat rigid across from CJ on a matching sofa, her feet flat and hands crossed. "As I told you, my husband's not here. I'm not sure how I can help."

CJ eyed a photo on the wall behind the puzzled woman—a man she recognized as Charles Ralston, Ava, and a girl who looked maybe ten. "That's a lovely picture."

The woman twisted around. "My husband, me, and our daughter at our clubhouse last year. We played in a golf tournament together." She frowned. "We were supposed to play today ... well, yesterday, but Charlie called and said he had to stay in Greenville. So, of course, our daughter was disappointed when we couldn't play."

"Oh, that's too bad," CJ said with a slight smile. "Work can be such a pain sometimes. So, what does Charles do?"

"He's a real estate developer. Communities like this one. He travels quite a bit." Her hand flew to her mouth. "Where are my manners? Would you like something to drink?"

"To be honest, I'd love a glass of water. It's been a long night."

Ava left her seat and went to the back of the room and a bar the same color as CJ's chair. "We have a couple of choices." She rummaged through a full-size refrigerator. "Hopefully, Perrier is okay." She returned, handed the bottle to CJ, and sat again. "I'm sorry if I've been testy. I'm so pissed off at my husband. His trip to Greenville on Friday was supposed to be for dinner, but he called me around eight thirty and said he was too tired to drive home."

"What did he say when you talked to him yesterday?" CJ asked.

"The bastard hasn't called me," she spat. "I called him several times and left messages. It's not the first time he's gone AWOL for a couple of days, but disappointing our daughter is different. He starts an enormous project and loses all sense of time."

"Mom, what's wrong?"

CJ turned to the voice behind her. A girl, a smaller version of her mother, stood barefoot in the doorway, wearing a long, white T-shirt.

Ava jumped up and rushed to her. "Nothing. Go back to bed."

The young girl pointed at CJ. "Who's she?"

"No one, sweetheart," Ava said. "Nothing for you to worry about. Go on now. Back to bed."

"Who are you?" the girl asked, her eyes narrowing.

"Uh, I'm a friend of your mom's. My name is CJ."

The girl approached, her honey-brown eyes wary, and stuck out her hand. "I'm Sophie. How come I've never seen you before?"

"Enough!" Ava snapped. Catching herself, she said, "Please go back to bed. We can talk about it tomorrow." She smoothed the girl's golden-brown locks and hugged her.

Reluctantly, the young girl turned and plodded up the stairs.

Ava paused before she turned back to CJ. Once the door closed upstairs, she wheeled around, fists clenched. "It's almost four o'clock in the morning. Why in the hell are you here?"

"Please sit back down, and I'll tell you."

Ava did as requested and stared at her, unblinking.

"I'm afraid I have some terrible news about Charles." CJ moved to the sofa and took her hand. There was no easy way to say it, or avoid it, any longer. "He's dead. We found his body in the Duncan House in The Boroughs last night."

Ava's brow furrowed, and she laughed nervously. "No. No. You're mistaken. Charlie went to Greenville. He's not in town."

CJ cleared her throat. "He never went to Greenville. The owner of the Duncan House said he checked in Friday night around seven thirty."

"But ... but ... he called me from Greenville around eight thirty and—"

"He lied to you, Ava. Do you know why he'd do that?"

The woman's eyes stayed fixed on CJ until she jumped up and walked toward the bar. "You're wrong. You've gotten whoever you found mixed up with my husband."

"I'm not wrong. I'm sorry, but the person we found looks identical to him." She pointed to the photo hanging behind the sofa. "Plus, the owner knows your husband. He's stayed at the Duncan House multiple times over the last two years. Do you have someone who can come and—"

Ava exploded and pointed to the door. "Get the fuck out of my house! You're a damn liar!"

CJ had more questions, but now wasn't the time. She stood up and moved to the door before turning around. "I'm so sorry for your loss. We can talk later." She opened the door and walked out into the rain, now steady. As she neared her truck, a loud, shrill scream pierced the night. Ava, now wailing, raced to her and threw herself into CJ's arms. Both women fell to their knees as a low rumble erupted in the distance, followed by a flash of lightning.

A little after 7:00 a.m., CJ opened her truck door and slid into her seat. She'd stayed with the destroyed wife and her daughter for three hours until a close friend of Ava's arrived. She'd then listened to the sobs and sniffles and barely audible conversations between the two of them.

She'd provided more details to Ava's friend so she could relay information when the time was right. Her earlier attempt at explaining to Ava why an autopsy was needed had gone over like a lead balloon, resulting in another ear-piercing invitation to get the fuck out.

Before starting the truck, CJ stared at the massive building. It was much more impressive in the early morning light. *I suppose I could have held off on the theory Charles had a woman with him.*

As she backed up and turned her truck around, her eyes caught Ava staring coldly at her from an upstairs window, her honey-brown eyes dark.

FIVE

Sunday, April 17
The French Quarter, Charleston, South Carolina

At 8:15 a.m., CJ trudged up the steps to her apartment. The party at Uncle Harry's, and Ben's arms wrapped around her as he kissed her softly, now seemed like weeks ago, not yesterday. She went straight to the shower and got the water running as she stripped off her clothes. She'd been wet and dried more times than she could count since midnight. Her auburn hair was tangled, and she stank like a wet dog.

She leaned forward in the shower and let the hot water caress her. She needed this—and some sleep, after being up for more than twenty-four hours.

After drying her hair and pulling on her comfiest sweats, she stretched out on her couch. A little food would be helpful, but the need for rest won out, and she closed her eyes. *Just a short catnap.*

Five hours later, her ringing cell phone startled her awake. Retrieving the noisy device from the floor, she answered to find Thomas on the other end. He told her he had done his autopsy and was confident Ralston hadn't died of natural causes.

She jumped up and stared out the picture window at the gloomy, gray sky. "So Ralston didn't have a heart attack? Why did he die?"

"No. It wasn't a heart attack. I haven't determined the official cause of death yet, but I'm certain it wasn't natural causes. We can talk through the details when we meet."

CJ stood fixated on a lone seagull cleaning his feathers on the roof across the street. "Okay. Thanks for updating me."

"I'm checking a few things and will call if I find anything else significant," Thomas said. "You can come for a debrief tomorrow."

She put her cell phone on speaker and thumbed to her calendar. "I'm scheduled to meet with Cap first thing tomorrow morning. Can I call you afterward and set up a time?"

"Sure," Thomas said. "I'll be here all day."

CJ hit the red circle and moved closer to the window. The seagull was finished cleaning himself and sat staring at her. "Well, Mr. Gull. It appears I have a new murder case." She pulled up her speed dial list and punched in a number.

"Hey, Unc. Wanna treat me to dinner?"

"You bet! How 'bout we meet at The Wreck at, say, six thirty?"

"Works for me. Meet you there."

She hung up, dug at the knot in her neck courtesy of the arm of the couch, and went to the bedroom to change. Dinner with her uncle Harry, who'd raised her, was always a welcome distraction. They'd talk about her work at some point, and he was an excellent sounding board that helped calm her. His thirty-plus years with the Boston PD, most of it as a detective, always offered her seasoned perspectives.

CJ crossed the Arthur Ravenel Jr. Bridge for the third time in twenty-four hours. The breeze caused her truck to sway as she crested the bridge's highest point and kicked up whitecaps on the river below. She cut through the white fog that had replaced the rain and dropped into the town of Mount Pleasant. After crossing the Shem Creek Bridge, she veered right before turning onto Live Oak Drive and winding along until she reached her destination.

The Wreck of the Richard and Charlene was a local favorite. Out-of-towners were able to find it, but it wasn't easy. The building was tucked in the back of the marina area and didn't stand out as a restaurant. The high-school-aged young woman who sat CJ at a corner table told her she'd watch for Harry, but she could help herself to a beer from the cooler in the meantime. Keeping her alcohol-free streak going, CJ opted for sweet tea instead.

Harry O'Hara rounded the corner and his hazel eyes, greener than brown, flashed when he saw her. Technically, Harry was her uncle, but he was more like her father. When a drunk driver had killed her family when she was eleven, Harry took her in without hesitation. He'd seen her through both thick and thin times, never wavering. So when he retired at sixty and moved to Charleston, she'd followed.

His arms wrapped around her, and she got a kiss on the forehead. "I'm happy you called and invited yourself to dinner," he said, chuckling. "It saved me from eating leftovers from the party yesterday."

After they'd ordered their usual fried grouper fingers, red rice, coleslaw, and a double serving of hushpuppies, Harry told her about the fishing trip to the Keys he was planning with her other uncle, Craig. Like a small child on Christmas morning, he was full of excitement. As he munched on a hushpuppy, he asked, "How about you go with us?" His eyes twinkled. "We can invite Ben too."

"Who?" she said, grinning.

"The tall guy you were smooching with last night on my back deck," he teased. "I thought I might need to grab the hose."

CJ stuck her tongue out at him, and they both laughed.

After they ate, their conversation turned to last night's call. Harry leaned in close as he listened to her. She gave him a rundown of the scene and her trip to Dunes West. She told him about the call earlier from Thomas and how it didn't appear the death was because of natural causes.

Harry exhaled, sat back in his chair, and ran his fingers through his short salt-and-pepper hair. "You said there were signs a woman was at the scene at some point. Would she be your prime suspect?"

CJ tilted her head from side to side. "Yes. I think so. The Duncan House owner acted shady, and I couldn't figure out the wife. She was distraught, but something about her was off."

"Hmm … the wife was probably caught off guard by losing her husband so young."

"Could be," she said, nodding. "Who knows?"

He put his hand on her shoulder. "Wait for the autopsy report. If it's a murder, I'll be happy to help you sort it all out." He clapped his hands together. "Let's have some banana pudding. You're too skinny."

After their sweet treat, they hugged and said their goodbyes, and CJ hopped back in her truck. Checking her cell phone, she saw she had a missed call from Ben. Her pulse picked up and her stomach quivered. *Am I excited or terrified?*

Ben Parrish was a great guy—she was falling for him, or already had. However, while he was an officer in the department, single, and in another unit, no matter how hard she tried, her guilt from the affair in Boston with a married superior still hung over her.

She put the truck in gear and crunched out of the gravel parking lot. Her fingers tingled as she hit redial. "Hey, Ben," she said when he answered.

"Hey, I was gonna call you earlier, but Dad and I took the boat out, and I knew you had a late night."

"Yeah," she said. "I didn't get home until after eight this morning."

"Ouch. Bad case?"

"It looks that way. I think we have a man who was murdered. We found his body over at the Duncan House. Some guy named Ralston."

"Wouldn't be Charles Ralston, would it?" he asked.

"That's the one. Do you know him?"

"I know of him. He's a regular at high society events, and a huge developer. Old money. I've met him a time or two."

"How about his wife, Ava?"

"I've met her once or twice as well. These big social gatherings bring everyone out."

As she drove, she told him more about the scene and her interactions with Larry Simpson's attorney, Percy Winston Ricardson III.

Ben paused before quietly saying, "Ricardson is bad news."

"How so?" she asked.

"I only know about him second-hand, but I've heard he's a major player in the Palmetto Men's Society and knows everyone. Everyone who can cause you grief."

CJ pulled her truck into her parking spot at home. "What's this society?"

"It's a men's group that's been around for at least a hundred years. Whispers are those with lots of money and power dominate their membership. Rumor has it you can only get in by invitation from at least three members. So I know it's extremely secretive."

She laughed. "What does this secret boy's club do? Sit around, smoke cigars, and sip brandy?"

Ben laughed feebly. "That, among other things—some are unsavory. Promise me you'll be watchful of Ricardson."

"Okay. I promise."

Before they hung up, she agreed to meet him for dinner on Wednesday night, then went inside. After she'd changed back into her sweats, she booted up her laptop and searched for the Palmetto Men's Society. Unfortunately, she only found a one-page website that merely told her a little about Charleston's history and the society's objective, "Men working as one to establish a better Charleston." There was nothing on its members, how to join, meetings, or any details on how the objective would be fulfilled.

SIX

Monday, April 18
The French Quarter

The buzzing of her alarm clock woke CJ at 5:00 a.m. She flipped off the bedcovers, changed into shorts and a T-shirt, and laced up her Nike running shoes. Armed with a thousand milliliters of water, she hopped on her stationary bike, which she'd nicknamed The Punisher, in front of the picture window. The early morning rays of the sun were making their entrance, and a flock of pigeons had replaced her lone gull on the roof across the street.

Within minutes, she was huffing and puffing and called it good after working up a sweat that got her thighs screaming. Swapping her water bottle for a mug of coffee, she headed to the shower.

By six fifteen, she had showered, dried her hair, and gotten dressed. Today's attire included black jeans, a long-sleeve tan blouse, and her usual chocolate-brown, high-ankle lace-up boots. She slipped her badge onto her waist, grabbed her Glock and credentials, and scurried out the door.

After a five-minute walk, the door chimed as CJ entered Sal's Coffee, and her favorite barista greeted her. "Good morning, beautiful! I swear you're more stunning every time I see you."

Pinkness spread across her cheeks, and she winked at him. "You're such a charmer. If you were only twenty years younger and weren't married."

Sal cheerfully said, "Fifty-five is fine! It's the married part that takes me off your list. Your usual, *cara mia*?"

"Yes, please." She pointed at the blueberry muffins behind the glass. "I'd like a dozen of those too, please. Stick a couple in a separate bag for me."

He handed her a large black coffee and filled a box with tasty treats. "Ah. Bribing the fellow officers."

"All the time. I have a meeting with the captain at eight, and it never hurts to feed him." She handed him two twenties and hustled back to her truck.

After the short drive to the Chief John Conway Law Enforcement Center that everyone called the LEC, she parked and raced up the steps. The keycard buzzed her in and she went to her office to prep for her meeting, stopping long enough to hand the box of goodies to a group of officers congregated near the coffee area—keeping the smaller bag for herself.

A few minutes before eight, CJ stood and grabbed her notebook, mug of coffee, and her surprise for the captain. Steps later, she waited outside the open office door as Captain Stan Meyers finished a call. She stared at the back of his head and his neatly combed dark brown hair. Her stomach fluttered. Her aspirin hadn't improved her headache. She heard him say goodbye and, with a spin of his chair, he turned to face her as he stood to his six-one height.

"Come in and have a seat."

She offered him a white bag. "I brought you muffins." She flinched as she realized she sounded like a schoolgirl bringing her teacher an apple.

He smiled as he took the treats. "Thanks. I skipped breakfast this morning, and my coffee is burning a hole in my stomach. The wife keeps telling me I need food first." He dropped into his brown leather chair and took a bite. After swallowing and licking his fingers, he pointed to the notebook in her lap. "I assume you're gonna brief me on the new case, right?"

"Yes, sir. I'll bring you up to speed on what we have, and plan to meet Thomas later today to get his autopsy report. He gave me a preliminary yesterday afternoon."

He nodded. "Before you do that, let's discuss your promotion to lieutenant."

CJ sipped her coffee and waited.

"Chief called earlier and wants to do the formal ceremony on Friday morning at nine. The mayor will attend. We'll pin you with your new badge and handle three other promotions." He took another bite and wiped his mouth with the napkin he found in the bag. "Will you tell Harry? I'm sure he'd like to attend."

"Yes, sir. I'll tell him."

"Also, thank him again for the party on Saturday for me." Stan pushed away the bag with the second muffin, folded his hands, and leaned forward. "One other thing. Effective immediately after the ceremony, Detective Jackson will begin reporting to you, and we'll assign a second detective to you soon. Jackson's a challenge, but it appears you two are on good terms. You okay with that?"

"Yes, sir. Does he know yet?"

"He does," he said. "Didn't say much either way. Jackson's been here a long time, and he should be the one getting the lieutenant slot on time served, but the sad fact is, he'll never be a lieutenant. That's not on anyone but him. Deep down, he knows it."

She nodded. "We'll be fine. We got off to a rocky start when I first arrived. He was less than pleased when I was given the Lowcountry Killer case the day I arrived. All but told me it was only because I was a White woman. In the end, though, I think I earned his respect. He even visited me in the hospital after Bryan Parrish damn near killed me."

Stan's eyes widened. "I wasn't aware you two had a run-in. If you had told me he—"

"No need, sir," she said, holding up a hand. "It hurt Jackson that he wasn't assigned the case. I've learned sometimes you gotta give a fellow officer room." She paused. "Besides, I'm no weak-ass female who can't stick up for herself. I'm used to being teased, picked on, and the occasional off-color comment. Men do it to each other all the time. I'll stop it or tell you if I can't handle it."

Stan crisply nodded, grabbed his notebook, and picked up a pen. "Okay. Let's talk about your new case." He leaned forward, and his brown eyes bored into her.

CJ liked her captain. He'd always been supportive. However, she'd have to adjust to reporting directly to him instead of Paul, with whom she had grown quite close in her short time in Charleston. She cleared her throat and covered her summary for the next twenty minutes. Stan listened intently, jotting down notes as she went. She finished and waited while his eyes scanned his notes.

"Okay. So we have a fifty-three-year-old man who died suspiciously in one of Charleston's oldest bed-and-breakfasts. I don't know Ralston personally, but he's a bigwig developer. You've got three persons of interest on your list so far—an unknown woman, the owner, and—a longshot—the wife." He tapped his pad with his pen and held up a finger when his phone rang. He checked the incoming number. "Hang on. I need to take this."

CJ sat, her knees bouncing as he took the call. The conversation was short, and his penetrating eyes returned to her.

Clearing his throat, he said, "We have a couple of little problems. That was the chief, and he's had two calls this morning. First, the attorney for the owner of the Duncan House called, raising hell about police misconduct. He says you harassed and intimidated his client, Larry Simpson."

"That's a lie," she said. "All I did was ask the squirrely little bastard some basic questions. You'd think he'd want to know why a dead guy was on his property."

Stan stared at her and paused while the redness left her face. "Second, the chief also got a call from the attorney for Ralston's widow demanding we don't perform an autopsy."

Her eyes narrowed. "You told him it was already done, right?"

"Yes, and the chief will tell her attorney." He sighed. "He's not exactly happy."

Rubbing her forehead, she muttered, "I'm sorry the chief is catching hell early on a Monday morning. I'll be happy to talk to him. Officer Jones can back me up on my questioning of Simpson. As for Mrs. Ralston, I did my best to explain to her friend why the autopsy was required, and it was the coroner's call under South Carolina law." She frowned. "We need the cause of death to determine if we have a murder." Her laugh was forced. "I'm not apologizing for the efficiency of Thomas in getting it done so quickly."

Stan raised his palms. "Nor should you. Don't worry about the attorneys or calling the chief. He'll call you if he wants. Simpson sounds like he's a drama queen, and I'm sure Mrs. Ralston was shocked and upset over losing her husband."

CJ's brow furrowed. "Was she not planning an autopsy?"

He shook his head. "Apparently not. Her attorney wanted the body released for cremation."

"Cremation." Her jaw went tight. "Why in the hell would a wife do that without discovering why their husband died?"

"Your guess is as good as mine," Stan mumbled. "I'll tell you what. You keep doing your job, and I'll handle any fallout. Your job is to find whoever murdered Ralston. After seeing Thomas this afternoon, let me know if he has anything new."

She nodded, thanked him, and left his office. CJ hated the political side of law enforcement and was more than willing to let the captain handle it. She slid into the chair at her desk and stared at her summary notes.

Do I have the priorities of the persons of interest wrong? Maybe the unknown woman isn't my top suspect.

SEVEN

Monday, April 18
Downtown Charleston

At 12:50 p.m., CJ turned left onto Ashley Avenue and into the Ashley-Rutledge Garage at the Medical University of South Carolina. She grabbed her notebook and hustled to MUSC's Medical and Forensic Autopsy Section. An autopsy assistant signed her in, gave her a visitor's badge, and asked her to wait while he told Thomas she had arrived. She dropped into an uncomfortable metal chair.

"I want the body released today, and a permit issued for cremation!" a loud voice in the back boomed.

CJ leaned forward and frowned. The autopsy assistant rolled his eyes at her and shrugged. "Who's back there?" she asked.

"It's some lawyer for the Ralston family."

She listened as the discussion became more heated before jumping from her chair. Rounding the corner, she saw Thomas being confronted by a short, stocky man with a beet-red nose in an expensive charcoal suit. Two burly men stood behind him.

"What's going on, Thomas?" she asked.

Thomas turned to her. "This is Mrs. Ralston's attorney, Richie Pickett. He wants us to release Charles Ralston's body and issue a permit for cremation. I've tried to explain to him we can't do that until we have the necessary information."

Pickett turned his wrath on CJ. "We demand the body be released *right now*. This is an overreach of the State's authority, and I—"

"Will take yourself and your friends out of here now," CJ interrupted, stepping nose-to-nose with him. "We will release the body as soon as possible, but not one minute before. This is an open case."

"Who in the hell are you?" Pickett fired back.

She dug out a card and handed it to him. "Detective CJ O'Hara of the CID."

He snatched the card out of her hand. "So you're the illustrious Detective O'Hara."

She smirked. "In the flesh."

"Well ... well ... I'll have your badge over this. I'm calling your chief, and I'm friends with the mayor."

"Good for you. Knock yourself out and call either of them, but the body stays until we release it. Now go."

"You don't understand—"

"Out! Now, or I'll be forced to arrest you for obstructing justice."

Pickett opened his mouth without speaking, then snapped it shut. Turning to the two men, he motioned for them to follow him.

"Jeez. Pickett's a piece of work." She turned to Thomas, who was visibly shaken. She put her hand on his arm. "You okay?"

He slowly nodded. "Yeah, I'm fine. Unfortunately, I don't handle bullies very well."

She smiled. "I'm accustomed to them, I guess. But, of course, we had a lot more like him in Boston than we do here. What's that saying? You catch more flies with sugar or something like that."

Thomas finally smiled and exhaled. "How about I give you my autopsy report?"

"Okay." She started for the changing room door. "Let me gown up so I don't stink of death all day."

"No need," he said. "I was going to use slides for my summary." He motioned down the hall. "Let's go to the conference room."

"Perfect. I hate those damn gowns."

Thomas opened the door to a small conference room with an off-white, eight-seater table and projection screen. He pointed to the tall Black man smiling up from the slide projector. "You've met my autopsy assistant, Byron."

"I have." She took Byron's hand. "Last time we were together, he was nursing me back to health after I passed out in your exam room."

"Good to see you, ma'am. I'm happy you're feeling better now."

And happy I won't pass out again, I'm sure.

Thomas flipped off the lights. "Byron, let's pull up the externals first, please." The projector hummed, and the naked body of Charles Ralston filled the screen. Clearing his throat, Thomas started. "I'll cover my external and internal exams, and we can discuss the cause of death. First, I did an external exam and checked for any signs of puncture wounds. Ralston had none on his body. The only unusual items are the rash and scratches on his back, which we've discussed." Photographs of Ralston's back appeared as the projector clicked. "The scratch pattern is indicative of fingernails."

CJ leaned forward and her eyes scanned the photographs. "Did you find any foreign substances?"

"None. The only substance on the body was dried semen. I've sent this to the lab for DNA analysis."

"Anything more on the rash?"

"Not yet. It appears to be some type of allergic reaction."

Byron slid a copy of Thomas's notes across the table to her. "Here's the report. I highlighted the key items for you."

Thomas continued. "I did the usual internal exam, covering all the organs. Tissue samples for forensic analysis were collected from the brain, liver, and kidneys. I also collected urine and blood; we'll analyze those."

"How about his stomach?" she asked.

"I extracted the contents of his stomach, and an initial tox screen showed no signs of recreational drugs. However, his blood alcohol level was over the limit hours after his death, so he'd consumed a considerable amount of alcohol. I've sent the stomach contents to the lab for further analysis."

CJ frowned. "What does all this mean?"

"Long story short, Mr. Ralston appears to have been a healthy, fifty-three-year-old man. He was six feet tall, weighing approximately one hundred and eighty pounds. I was able to access his medical records. He has been religious about getting his annual physicals and nothing in his file jumps out at me. He doesn't take any prescribed medications, had no significant illnesses or surgeries, and his scans and tests are all within normal ranges."

CJ stared at him and he sighed. "I can't give you a cause of death at this point. We need the results of the battery of tests before I can nail it down."

Nibbling her thumb, she asked, "He didn't die of a heart attack though?"

"No. We usually find an enlarged heart, dilation of the heart chambers, and damaged blood vessels if someone dies of a heart attack. This happens when some form of blockage or blood flow restriction occurs, and I found none of that. So, based on what I have found, I believe he had a cardiopulmonary attack."

Her face went blank. "Wait ... I thought—"

"I'm sorry," Thomas said, smiling. "I've confused you. A cardiopulmonary attack, also called a sudden cardiac arrest, differs from a heart attack. His parasympathetic nervous system was disrupted, causing the heart to stop beating. As a result, he lost all blood flow and stopped breathing."

She squeezed her chin. "So, he basically shorted out and suffocated."

"Yeah, that's one way to describe it. Now we need to determine why."

She thumbed through the preliminary report and circled the information for the heart. "When will we have the tests back?"

Thomas cleared his throat. "Some results will arrive sooner, but I'd estimate three or four weeks to complete everything."

Her eyes went wide. "Jeez. That long?"

"Unfortunately, yes. It's tougher when you don't have something specific you suspect."

Scanning the report Byron had handed her, she asked, "Are there signs of foul play?"

Thomas stood and walked to the screen. "Yes and no. There's nothing external to indicate a murder, but nothing internal to point to a death by natural causes. Since he's an otherwise healthy man, I'm suspicious."

Her head snapped up. "Of what?"

He motioned, and his assistant turned off the projector. Thomas flipped on the lights and sat down across from her. "It could be a drug, and we'll analyze for all the common ones—antidepressants, antihistamines, stimulants, cocaine, and narcotic analgesics. I've also added barbiturates, GHB, and LSD to the list. Maybe our guy got tangled up with the wrong person."

"Didn't you say you've already screened for drugs?"

"We did a screen for some, but the lab will analyze a more extensive list and confirm those screened." He sat looking down, tapping a pencil on the table. "How much do you know about poisons?"

She shrugged. "Not much."

He nodded. "Fair enough. I'm not an expert, but I've dealt with a few poisoning cases over the years. There's a long list of them, but I group them into slow and fast acting. We have a fast-acting type here, but I've asked for tests for all the common types."

"If Ralston was poisoned, what kind would they use?"

"Hard to tell. People have used numerous poisons to murder someone ... arsenic, cyanide, strychnine, antifreeze, snake venom, Atropa belladonna, or conium maculatum, to name a few."

CJ rubbed her forehead. "I've heard of the first four, which are rather easy to obtain, but I'm unfamiliar with the last three."

"That's because they're so rarely used. Snake venom is a low probability, since few people want to milk a venomous snake. Atropa belladonna is a plant sometimes called deadly nightshade. Conium maculatum, also a plant, is known as poison hemlock. You can find the hemlock in the US, but deadly nightshade isn't common."

She exhaled. "Will we test for all of these?"

"We'll look for the most common first," he said. "If we don't get answers, we'll extend our analysis."

"This is quite a list of possibilities," she groaned. "Please keep me posted as results come in."

They were quiet before she spoke. "There's one last item we need to address. Since Pickett was such an ass, I'm tempted to stall, but should we release the body?"

He nodded. "We can. I have all the samples we need to analyze, and there's nothing else to glean."

"Okay. Let's call Mrs. Ralston and advise her. Any reason to deny a cremation permit?"

"No," Thomas said as he shook his head. "We have what we need."

She stood and paced the room. "I don't like having the body cremated. I'm worried we won't be able to exhume Ralston once this happens. But it's fine by me if you're confident you have what we'll need."

They said their goodbyes, and CJ returned to her truck. She climbed into the seat and stared blankly as her fingers gripped the wheel. She still had a dead man with no answers about why he'd died. Thumbing through the autopsy report, she stopped on the last page and the list of poisons. *What the hell did you ingest?*

EIGHT

Tuesday, April 19
The Boroughs

CJ had spent the evening before sitting cross-legged in her side chair under the picture window, reviewing her notes and prepping for her meeting with Larry Simpson and his high-priced mouthpiece. Having his attorney present was the only way Simpson would agree to meet with her. She had questions, and she was sure he had more answers.

At a few minutes past nine, she pulled into a visitor's parking space in front of the Duncan House. She had some time before their agreed nine thirty meeting, so she called Johnny and reviewed her notes. This could be her best shot at filling gaps, and two heads were always better than one.

He offered to join her but she declined, as she wanted to make this visit as low-key as possible.

CJ climbed out of her truck, hit the key fob, and stood staring at the impressive three-story building before her. Saturday night had been dark, and there had been no way to appreciate one of Charleston's top bed-and-breakfasts. The place oozed charm and history with light, steel-blue paint accented with white trim and highlighted with bold, black shutters.

The pristine main house was surrounded by a perfectly groomed landscape with multicolored flowers and palm trees of various heights sparkling from the early morning shower. Red brick, well-weathered by the salty sea air, covered the parking lot and walkways. Her research told her the place was built in 1790 and had been refurbished numerous times over the years—it was old, but new.

Taking a deep breath, CJ made her way up the four steps onto the porch and through the dark cherry double doors. Like the exterior, the lobby area screamed elegance. She stood on a light oak floor, and the room had to be a thousand square feet, tastefully decorated with a gold sofa and two matching chairs. Expensive-looking paintings of various parts of the city adorned the walls.

A stunning woman in her mid-twenties smiled at her from where she stood by a desk in the corner. "Welcome to the Duncan House. I'm Mary Beth. How can I help you?"

"I'm here to see Mr. Simpson," CJ said, self-conscious of how she was dressed compared to the young woman's pleated olive-green skirt, black blouse with flowing sleeves, and matching black heels.

As she reached for the phone, the young woman asked, "May I let Mr. Simpson know who's here to see him?"

She nodded. "Yes. I'm sorry. I'm Detective CJ O'Hara, and he's expecting me."

The young woman's smile faded. "Thank you. Please have a seat and I'll ring him for you."

Picking a chair in the opposite corner, CJ sat and waited.

Mary Beth hung up the phone, and approached. "He'll only be a couple of minutes. Can I bring you something to drink? We have coffee, tea, water, and sodas."

"Thank you, I'm fine," CJ said as Mary Beth stood staring at her, biting her bottom lip.

In a low voice, the younger woman leaned in closer and said, "It was terrible what happened to Mr. Ralston."

CJ gazed into her green eyes closely. "Yes. It was. Did you know him?"

"Uh. Well … I—"

"Mary Beth!" Simpson snapped as he entered the room. "Let's not bother the detective."

She winced. "Sorry. We were—"

"Go back to work." He motioned toward her desk. "We have guests you need to be mindful of."

Her eyes wet, the young woman turned for her desk. "Yes, sir."

Simpson's glare followed her before turning back to CJ. "Hello again." He offered her a hand but barely shook. "Let's go into my office. My attorney's waiting for us."

Passing the desk, CJ smiled at Mary Beth when she glanced up. It was clear the young woman had something to say. Making sure to not let her boss notice as she walked behind him, CJ dropped her business card on the desk and kept moving.

Once they reached his office, Simpson reintroduced her to his attorney, Percy Winston Ricardson III, who did not shake her hand. The three slid into chairs around a four-seat walnut table.

"I'd like first to thank you both for meeting with me. As you are aware, I'm working to resolve any issues with the unfortunate death of Charles Ralston," CJ began.

"Nothing to resolve," Ricardson snapped. "He had a damn heart attack."

Resisting the urge to go eye-to-eye with him again, she opened her notebook. "According to the ME's autopsy, this doesn't appear true. Ralston died from—"

"I thought an autopsy wasn't planned," Ricardson said, his voice sharp. "I understood the family didn't want one."

She cleared her throat. "I'm sure you know the coroner makes that decision under our state laws in case of a suspicious death."

A forced smile crossed his lips. "I'm well aware of the laws in this state, young lady."

"Yes, sir. I'm sure you are," she said.

He waved the back of his hand at her, dismissing her. "No matter. My client had nothing to do with it and has nothing to hide."

"I understand," she smiled, "but I have to find out what happened and if someone was involved."

Ricardson leaned back and folded his arms across his chest. "Is my client a suspect?"

CJ shrugged one shoulder and focused on Simpson, who sat with his head down. "No. He's a person of interest, meaning he may be helpful in sorting this out." She turned back to Ricardson. "With your years of experience, I'm sure you know sometimes people can help even if they're unaware of it."

The owner spoke up. "How can I help—?"

"Let me make the decisions here," Ricardson scolded as he put his hand on his client's arm.

Simpson slowly nodded and dropped his head.

"I'll tell you what," she said. "How 'bout we do this? I'd love to tour this beautiful place, and then I'll ask a few questions I'm sure can be easily answered. We don't need the formalities of subpoenas or warrants."

The two men were quiet until Ricardson broke the silence. "Let me have a few minutes alone with my client."

"No problem," she said as she stood. "I'll go wait out front." She left the office and went back to an empty lobby. Mary Beth was nowhere in sight.

Ten minutes passed before Simpson emerged. "I'll give you a tour and only answer questions about my place. We'll rejoin Percy afterward, and you can ask anything else. I want him present."

"Fair enough. Would it be okay if I took a few photos? I'll let you and your attorney approve them before I leave."

He ran his fingers through what was left of his hair. "Uh—yeah—I guess."

"Excellent. Let's start outside, and I'll grab my camera from my truck."

For the next hour, they went room by room through the main house, which offered guests three bedrooms and one suite on each of the second and third floors. The first floor included the lobby, the kitchen, the laundry room, the storage room, and the owner's one-bedroom suite. Only two guest rooms were occupied, so she got to see most of the rooms.

Each guest room, named using Charleston's rivers, was similar in layout and amenities, yet different—the floors were various types of wood, light and dark, and the furniture varied. The only thing that stayed the same was the white bed linens.

CJ ran her finger down her notes. "Guests enter the main house to reach their rooms, correct?"

Simpson nodded. "Yes. My suite does have a private entrance."

"Has it always been used by the owner or manager?"

He pressed his lips together and said, "Uh, I'm not sure. I think before the suite in the carriage house was opened, it was used for guests."

She nodded as he fidgeted. "Okay. Let's see The Ashley since it was too dark on Saturday night to fully appreciate."

Simpson led her to the carriage house where Charles Ralston's body was found. It had been converted into a one-bedroom suite nine years ago. This building was detached and secluded from the main house with its own two-car parking area.

As he fumbled to unlock the door, Simpson told her the room would be emptied and cleaned before it was re-opened. "We'll take everything out and sanitize things. I plan to buy a new mattress, curtains, and bed linens."

CJ snapped several more photos and followed him along the brick walkway and back into the main house.

Her last thirty minutes were maddening. Ricardson approved her photos but cut in with, "We don't have an answer for that," more times than she could count. She knew Ralston had stayed there ten times since Simpson had bought the place. Somehow, the guest records before that had been *lost*.

She returned to her truck and stared at her notes. Finally, she added one last item.

Cover-up!

———

CJ glanced up at the clock over her desk—5:23 p.m. She picked up her notebook and headed down the hallway and out the door. Heavy black, gray, and white clouds floated overhead. She hoped the rain would hold off until she got groceries and lugged them up her stairs.

She parked, grabbed a cart, and pushed through the automatic sliding door at her favorite Piggly Wiggly. As was her usual luck, she managed to pick a cart with a wobbly front wheel. Rattling and squeaking, she made her way up and down each aisle, grabbing the items on her list, plus a few things she couldn't live without.

She stopped as she rounded an end aisle before bumping into a mother and her two sons. The youngest boy, maybe two, sat in the cart, snacking on Barnum's Animal Crackers. His little lips curved into a smile at her as crumbs dropped to his gray shirt bearing the words *Mommy's Little Angel*. She beamed when he stuck out his tiny hand and offered her a bite of his soggy cookie.

"Thank you, sweetie, but you better keep that for yourself."

The older child, who appeared to be maybe four, busily helped his mother with their shopping. About CJ's age, his mom pointed at what to take from the shelves he could reach, and the little guy grabbed the item and dropped it into the cart. This process went on as they worked their way down the aisle. At one point, the woman asked, "Would you like to go around us? We're a bit slow."

"No," she smiled. "I'm fine. Please take your time. I'm enjoying the show."

CJ turned too sharp at the end of the aisle, resulting in cartons of vanilla wafers all over the floor. "Crap!" She winced and kneeled to gather the spilled items. A small voice behind her caused her to turn to face Mom's little helper.

"I can help you." The four-year-old quickly picked up the boxes and placed them on the cardboard stand. "I'm a really good shopper, and these things happen sometimes."

"Thank you," she said. "You're good at this."

Mission accomplished, the little guy hugged her and returned to his mom, who smiled proudly at him. CJ's gaze followed them as they continued—all three with matching sandy blond hair and light blue eyes. A heaviness engulfed her. *If I ever have kids, will they look like me?*

NINE

Wednesday, April 20
Downtown Charleston

At 8:30 a.m., CJ opened the gray metal door to the forensics laboratory.

A middle-aged technician with black-rimmed glasses smiled at her. "Eddie's in the back. He told me to have you join him when you arrived."

CJ thanked her and wound her way to the lab, where the CSI stood scribbling notes on the whiteboard.

He motioned her to a tan, eight-foot folding table stained with coffee rings. "Let's sit here, and I'll bring you up to speed on where we are so far." The metal chair squeaked when she sat. "I've made a list of the items we collected at the scene." He pointed to the list on the board.

"First are the two empty wine bottles and glass. Our victim's fingerprints were on the glass and one bottle. The only other item of interest is a residue in the bottle that was wiped clean. It's gone for analysis."

"Could it be from the wine?"

He shook his head. "I don't think so. It's from some other substance."

"What about the bathroom print?" she asked.

"Simpson's. He said he cleaned the room."

CJ slowly nodded and added a note to her notebook.

Eddie pulled a photo from a folder. "We've also sent the two stains to Columbia for analysis. I'm confident one is vomit." Then, holding the image up, he said, "I'm pretty sure we'll be able to obtain DNA from the other."

She leaned in closer. "Do you think the stain under Ralston is from semen and vaginal fluids?"

"That'd be my guess," he nodded. "It's not blood."

She stared at her notes and nibbled on her thumb. "We also found a hair and minty vanilla odor on one pillow."

"No luck on the odor. I guess it's a perfume, but we couldn't extract a sample."

She sighed, circled the words *minty vanilla odor* and added a question mark.

"As for the hair, we won't be able to run DNA, but we've confirmed it's human hair and brown. I've asked the hair expert at SLED to examine it for anything more," he said, referring to the State Law Enforcement Division.

"Okay. I appreciate the update." She stood. "I'll check on how I can expedite the analytical reports."

After she left Eddie, CJ sat in her truck, flipping through her notes. On a clean page, she wrote down some bullet points.

- *Residue in wine bottle?*
- *Stain on bottom bed sheet?*
- *Stain by vic's head, vomit?*
- *Dried fluid on vic's privates?*
- *Fingerprint on wine bottle and glass, Ralston's*
- *Fingerprint on mirror, Simpson's*
- *Brown hair?*
- *Odor on pillow?*
- *Missing bath linens?*
- *Missing personal items, wallet, keys, cell phone?*

She turned the key to start the engine and headed for the LEC. She planned to spend the rest of the day reviewing the evidence she had so far. Her date with Ben was at six thirty, so she needed to leave in time to change. *Why am I so damn nervous?*

———

Ben Parrish eased the throttle back and glided along the edge of Shem Creek's green sea grasses to a stop. He was happy to have the day off and a chance to take his black Labrador Retriever, Jake, out on his boat. The dog loved fishing more than chasing his tennis ball in the waves at the beach.

The Lab stood on the bow beside Ben, his cognac-brown eyes fixed on the line his master tossed in the water. "We'll catch one soon, boy. Be patient."

Ben stretched his six-foot-four frame and pulled on an Isle of Palms Marina hat, causing his dark brown hair to stick out at the back. The heat climbed as it crept toward noon, and the sun beat down. A brief morning shower had bumped up the humidity in the air.

He had just celebrated one year as an investigator in the Charleston PD's Homicide Investigation Unit, but this wasn't the anniversary on his mind. It had also been a year since CJ O'Hara had arrived from Boston and joined the department. From the moment they'd met, Ben had been smitten.

Her natural beauty drew him in first—an athletic body, wavy, auburn, shoulder-length hair, a heart-shaped face, and a slim, small nose. Her eyes were a color of green he'd never seen, and the sun's rays picked up tiny flecks of yellow in them. He'd only seen her in a dress once, at a gala, but she was feminine even in jeans and boots. It didn't take long for him to realize that wasn't why he had fallen for her.

She was intelligent, passionate, strong, and able to handle any situation. She reminded him of the latter when he'd screamed at her for chasing down and subduing a suspect. But the best part was she didn't know how beautiful she was, inside and out.

Jeez, calm down.

Like everyone, CJ wasn't perfect. Her biggest struggle came from the guilt she carried over her parents' death, for which she blamed herself. When it overwhelmed her, she'd turn to alcohol to escape. Sometimes, she struggled with self-confidence and didn't trust her instincts. When a perfect storm of guilt and self-doubt from a complex case hit her, she would crack and become self-destructive.

Am I blind to things I can't change?

Then there was his arrest. Ben knew she was doing what any good cop should do by arresting him when the physical and forensic evidence pointed squarely at him. Who could have imagined his twin brother was alive and had returned to Charleston for revenge? At least she'd followed her instincts and kept investigating even after the Lowcountry Killer case was "closed" and had taken his brother down. But it took until he'd thought he lost her to Elias Lewis, a young man the press ultimately dubbed the Hoodoo Man, for him to know he had to have her in his life—scars and all.

Loud barking broke Ben's train of thought. He'd hooked a fish, and his furry partner was running in circles on the deck, barking like crazy. "I'm reeling as fast as I can!" He dropped to a knee, leaned over, and eased the fish into the boat—a nice-sized redfish. Jake began his we-got-one! dance, sniffing and snorting, with his tail going a hundred miles an hour.

Ben held the water creature up. "Whaddaya think, boy? Keep him or let him go?" Jake gave a whimper, followed by a stare. "Okay. We'll let him go."

This process continued for another two hours. Ben would catch one, his dog would go nuts, and the fish would swim away. When he fished with Jake, he rarely kept any of his catches—the big dog wouldn't allow it. He'd only save a badly hooked fish that would die and fool Jake by throwing his ball in the water while he slipped it in the cooler.

Ben checked the time on his cell phone, patted Jake's head, and started packing up. "Time to go home, buddy. You and I have a date tonight, and we gotta get cleaned up."

"*Woof!*"

"Yep, the pretty lady who gives you treats, and lets you sleep on her bed." Jake climbed to his usual position on the front of the bow. Ben pushed the throttle forward and made his way back out of the creek.

TEN

Wednesday, April 20
The French Quarter

At six thirty, there was a knock on her door, and CJ peeped through the door viewer before opening it to Ben in tan khakis and a pale blue button-down. He had a leash connected to Jake in one hand and a bouquet of brightly colored flowers in the other. His amber-brown eyes flashed at her.

"Wow. You look unbelievable."

She smiled as she took the flowers and dropped to one knee to pet the black block head of her furry friend. "You two guys look handsome." Jake did his usual routine and laid his head on her shoulder and nuzzled her ear. She stood and ran her free hand down her pistachio green dress with a small floral pattern. "Is this okay? I wasn't sure where we were going. I don't wear dresses much, but the lady at the shop said this was versatile."

"You look great, and it will be perfect for where we're headed."

"Okay. Let me grab a sweater, and I'm ready to go. Remember, our deal is Jake gets to go on our first official date. Not sure what places let dogs in."

He smiled. "I have a place."

She cocked her head. "You're still not gonna tell me where we're going, are you?"

"No, ma'am. It's a surprise."

Ten minutes later, Ben turned onto Queen Street and pulled to a valet stand for Poogan's Porch—a yellow and white-trimmed Victorian townhouse converted to one of Charleston's best eateries.

"They won't let Jake in here," she said, shaking her head.

"Au contraire. Of course they'll let a dog into a restaurant named after one. We'll sit right up front on the porch, just like Poogan did."

Ben was right. The young hostess, with a navy dress and dark hair in a bun, sat them at a two-seater glass table with black wrought-iron chairs. She scratched Jake behind his ears and told them she'd bring him a water dish. Dutifully, the ninety-pound ball of fur laid down along the white porch railing and rested his head on CJ's foot.

After scanning the menus, they decided on fried green tomatoes for an appetizer—new for CJ. Ben ordered the chicken fried pork chop, and she couldn't resist trying the salmon glazed with sweet tea.

"It has to be delicious if it has sweet tea on it," she said.

While finishing their after-dinner coffees, a little girl in a navy-blue dress and white shoes walked past them and through the front door. A ribbon that matched her shoes held her black hair in a ponytail. CJ's eyes trailed after her as she and her parents sat at a table inside the window.

"She's a cutie," Ben said, breaking her from her trance.

"Uh—yeah, very cute. How old do you think she is?"

He glanced at the girl. "Maybe five. I've never been good at guessing ages."

CJ stared at her coffee.

"Do you wanna have kids?" he asked.

Her eyes glistened under the overhead lights and she nibbled her lip. "I do, but …"

"But, what?"

"I'm not sure I ever will." She lifted a shoulder. "According to my doctor, I'm physically fine to have children …"

Reaching and taking her hand, he said, "Tell me."

CJ pursed her lips. "The job makes it tough between the time commitment and all the crap I see daily—plus, it's dangerous as hell. How can I raise a child with this job and not be terrified for them every second?" She sighed. "I'm not sure I'd even be a good mother. And I'm not getting any younger."

He stopped her fingers from twiddling with her cup and squeezed them. "I'll be honest. I worry about the same things." He chuckled. "Not the good mother part, of course, but being a good father. For me, it's about choices … and you're still young."

She pinched her eyebrows together. "You don't worry about your job getting in the way of being a parent? I mean, look at how many cops are working half the night, divorced, and living away from their kids, or—"

"No. I may be delusional, but we'll figure it out together if I marry the right person. I know you'd be a good mother, and yeah, the world sucks sometimes, but the real question you have to ask yourself is, how bad do you want children?"

Her eyes returned to the girl, who smiled at her through the window. Then she turned back to Ben and said, "Nothing would make me happier. I've always dreamed of having a husband and a family—"

"Can I pet the doggy?"

Both turned to find the little girl standing beside them.

"I love doggies. Pleeease?"

Ben smiled. "Sure. He'd love it. His name is Jake."

Jake's tail thumped the floor, and he sat up. They watched as she rubbed the big dog's head and scratched him behind his ears. Then, after a couple of minutes, she hugged Jake, thanked them, and headed back inside.

"Are you getting chilly?" he asked.

"A little. I'm not used to having my bare legs exposed." She rolled her eyes and chuckled. "The perils of a dress."

He motioned to their waiter. "How 'bout I pay the tab and we head out?"

Ben drove home and parked behind the apartment alongside her truck.

They sat there silently until she broke it. "I'd invite you up, but it's a school night, and we both have early starts tomorrow."

He slowly nodded. "Yeah. That's probably best. Plus, I have Jake …"

She read the disappointment on his face. Truth be told, she felt the same.

He opened his door. "Wait, I'll walk you up."

She wasn't accustomed to having someone open her door, but she liked it. *I guess not all chivalry is dead.* At the top of her steps, she hugged him. "I had a wonderful time."

He gave her a squeeze. "Me too." He eased her back and stared at her. "You think I've earned a second date?"

"Yeah. I think so," she said with a flirty smile.

He leaned in and kissed her as she melted against him. "Well, good night," he said. "I'll call you tomorrow. I'll be working on a case in Harleston Village and doubt I'll be at the station."

Her eyes followed him down the stairs. "Ben. Wait." He stopped, turned around, and climbed back up to her.

Nibbling her lip, she said, "I'm scared."

"You don't have to be, but I'm a little scared too. There's no rush. We can—"

She pulled him to her, pressed her lips to his, and whispered in his ear, "Go get Jake."

ELEVEN

Thursday, April 21
The French Quarter

It was the first time she hadn't woken up alone in a long time. CJ's eyes fluttered as the morning light streamed in the partially open blinds. Her head rested on Ben's bare chest, and his arm was around her. His breathing was slow and steady, and she sensed his every heartbeat.

Shit! I gotta pee.

She raised her left leg, which she had draped over him, as slowly as possible, and tried to slide from under his arm without waking him. It didn't work.

"Good morning," he half-groaned and half-sighed as he squeezed her tight against him. "Where are you going?"

She pressed her lips to his cheek. "Hate to spoil the mood, but nature calls."

He laughed and opened his arm.

She managed to untangle herself from the sheets, avoid stepping on Jake sprawled out on the floor, and headed to the bathroom. After she'd relieved herself, she stared into the mirror ... and smiled. She splashed some water on her face and brushed her teeth. When she opened the door, Ben had pushed himself up on an elbow and gave her a goofy grin. "Better?"

"Much. I'm sorry I woke you." She tugged at the oversized Boston Red Sox T-shirt she'd slept in. "What time is it?"

Ben rolled over and pulled his shirt off the clock. "A little after six." He popped out of bed. "I need a minute, and we can snuggle if you'd like." He walked past her in his navy-blue boxers to the bathroom, giving her a peck on the cheek.

She climbed back into bed, and with a pat, Jake joined her. "Okay," she called to him, "but we gotta get moving soon. Busy day."

"What the hell?" Ben returned with a chuckle and stood with his arms spread. "Jake. What are you doing?"

CJ rubbed the big dog's belly as his legs pointed to the ceiling. "I invited him. He looked cold on the floor."

Ben took what was left of the bed and wrapped his arms around her.

Thirty minutes later, he left her with a heart-fluttering kiss and she raced to the shower. She was running later than she'd wanted, but didn't care. Her night with Ben had left her tingling. As badly as she wanted him, she was glad they'd not had sex ... just lots of heavy petting. She was still terrified, but unbelievably happy.

Her cell phone buzzed as she laced up her boots. She looked at the screen and answered, "Hey, Thomas."

"Good morning. Sorry to call you before eight, but I have some news. Our tests indicate Ralston didn't have drugs in his system."

She grabbed her notebook. "Meaning?"

"He was poisoned. With what I'm not sure yet, but I have my ideas."

"What are your ideas?"

Thomas cleared his throat. "I'd rather wait until the lab confirms."

She frowned. "Okay. When will that be?"

"Couple of days," he said. "I'll call you as soon as I hear anything."

She added *no drugs* and *poison* to her notes and finished tying her boots before she left for work.

CJ pulled off Lockwood Drive into the LEC parking lot at 8:10 a.m. She hustled up the stairs and through the door a young patrol officer held open for her. She remembered him and smiled. "How's it going with the new baby?"

"Other than him waking us up every few hours for a bottle, it's great." He beamed, pulled a photo from his breast pocket, and held it up.

"He's a cutie," she said. "I love his blue eyes."

He nodded, stared proudly at the picture, and followed her.

She bypassed any more stops as she hurried past the boisterous bullpen. She checked her desk for any messages or incoming mail and headed down the hall. Stan was reading a report when she knocked on the doorframe.

"Do you have a minute, sir?" she asked. "I'd like to update you on the Ralston case."

He closed the file and motioned her in. "Have a seat. I was going over the financials—so damn boring. I have another item for you as well. You go first."

She dropped into the chair across from him. "Thomas called earlier and said our victim was poisoned. He was reserved about the method, but told me he expected the lab to have an answer in the next couple of days."

He leaned forward with his elbows on the desk and folded his hands. "Hmm, interesting he didn't tell you what he thought. Do you know any reasons why?"

CJ shrugged. "No clue."

He frowned. "I guess we'll wait on the lab. Anything else?"

She opened her notebook and scanned her scribbles. "Forensics expects to be able to run DNA for the stains at the scene. Besides our vic and the owner, who told us he cleaned the room, we found no other prints." She paused as she stared at her notes. "We also found a residue in one of the wine bottles, and Eddie hopes they can identify it."

"Poison," he said.

"Excuse me?"

"The residue in the bottle may be from the poison used," he said. "Have Eddie call Thomas to coordinate with the lab. If Thomas thinks he knows the poison, ensure the lab tests for it in the residue sample."

"Good idea. Will do." *I should have thought of that.* She closed her notebook. "Your turn."

"How is Sam Ravenel doing after the incident?"

Her mind recalled the night she'd saved Sam from Elias Lewis after he'd kidnapped her and planned to take her heart for his warped hoodoo ritual. The hair on the back of her neck stood up. "She appears to be fine. She's a strong woman."

"Fair enough." A smile slowly crossed his lips. "I've got good news for you and the whole CID. I was able to find the money to keep her here with us."

"That's great! She's so much help, and this is where she wants to work. Have you told her?"

He stood, and she joined him. "Not yet, but she's headed our way. I asked her to swing by at eight thirty. Let's grab more coffee, and when she gets here, let's tell her together."

"I'd like that."

The face of a young woman with golden-brown hair and baby-blue eyes peeked around the edge of the door right on time. Her face brightened when her eyes met CJ's.

Stan waved her in and pointed to his detective. "Come in, Miss Ravenel. I've asked Detective O'Hara to join us." Sam lost her smile, and he burst out laughing. "Only kidding with the formalities. Have a seat."

The young woman blushed, pulled a chair up next to CJ, sat, and folded her hands in her lap.

Stan's eyes went back and forth to each of the women. "Sam, I'm aware you requested to become a permanent member of the CID, but it was denied due to funding. However, the detective has an update for you."

"What the captain is saying is, he found the money to bring you on here with us."

Sam sat rigid before she wiped her eyes and sniffed. "I … I'm pleased about that. Thank you so much, sir."

He grinned at her. "Here's the deal. With CJ being promoted to lieutenant, I'd like to give her your day-to-day management responsibility. Everyone in the CID can share your research expertise, but she'll make sure it all works. I've commandeered the small conference room three doors down, and you two can share it. That work for you, ladies?"

In unison, they said, "Yes, sir."

His phone rang, and before he turned to answer it, he said, "Now, go catch some bad guys."

CJ and Sam left his office and waited until they were out of sight before they hugged.

TWELVE

Thursday, April 21
Downtown Charleston

After leaving Stan, CJ and Sam sequestered themselves in their shared office, and CJ briefed Sam on the Ralston case. The younger woman made notes on the whiteboard, and they agreed on the items she could help with—backgrounds of the victim, his wife, and the owner of the Duncan House.

CJ stood and joined Sam at the board. "I have one more item I'd like you to look into … the Palmetto Men's Society."

"Oh," Sam said as her eyes widened. "Having lived here all my life, I've heard of them enough to know they're secretive. I'll do some digging."

Shrugging, CJ said, "That's all I can ask." Her eyes glanced at the digital clock on the wall. "Listen, I need to visit Ava Ralston 1:00 p.m., so I'd better leave. I'll call you after I'm done."

"Sounds good. In the meantime, I'll set up the room and start my research."

———

CJ parked her truck in front of the Ralston home and stared at their daughter, flying back and forth on a rope swing hung in a massive oak tree in the side yard. The little girl stared blankly at her—no smile or acknowledgment of her presence, even after she gave her a little wave. Notebook in hand, CJ climbed out and reached the door.

Ava Ralston answered her knock on the door. The victim's wife didn't appear any worse for wear in her yellow pantsuit and made-up face. There was no sign of tears. CJ thanked her for agreeing to meet and followed her into the same ballroom-sized den they'd been in on her first visit. Attorney Richie Pickett and his beet-red nose sat cross-legged in a black leather chair in the corner.

"Detective, I believe you've met my attorney." Ava pointed to the stocky man, who tipped his head. "I've asked him to join us." She motioned to a chair. "Please have a seat."

"That's certainly your right," CJ said with a stiff smile as she dropped into the expensive leather chair. "I think you'll find there's nothing to fear. I'm just hoping to resolve things with your husband's passing. Let me say again, I'm sorry for your loss."

Ava nodded without saying a word.

Opening her notebook and clearing her throat, CJ said, "I don't have too many questions. First, you said your husband told you he was going to Greenville for a dinner meeting. What time did he leave the house on Friday?"

"In the morning, around eight thirty. Charlie was going to the office and heading upstate later in the afternoon."

"And you didn't speak to him again until around eight thirty that night, correct?"

"Right."

She added a checkmark to her prior notes and refocused on Ava. "As you are now aware, your husband didn't leave town. Instead, according to the Duncan House records, he checked in around 7:30 p.m." There was no response or movement from Ava, just an icy stare. "Are you aware of him staying there at least ten times in the last two years?"

Her lips pressed together, then Ava said, "No. And I don't believe you, or the records."

CJ pulled a sheet of paper from her notebook. "Here are the days, maybe—"

"That's enough, Detective!" Pickett snapped. "My client is a loving wife sick with grief and knows nothing about your allegations. She had her poor husband cremated this morning, and here you are with all your innuendos. All you're doing is slinging mud at a wonderful man who had a heart attack. I don't—"

"Mr. Pickett, your facts are wrong. Charles Ralston died from sudden cardiac arrest, not a heart attack. Something caused this, but the ME who did the autopsy told me the death was not from natural causes. You were informed of this as well when you went to MUSC."

He frowned and flipped his hand at her. "More lies and speculation." He turned to Ava. "I think we've answered all the questions we need to. Charles died of a heart attack. Maybe he went to the Duncan House instead of going north or coming home because he was ill?"

CJ cocked her head at him. "Who's speculating now? If Charles Ralston stayed at the Duncan House because he was sick, wouldn't he have told your client when he called her at eight thirty? The evidence shows he was there, and so was a woman. For some reason, he then went into sudden cardiac arrest, and that's what killed him." She turned back to Ava. "Were you aware of anyone your husband was seeing?"

"You bitch!" Ava jumped up and moved beside Pickett. "I'm going to sue you and the damn police department for slander. Hon ... er, Richie, make her leave."

The short, stocky attorney stood.

CJ put up her hand. "Okay. One last question, then I'll show myself out. Where were you on Friday evening?"

Ava's face went crimson, and she balled up her fist.

Before she spoke, Pickett put his arm around her. "She doesn't need to tell you where she was. It's none of—"

"I was home!" Ava stepped forward, pushing past her attorney's arm who was trying to block her. "I was right fucking here all night with my daughter."

Pickett grabbed her arms and finally got control of her.

"Okay," CJ said. "Fair enough. Would you mind if I confirmed this with your little girl?"

"Don't say anything else," Pickett said. "This is a ridiculous miscarriage of justice." He glared at CJ. "The chief is a friend, and I will be calling him."

CJ was sure she tasted blood when she clamped her teeth down on her lower lip to contain her response. She closed her notebook, stood, and headed for the foyer. "Thank you again for your time. We'll be in touch once the ME gets the lab report on what caused your husband's death." She twisted the knob and let herself out.

An old Black man in worn, blue overalls and a white T-shirt was on his hands and knees in the flower bed at the bottom of the steps as she exited. His head was down as he clipped dead foliage and dropped it into a burlap bag. He glanced up when her shadow crossed and smiled warmly. He was missing a front tooth.

"Hello, miss." He stood and removed his white straw hat with a noticeable stain ring around the rim.

"Hey," CJ said as she returned the smile. "Those are beautiful." She pointed to the multicolored plants. "What are those?"

He glanced down. "Oh, we have a mix of shrubs and flowers—anemones, lilies, jessamine, camellia, and such. I change the flowers out several times a year to keep 'em fresh. Mrs. Ralston likes her variety."

"Lovely. Do you do the landscaping at other houses too?"

"Ah, no, ma'am. I spend every day here. It's a big yard, and Mrs. Ralston wants everything to be perfect."

"Wow." Her eyes went wide. "You're their personal gardener."

"Yes, ma'am. It takes me all week to keep the place up how I'm s'posed to. Sometimes, I work on Saturdays when we get lots of rain. Makes the grass grow like crazy, and I use a manual push mower to cut it. Mrs. Ralston hates the noise of gas power tools."

CJ scanned the grounds. "You been working here long?"

The old man twisted his lips. "Well, lemme think. I've been here about eight years or so. Ralstons hired me after they married and moved in once the house was finished."

"Sounds like they like having you here."

"I s'pose so," he smiled. "Been good to me. Always pay me on Friday. Pay me in cash, too," he said, winking. "Don't tell the IRS. Tax-free, ya know."

"Oh, I won't," she said, winking back.

"Mind if I tell you something?" he asked.

"No. Of course not."

"You're a handsome woman, uh … I mean, pretty." He winced. "Them green eyes sparkle in the sun."

"Thank you." She gave him one more big smile. "Well. I'll let you go back to work." She started down the red brick walk, stopped, and turned back. "By the way, did you see the Ralstons last Friday?"

"Well, lemme see." He rubbed the back of his neck. "Mr. Ralston left for work early, and I didn't see him no more. Mrs. Ralston paid me as always before she left to go downtown."

"Left … what time was that?"

"Late. Maybe five o'clock."

"I assume by downtown, you mean downtown Charleston?"

"Yes, ma'am. She said she—"

"Reggie! Quit talking and go back to work." Ava raced down the steps, her eyes blazing as the old man flinched. She turned to CJ. "Damn you, Detective. You need to leave and stop bothering my family and staff."

CJ nodded, mouthed a *sorry* to the old man, and turned for her truck.

Behind her, Ava continued to scold her gardener. "Men are worthless! You open your mouth again, and I'll fire your black ass."

CJ stopped short, wheeled around, and raced back up the walkway towards Ava. "Hey! Keep it up and I'll arrest you," said CJ.

Ava stepped toward her and put her hands on her hips. "Yeah. For what?"

"How about disturbing the peace, assault, or being a fucking racist?!" She knew the captain would call her on the carpet for her outburst, but *protect and serve* was in her oath.

Ava glared at her as she opened her mouth, but stayed silent. After a tense stare-down, CJ turned and walked away.

She sat in her truck, staring down at her lap as her chest heaved. She hated losing her cool, but there was no way she would let someone be verbally abused, reprimand be damned. Finally, she lifted her head and stared at Sophie, still swinging back and forth, back and forth, with a devilish smirk on her face.

As she climbed the Arthur Ravenel Jr. Bridge, her cell phone rang. *Thomas.* She hit the speaker button. "Hey, Doc."

"I got the lab report and wanted to tell you about the poison," he said. "Ralston ingested a significant amount of the Atropa belladonna, deadly nightshade."

Her brow furrowed. "I thought it was rare. Where the hell did that come from?"

"Not sure, but that's what it was. It acts fast and disrupts the nervous system. I'll call Eddie and see if the results he gets for his samples match. I wanted to update you ASAP."

She steered off the ramp into downtown. "Do you think it was an accident?"

Thomas exhaled. "I don't see how."

"Suicide?"

"Well … that's possible, but again, remote. It'd be an awful way to go. Fast, but far from painless."

"Can you send me the report so I understand more about this poison?"

"Byron's already emailed you one. By the way, are you excited?" he asked.

"Huh?"

"You're being promoted tomorrow. I'll be there."

She absentmindedly stared at the darkening clouds, lost in her case. "Oh, yeah. Sure, I'm excited. See you tomorrow."

THIRTEEN

Friday, April 22
Downtown Charleston

CJ was already awake as the fingers of the sun slipped through the window and crawled across her bed. She focused on the dust particles dancing merrily in the slivers of light.

It's promotion day.

She flipped off the sheet and went to the kitchen to grab a coffee. CJ sipped the black liquid as she stared out her picture window—there were no feathered friends on the roof across the street this morning. She shifted her eyes beyond the roofline to the fuzzy image of Fort Sumter looming in the distance.

Showered and dressed in her formal uniform, she flew down the stairs, jumped in her truck, and headed for the LEC. It was 7:00 a.m., so she had two hours before her promotion ceremony. She had too much work to do to spend it on niceties. She was delighted to be a lieutenant, but saying the word reminded her of Paul.

As she traveled along Calhoun Street, she pulled out her cell phone and hit the speed dial number for Sam. "I was hoping you could come in a little early today. I've got some more info I need you to run to ground for me."

"I'm already here," Sam said.

CJ laughed. "Why am I not surprised? I'll see you in ten." She hung up and eased around an ancient Ford pickup taking its sweet time.

She got parked, through the door, and raced past the bullpen to whistles and claps. Wearing her formal uniform was uncomfortable all the way around. When she arrived at the conference room, now turned office, she knocked when the door wouldn't budge.

Sam swung the door open. "Sorry. I got a new lock installed. I have a key for you." She handed it to her new boss. "I didn't want a repeat of someone stealing information from the files like we had in the Lowcountry Killer case."

The two women settled at the brown, six-foot table after CJ had added bullets to the whiteboard. "Okay. Let's review what we have and set the next steps." She squirmed, stood, and went back to the board. One by one, she covered the bulleted items.

"You're antsy this morning," Sam said. "You all right?"

CJ blew out a long breath. "I'm fine. I slept like shit. Every time I answer one question, two more pop up. It's like swimming upstream." She turned and stared at the list of possible suspects. "I still have the mysterious unknown woman, as well as Ralston's wife and the Duncan House owner. I don't trust the attorneys involved." Her cell phone buzzed, and she checked the screen—8:45 a.m. "Great. I need to go get badged for my new job. I'm buried with this case and still haven't met with Jackson or whoever else they assigned me."

Sam stood and joined her. "Okay. Let's calm down. We'll go to the ceremony, celebrate your promotion, and we can resume things. I'll help you. Maybe you need to bring in other officers too."

"Yeah. Maybe." She shrugged. "Jackson's underwater with his cases, so he can't help, and I have no idea about the other detective joining our team."

CJ and Sam entered the press room. It was packed with people from both the department and the public. Charleston Mayor Margie Sellers was canvassing the room, smiling and shaking hands. She was dressed in a three-button charcoal skirt suit and beige pumps.

When the mayor's eyes met CJ's, she beelined over to her. "Detective O'Hara! I'm so pleased you've been promoted. We've got you moving up in the ranks, and our second female detective starts Monday. Isn't it great you two will be working together?"

"Uh ... yes," CJ replied. "That's wonderful."

The mayor patted her on the shoulder. "Well, it's almost time to start. Let's take our places." With that, she turned and hustled to the stage.

Sam whispered, "Mystery solved. Your second detective is a woman."

"Uh-huh."

CJ spun around when a familiar voice behind her said, "Hello, sweetheart." Harry gave her a quick hug, and he and Sam found chairs in the back as Chief Walter Williams took the podium and the room went silent.

CJ crept across the room and dropped into a chair by Stan. She leaned over and whispered, "Cap, I need to update you on the Ralston case."

He nodded without turning his head. "Later."

Chief Williams briefly introduced the day's planned events and asked the mayor to join him. Her five-foot-two frame only made him appear taller. At six feet six, he towered over everyone. The overhead lights made his bald head shine and his dark brown eyes darker. CJ focused on the scar on his right cheek.

At his assigned time, Stan stood and went to the podium. First, he described CJ's accomplishments in her first year with the department. Then, somberly, he said a few words about Lieutenant Paul Grimes, the man she would replace. She wiped her eyes at the mention of how proud he would be of her—and she wasn't alone.

"Detective. Please join me."

Her legs wobbled before she collected herself and approached him. Stan congratulated her, and the chief and mayor shook her hand as cameras clicked. Harry beamed from the back row, and everyone clapped after she was pinned with her new badge. Ben, who had slipped in late, whistled.

After the ceremony ended, everyone moved to the hallway for refreshments. CJ spent the next forty-five minutes thanking those congratulating her, wishing she could sneak away. Harry and Ben wanted to take her to an early lunch, but she begged off. However, they refused to take no for an answer on dinner and agreed to rendezvous at the Boathouse at Breach Inlet on the Isle of Palms.

Detective Vincent Jackson, who now reported to her, strolled over. "I'm happy for you," he said, and stuck out his hand.

She took it. "Thank you. That means a lot. You've been with the department a long time and applied for—"

"I guess you beat me out. It's the way it goes, I guess." The Black man, ten years her elder, shot her a weak smile. "Shoot me a text when you're ready for us to meet."

She nodded. "Thanks. We'll sit down real soon."

"Lieutenant?"

CJ turned to find Stan with a Black woman of about her height. She appeared slightly younger than CJ, with jet-black hair she wore in loose curls and bright, cocoa-brown eyes. Her face carried a warm smile.

Stan smiled as well. "I want to introduce you to Detective Janet Wallace. She starts on Monday, joining us from North Charleston. She'll be on your team."

"It's so nice to meet you, Lieutenant O'Hara. It's such an honor to work with you."

CJ smiled, and the two shook hands. "Thank you. We're excited to have you."

The three spent a few minutes discussing the department before Stan pulled CJ aside. "I have another item I need you to handle." He held out a file. "We have something you'd be perfect for. I know you're adjusting to officers reporting to you and the Ralston case, but the Special Victims Unit asked me for a favor."

She opened the file and scanned the contents. "This is a sexual abuse case."

He nodded. "Yes. A twelve-year-old girl showed up at Roper complaining of pain from a fall. The ER doc checked her out and reported it as a possible sexual assault. The girl denies this, but the officer who spoke to her is convinced she's lying."

"Okay. Can I ask why we're getting this in our unit?"

He rubbed his chin. "The SVU is busy chasing down a human trafficking ring. Plus, we need a female detective on this, so the girl will be more open. As you're aware, we only have two in the CID. So that's you ... or Janet, if you choose. Can I count on you?"

"Yes, sir."

"Oh. By the way, Thomas had to leave, but he asked me to have you call him." He handed her a note, turned, and walked away.

She unfolded the piece of paper, scanned it, and frowned. *Call me about a man named Wilkins. Thomas.*

She was almost through the side door when Mayor Sellers approached with the chief in tow. "Lieutenant, I need to speak with you."

The three of them moved to a quiet corner. Mayor Sellers stood close to CJ. "I understand Charles Ralston may have been murdered."

CJ nodded. "Well, yes, ma'am. That's what the autopsy appears to show."

The ordinarily jovial woman leaned in closer, her eyes fiery. "You find out if it was murder, and if so, whoever did it better be locked up sooner rather than later. Charles Ralston was a pillar of this community." She walked away, but stopped and returned. "By the way, I'm friends with Ava Ralston, and she's distraught at how unprofessional you've been to her. I can't begin to tell you how disappointed I am in you."

CJ's eyes went wide. She opened her mouth to defend herself before she caught the chief shaking his head behind the mayor. So, instead, she took a deep breath and replied, "Yes, ma'am. I'll find out who murdered Mr. Ralston, and if needed, I'll apologize to his wife."

Sellers gave her one last glare and stormed off.

Chief Williams leaned over and whispered in her ear, "You need to do your damn job, Lieutenant." He wheeled around and walked away.

She stood frozen with a flat gaze before she slipped out the side door, a crushing weight smothering her. *Happy fucking promotion day to me.*

PART TWO

HISTORY REPEATS ITSELF

FOURTEEN

Friday, April 22
Downtown Charleston

*T*hurmond Wilkins died of deadly nightshade poisoning at
the Duncan House ten years ago.

CJ sat rubbing her temples at the news Thomas had
given her. He remembered the deceased man and had done
the autopsy. But the case had gone cold and remained un-
solved. His notes suggested it was identical to the recent
death, except the man was found in the first-floor suite
of the primary house—the room now occupied by Larry
Simpson.

Am I gonna need to solve this old case too?

She stood and stared out her office window at the
seagulls riding on the breeze. The Ashley River Memorial

Bridge traffic had stopped, and the red flashing lights indicated a wreck. She turned, dropped into a chair, and picked up the file labeled *Ralston Case*.

She thumbed through the contents, placed it back on the table, and picked up the folder Stan had given her for Jolene Mason. Her experience with sex crimes was limited, but she'd promised to sort it out. Exhaling, she put the folder down and rubbed her eyes. Then, a lone sheet of paper with the words *Wilkins Case* scrawled across the top caught her attention.

The door lock clicked, and Sam entered. "I grabbed some lunch for us. I wish you'd let me take you somewhere to celebrate."

"No. I have too much work to do."

"All right." The younger woman handed her a to-go container. "I went to Sully's and picked up your usual— baked chicken, mashed potatoes, and green beans."

"Uh-huh." CJ left the container untouched and picked up the sheet with the name Thomas had given her for the man murdered ten years ago. "I need to go to Cold Case and pick up the file on an old murder." She held up a sheet. "This gives me the highlights, but there has to be more."

Sam eyed her. "I'll take you down … after you eat. I'm sure Jimmy can help."

Furrowing her brow, she asked, "Who's he?"

"He's in charge of the records and evidence for unsolved cases, and he's been here for at least thirty years. Most of it is down in the basement. He's super smart."

"And, of course, you know him," she chuckled.

"Yep, I've met him once or twice doing my research. Finish your lunch and I'll introduce you." Sam stood and went to her desk. "I'll tell him we're coming."

———

At 1:00 p.m., Sam opened the gray steel door labeled *Cold Case Evidence Room* and motioned CJ in. A man with curly gray hair, who had to be close to sixty, looked up from a brown wooden desk that'd seen better days. A crooked smile crossed his lips when he saw Sam.

"Hey, Sam. It's been a while. How're you doing?"

She smiled. "Doing wonderful, Jimmy. How's the cold case business?"

He stood and spread his arms. "Same old, same old. Boxes and more boxes. I've been transferring information to a new electronic system, but it's slow since I'm the only one doing it. Unfortunately, the budget won't allow for help." He limped toward them. "Who have you brought to see me?"

Sam hugged him and pointed to CJ. "This is Lieutenant CJ O'Hara. She's my new boss in CID."

"Nice to meet you." Jimmy stuck out his hand, and they shook. "Sam tells me you need my help."

"I do. There's a case from ten years ago mirroring a recent one, and I'd like to see what we have on it—Thurmond Wilkins."

He nodded. "Poisoned with deadly nightshade, if I remember correctly. I think they found him at the Duncan House."

She glanced over at Sam, who winked. "Told you he was smart."

Jimmy laughed. "Not sure about that, but one learns a thing or two over the years. Plus, when bored, I read through old cases and try to figure out what happened." He sighed. "I'm sorry I haven't transferred that file to the new system yet, but I can show you the boxes."

"That'd be great," CJ said.

He turned and hobbled toward two rows of metal shelves crammed with boxes. "Let's see if I can find the dang thing."

CJ followed him while Sam waited. "How did you hurt your leg?" she asked.

"I took a bullet over in the Business District when I was twenty-five during a robbery gone bad. Couldn't work patrol anymore, so here I am in the basement."

"I'm so sorry."

"No worries. I'm glad I could stay on and have a spot." He stopped as his eyes scanned the rack. "Ah … here we go, Thurmond Wilkins Case, May 2001." Two white cardboard boxes, yellowed from time, sat on the shelf. "I'll take these out front for you. One box has paperwork, and the other has items collected at the scene."

"Can I take it back to my office?" she asked.

"Well, folks normally review things here unless they're officially assigned a case, but I guess I can let you sign it out. I'll need to make a copy of the contents list first." He smiled at her. "I need to make sure everything comes back. I got my ass chewed a time or two when evidence got misplaced."

She nodded. "Okay. I'm not sure yet if I'll be assigned this one."

"We can review it here too, and I'll make copies," Sam called out. "I'd hate to cause you trouble."

"That works fine too," CJ said. "The key thing I'm after is the officer's report."

"Works for me." Jimmy grinned. "It might be a good idea to make you girls work here, so I have some company." He placed the boxes on a six-foot folding table and opened two metal chairs. "Have a seat here. The lighting is better." He pointed to a copy machine in the corner. "My copier ain't much, but it works."

CJ pulled on surgical gloves and popped the top off the first box. "Let's see what we have."

"Let me know what you want me to copy," Sam said. "I'll be sure we get the contents list, and I can snap photos of the other evidence."

For the next two hours, they reviewed the information. CJ handed various paperwork to Sam, and she copied them. He was right. The copier worked, but it was slow. They photographed the items forensics had collected—most noteworthy was a stained pair of men's boxers.

CJ stretched her arms over her head. "That looks like it for now. The file's pretty thin." She picked up the contents list and scanned it. "Are you aware if they ran DNA on anything?"

Jimmy leaned down and rubbed his chin. "I don't remember any DNA reports … there's none shown on the list." He sighed. "Frustrating thing about these old cases, they aren't evaluated often enough with fresh eyes or new techniques."

They thanked him, picked up what they'd copied, and climbed the stairs.

"We got a second whiteboard," CJ said as they entered their office.

Sam smiled. "Yeah. I convinced the maintenance guy we needed two. One four-by-six space isn't large enough. This way, we can use one for each case."

"Thanks for being on top of things."

CJ spent the rest of the day reviewing the Wilkins file and jotting pertinent notes on the board. Sam stayed busy preparing a file for the second murder case and the sexual abuse case.

"Don't forget you have your dinner tonight," Sam said.

"I know," CJ said as she sighed. "I'd rather stay here and see what I can put together. I—"

"No! You're going to dinner. Harry invited me too, and I'm hungry." She shut her computer down. "It's almost six, so we need to go. I promised you'd be there by six thirty."

"Okay. Okay," CJ grumbled, and grabbed the Mason file as she headed to the door.

———

Scarlett rolled off his sweaty body. She climbed out of bed and seductively walked to the bathroom—giving him a good view and his money's worth. "I'll be right back, dar-ling." She stopped and turned around. "I need to freshen up."

"No problem," he said with a stupid grin. "I need a break, anyway. Damn, baby, you're exhausting."

She gave him her best flirty smile. "You're not so bad yourself." *What a fucking joke. You're the worst lay ever.*

Scarlett wasn't sure why she'd agreed to meet him. She had what she wanted from Ralston and didn't need the cash. Maybe it was just habit. She leaned in close to the mirror and cleaned off the smeared blush lipstick.

She had seen little on the news about the death of Charles Ralston. It was reported as a heart attack, but one reporter mentioned the police were looking into foul play. She smiled at herself in the mirror and whispered, "Poor ole Charles. He must have had some bad wine."

"You wanna go again?" she called from the bathroom. *If you can get it up.*

"Oh, wow, honey. I'd love to, but I think you wore me out. Besides, I promised the wife I'd be home by midnight."

She peered around the doorframe. "Where did you tell her you were?"

He laughed. "I told her I had an important client in town and had to take him to drinks and dinner. She'll be drunk, anyway. Damn bitch drinks like a fish."

"Okay, baby. I'm disappointed, but I understand." *I understand you're a lying piece of shit … men are worthless.* When she stepped out of the bathroom, he was almost dressed. "Listen, is it okay if I stay a bit and grab a shower?"

"Fine by me. The room's paid for till noon tomorrow." He leaned in and kissed her. "I'd stay and join you, but I have to get home."

"That's okay. I'll miss you, though." She took his hand and rubbed it on her breast. "Be careful driving home, and think about me."

She pressed her mouth to his and ran her nails down his back, and he moaned. Once she released him and he left, she headed for the shower.

FIFTEEN

Saturday, April 23
Downtown Charleston

The sun was still hidden when CJ pulled into the LEC parking lot. Sleep had eluded her—her mind was cluttered with questions. She'd enjoyed the dinner the evening before, but the distraction was short-lived. She'd declined Ben's offer to take her with him to visit his dad the next day. As much as she'd enjoy seeing him, she had to wrap her head around her cases and sort out how she'd handle her new reports.

She opened the door to the office lit by the pre-dawn dimness creeping in the window. A flip of the light switch made it less unsettling, but the low hum of the overhead bulbs was irritating. She exhaled and spread the files for the three cases across the table. Once she'd erased both whiteboards, she began listing critical facts for the two murders again and marking which matched.

She sat and stared at the boards. They'd found two local men in their early fifties dead at the Duncan House. In both cases, deadly nightshade had stopped their heart. She thumbed through the officer's report for Wilkins and paused. A handwritten note was in the margin with three words, *Palmetto Men's Society.* She flipped to the last page to find out who was responsible for the investigation. *Detective Vincent Jackson.*

"Vincent was the detective in charge of the case," she mumbled. The only information she found listed for suspects was an "unknown intruder." *What the hell! Did Jackson honestly think someone broke into the room and poisoned the victim? How the hell would that happen?*

She grabbed her cell phone and sent a text: "Vincent, sorry to bother you on a Saturday. Can we meet on Monday right after the morning roll call?"

She went back to the notes from the first officer at the scene. There was no sign of a break-in in his field notes. Her eyes froze at the name of the person who'd called in the incident. *Well, what do you know?*

At noon, she finished what she could do on the two murder cases. She stared at the Mason file, picked it up, and flipped it open. She dialed the number on the first sheet of the report.

"Hello, this is Detective CJ O'Hara of the Charleston Central Investigations Division. May I speak to Cathy Mason, please?"

"Uh … this is her."

"I'm sorry to bother you on a Saturday, but I was trying to close up some files and wanted to see if I could get some help." No response. "Would it be possible for me to swing by and talk to your daughter, Jolene?"

"Umm … why?"

"I want to be sure I have my report complete. It shouldn't take long."

"My husband's not here."

"Oh, that's fine. I only need a couple of minutes with Jolene."

"Well—I'm not sure. My husband won't like it."

"Speaking with your daughter would help me, and I'm sure you know how paperwork is … I don't wanna have an incomplete file. I could get in trouble with my boss."

"Well … I guess it'd be okay if it doesn't take long."

"Thank you. It should only take a few minutes. Would one o'clock work?"

"Yes, one is fine."

CJ ended the call and frowned. *That woman is terrified of her husband.*

———

Ben pulled up in front of his father's home in Johns Island. The white, single-story house sat on the Wadmalaw River with a massive back deck and a dock where his father kept the smaller of his two boats.

"Hey, Pop," Ben said as he stepped onto the deck.

Bill Parrish hugged his son. "Couldn't talk CJ into join-ing you?" he asked, grinning.

"No. She's working today."

Ben grabbed a Corona from the blue Igloo cooler and the two men dropped into Adirondack chairs. For the next several minutes, they talked about Bill's latest fishing trips, how his older brother, Will, was handling his upcoming wedding to Sam, and how Ben's work was going.

"So, how are things with you and CJ?" Bill asked.

The younger man offered a half-shrug. "I'm not sure ... we're doing okay."

Bill eyed him. "I know you care for her ... the real question is, how much?"

Ben pushed himself up, walked to the railing, and stared at the sparkling surface of the Wadmalaw River. "I love her," he whispered.

His father joined him and they both gazed at the water. "I like that one. She'd make a wonderful daughter-in-law."

Ben's head snapped around to face him. "You jumped there damn quick. I—"

"It's only natural. I got eyes and can see. After thir-ty-two years of watching you become the man you are, I can read you." He patted his son on the shoulder and talked about how proud he was of him—his time in the Marine Corps because he wanted to serve his country, his graduation from The Citadel with honors, and his job with the Charleston PD.

"You've always put others ahead of yourself. A noble trait, but ..."

"But, what?"

The older man shrugged. "I don't want you to be alone. You've dated several girls you cared about—CJ is more than that to you." He turned and stared at his son. "I can only remember one other girl you told you loved her."

"Yeah, of course—Kelly France."

"And how does your heart compare the two?"

"Not even close. I was barely twenty with Kelly, and while I thought I loved her, it's nothing close to how I feel now."

"Have you told CJ about her?"

"You mean …"

"That's exactly what I mean. If you love her, she deserves to know."

Ben walked to the other side of the deck, his eyes fixed on a red-wing blackbird swaying at the top of a reed. He knew his father was right, and he would tell her. *I should have already.* He wiped the wetness from his cheeks.

Bill eased up beside him. "I'm not trying to dredge up something painful from your past or cause problems. I'm sorry."

"You're right, Dad. If I love her, she needs to know."

SIXTEEN

Saturday, April 23
Harleston Village, Charleston

The Mason home was in Harleston Village, close to the LEC. CJ took Lockwood Drive until she reached Beaufain Street, where she took a left. A short distance later, she turned left again on Gadsden Street and parked her truck at the Sumter Court entrance. She picked up her notebook and walked to the yellow, single-story home with white shutters. The place appeared well-kept—normal.

As she approached the house, she saw the outline of someone in the window. She knocked on the door and waited. It was 12:55 p.m. *Come on. Let me in.* She raised her hand to knock again when the door cracked open and a woman in her late thirties with stringy brown hair peeked at her. CJ smiled. "Are you Cathy Mason?"

"Yes. Are you the detective?"

"I am," she said, holding up her badge.

"If I let you in, do you promise you won't stay long? My husband will be back soon …"

"It shouldn't take me long at all. Is your daughter here?"

"She's in her room." The woman opened the door and stepped back.

CJ shook her petite hand, slipped inside, and eyed a faint black bruise under the woman's right eye. "Thank you for letting me come by. I'm eager to get this pesky paperwork finished. Would it be okay for me to talk to Jolene, and I'll be on my way?"

"Uh … I guess that'd be okay, but I'd rather be with you when you speak to her." The woman, who couldn't have been over five feet one, led her down the hall to the closed door of the young girl's bedroom in the back corner of the house. "Jolene, honey. A detective is here to speak to you."

"Tell her to leave. I don't wanna talk."

"I promised she could speak to you to complete her report."

There was a rustling sound, and the door creaked open. A girl about her mom's height with the same brown hair faced her. Her dark brown eyes were red and watery, and she had a faint bruise on her neck. CJ followed her into the room and dropped into a wooden chair as the girl and her mother settled on the bed.

"I told my mom there's nothing else to talk about. I already told the policeman what happened."

CJ smiled at her. "I know, but I wanted to be sure we had everything in the file."

"You talk funny," the girl said.

"Sorry, I'm from Boston."

Jolene's eyebrows rose. "That's far, right?"

"It is. I moved here last year to be near my uncle. My apartment's near here. I live above the Watkins Clothing Shop in the French Quarter. Do you know where that is?"

The young girl shook her head and dropped her chin.

CJ opened her notebook. "You said you fell, right?"

"Yes, ma'am."

"I hope you're okay now."

"I'm fine," the girl said in a shaky voice.

"How did you fall?"

She glanced at her mother. "I—uh—tripped in the backyard. I'm kinda clumsy."

CJ gazed past the girl, left her chair, and approached the window. "You fell back here?" The yard was tiny and only had a patch of grass and a few shrubs.

"Yes, ma'am."

"Your yard is rather small. How did you trip?"

"I—I don't know. I forget."

CJ returned to the chair. "Well, the important thing is you're fine now. Are you sure you're okay?"

Jolene glanced at her mother again and hesitated before answering. "Yes, ma'am."

Cathy spoke for the first time. "She's fine. Kids are always skinning a knee or getting a bump or bruise somehow."

CJ's eyes narrowed. "Oh yeah. Accidents happen. I've had them myself." She leaned down and pulled up her pants leg, revealing a scar on her left calf. "Then sometimes, some nasty man hurts you."

Jolene's eyes bulged. "What happened?"

"I was trying to help a homeless man not freeze to death, and he got upset and stabbed me with a piece of metal."

The girl's mouth dropped. "I bet that hurt."

"Yes, it did."

"Did you shoot him?"

"No," CJ said. "I arrested him, though."

The girl nodded. "He deserved it."

"Yes, he did. If a wicked man hurts someone, he should be arrested."

Jolene's brown eyes cut to her mother, then back to CJ. Her bottom lip trembled, but she stayed silent.

"How did you get to the hospital?"

"I rode my bike. It's not far."

"She's not supposed to ride that far," her mother interjected. "Her father and I weren't happy."

"He's not my dad," the girl sneered. "He's my stepfather, and he's—"

"He loves you like—"

"Yeah, right."

The three sat silent for a couple of minutes before CJ spoke up. "Jolene, is there anything else you'd like to tell me for my report? I wanna do a good job, so my boss is happy."

The young girl glanced at her mother, then dropped her head again. "No, ma'am. I have nothing else to say."

CJ patted her on the leg and stood. "Okay, I guess that's it." She followed the mother out of the room and down the hall. As she got to the front door, she stopped. "Give me a minute. I forgot to thank Jolene." She hustled back down the hall.

The teary-eyed girl looked up when she opened the door.

"Here's my card with my cell phone and address on the back if you ever need to talk to me," she whispered. She dropped the card on the bed and backed into the hallway. "Thanks again, Jolene."

The girl grabbed the card and shoved it under her mattress.

CJ returned to her truck and sat numb until she pounded the steering wheel with her fists. Then she took out her notebook and scribbled in it.

Her stepfather is abusing her. The mother knows.

CJ finished drying her hair. She'd had a long day but was happy she'd agreed to let Ben come over and bring her dinner. A low-key night at home was in order. She had an empty feeling in the pit of her stomach. *Am I hungry or nervous?*

At a little past six, she kissed Ben as he came through the door.

"Dinner has arrived," he announced with a smile.

"Smells delicious."

"Pizza with the works. Well, no onions."

She headed to the kitchen and grabbed two plates, silverware, and a roll of paper towels. "Perfect. You want a beer?"

"You having one?" he asked.

"Nope." She held up a tumbler. "Sweet tea."

"I'll have the same."

"Ben, you can drink in front of me."

"I know, but tea is fine, since we've converted you to a sweet tea drinker."

As the two of them sat on the couch eating, she couldn't put her finger on it, but their conversations were easy—back to how it was before she arrested him as the Lowcountry killer. It was a welcome change from the awkwardness they'd experienced at the time.

"Where's Jake tonight?" she asked.

"My dad has him. He loves to keep him, but I fear he's a worse influence than you."

"Hey!" she laughed. "Can I help it if the dog likes to sleep in my bed?"

Ben rolled his eyes.

She snuggled against him and he slipped his arm around her. They stared at the TV screen for several minutes before she turned to him. "Since Jake has a sleepover, do you think you'd like one too?"

He took his arm from around her and leaned forward, his elbows resting on his knees. "CJ, I need to tell you something … and it's not good."

She nibbled her bottom lip, and her body tightened. "Okay." She adjusted herself so she was facing him. "Go ahead."

"It's something about my past I should have told you long ago. You've been open with me and, for the most part, so have I, but there's one—"

"Ben, you're scaring me. Just tell me."

He exhaled, turned to her, and started spilling. When he was twenty and at The Citadel, he began dating a young woman, Kelly France, and after about a year, one night after dinner, she told him she was pregnant. They were exclusive, so he knew the child was his.

"It wasn't what either of us planned for as college students," he said as he wiped his eyes. "She had picked me up, and we were sitting in the parking lot on Friday night before one of my football games …"

"Go on, Ben," CJ said.

"I was stunned. For several minutes, I couldn't respond. We'd both said we loved each other, and we had talked about getting married after school, but I just sat there." Wetness crept down his cheeks. "Finally, I managed to respond, but in a way I'll never forget and am ashamed of to this day."

She shifted and waited. When he stayed silent, she asked, "What did you say?"

"I simply told her I needed some time to figure this out, got out of the car, and went inside." He sniffed. "I'm not sure why, but it was cruel, thoughtless, and selfish," he said, wiping his eyes. "I abandoned her when she needed me the most."

"What happened then?"

"I laid in bed awake all night … and realized she needed me, and so did our unborn child. I called her early in the morning, but her roommate said she wasn't there. I kept calling but got the same answer. I knew this was a lie, so I skipped playing in the game and went to her apartment that evening, and she wouldn't let me in."

He paused, rubbing his face. "I slept in my car in the parking lot, and she finally let me in the next morning. Unfortunately, she told me it was too late—she'd had an abortion the prior afternoon. Apparently, she'd planned it before she told me." His shoulders shook as he cried. "I never had the chance to give her the ring in my pocket or …"

"It sounds like she had decided—"

"I could have stopped it if I hadn't been such an insensitive jerk," he said. Ben managed to compose himself and studied CJ. "I understand if this ends whatever we can have, but I couldn't go any further in our relationship without telling you. So all I can do is ask you to forgive me for waiting this long."

She stood and went to the picture window. The night sky was crystal clear, the moon hung over the harbor, and stars twinkled. *So he's not perfect after all.* Without turning back to him, she asked, "Ben, why are you telling me this now after all we've talked about in the past year?"

"Because I love you."

She stood frozen as her heart raced.

"I'll go," he said, standing and heading for the door.

"Ben, wait." She turned and motioned him to join her back on the couch. "Look, I can't pretend to understand how you or the young woman felt, and you're right. Your initial response was well … fucked up." She took his hand. "I also don't think I'm in any position to judge you. Hell, my past isn't any fairy tale—I've used sex and alcohol to cope, and had an affair with a married man. But good and bad, my past has made me who I am today, and I've learned from all my mistakes." She pulled herself to her knees, leaned forward, and rested her forehead against his. "You've never judged me, and I won't you. So if the past stays in the past, let's leave it there. Is there anything else you need to tell me?"

"No," he whispered.

"Thank you for telling me." She stood and pulled him up. "It's 1:30 a.m. and time to go to bed. You can stay, but the same rules apply as before. No sex."

SEVENTEEN

Sunday, April 24
The French Quarter

"We found Ralston's vehicle," Officer Johnny Jones said on the end of the line.

CJ wiped the sleep from her eyes. "Where?"

"Over by the cruise ship terminal, parked in the lot right past the North Market and Concord intersection," he said. "I swapped a shift with a buddy who patrols the Quarter and found it on my rounds of the docks."

She checked the time—5:10 a.m. "I'll be there in fifteen minutes. Have you called the CSU?" She flipped on the bedside lamp, trapped her cell phone against her ear with her shoulder, and struggled to pull on her jeans.

"They're on their way. I haven't opened it up yet, but it's a charcoal Range Rover, and the plates match what the DMV gave us."

"Good. Let's have our forensics crew handle the search. Anyone around?"

"No. No one."

"I'm on my way."

Ben, now alert, sat up in bed and stared at her. "What's up?"

"Johnny found Ralston's vehicle. I gotta go."

He hopped out of bed and grabbed his clothes. "Give me a minute, and I'll go with you."

"No," she said. "Go back to bed."

"You sure? I'm happy to—"

"I'm positive." She gave him a peck on the cheek. "You decide where you're taking me for brunch."

He nodded and climbed back into bed.

She pulled on a navy-blue sweatshirt with *Charleston, South Carolina*, written in white lettering, pulled her hair into a ponytail, and added her Boston Red Sox baseball hat. She laced up her favorite boots, grabbed her credentials and Glock, and raced down the steps to her truck.

Crappy morning for an early morning wake-up call.

The pavement glistened from the overnight mist, and her headlights cut into the haze. The city was asleep, so she was the only vehicle on the road. Her destination was less than a mile from her apartment, and she pulled in beside Johnny's squad car in the cruise ship terminal faster than she'd thought.

Johnny was leaning against the hood of his car. "Good morning. Sorry to drag you out of bed at this hour."

"No problem," she said. "Damn. This is right under our nose."

He chuckled. "It's hard to imagine it took us this long to find it. We put the APB out last Saturday night."

She stared into the Range Rover using her Maglite. "You think it's been here the whole time?"

"I doubt it," he said. "Something tells me it hasn't, or we'd have found it sooner since this is part of the standard patrol route."

CJ turned as the CSU van approached. An unfamiliar CSI emerged as the mist turned to rain and she introduced herself. "We need to scour every inch of the interior for prints," she said. "Search for clues to the driver's identity."

"Yes, ma'am. We'll work outside in. I'm Dan, by the way." He signaled to his partner, and they began their work.

"How 'bout I fetch us some coffee?" Johnny asked. "It's gonna take these guys a while."

"Sure," she said as she locked her eyes on the CSI as he slid under the truck.

By seven, the forensics crew had finished. They'd collected several fingerprints and found a Rolex and wedding band in the locked glove box. Johnny held a navy-blue umbrella over her as she wrote notes, struggling to keep her notebook dry.

"Did you find a cell phone?" she asked the CSI.

"No," Dan said. "We found a tube of lipstick on the floor under the driver's seat though."

She squinted. "What color?"

He thumbed through the photos on his digital camera. "Ah … here we go. Maybelline Sensational Red. We bagged it and will examine it for prints or a DNA sample."

She nodded. "I can't imagine the lipstick is our vic's, but it may be his wife's."

He shrugged. "We'll let you know what we find. I'll email you the list of what we've collected."

She handed him her card with her email address and cell phone number.

Johnny called for a tow truck and told her he'd have the vehicle held in case forensics needed it for anything else.

"I'll tell his wife we found it," she said. "She can pick it up once we're sure we don't need it."

———

CJ hustled up her stairs, eager to escape the dampness and return to Ben. She laughed as she slid the key into the lock and opened the door. "Honey, I'm ho—"

Ben sat rigid on the couch beside the slender frame of Jolene. The girl was bent over, her face in her hands, whimpering.

"Uh—Jolene. Are you okay?" She rushed over and dropped to her knees in front of her. "Sweetie, look at me."

The girl shook her head without raising it.

She glanced at Ben. "How about you find us some breakfast? Sal's should be open. Grab some doughnuts and hot chocolate."

Without speaking, he got up and left.

"It's just you and me now," she whispered. "Tell me what's going on."

Jolene lifted her head, and CJ tried not to gasp at the bright-red mark on the girl's cheek. Her eyes were bloodshot and puffy; wetness dripped off her chin.

"I'm sorry I came here, but didn't know where else to go. I used Mom's computer to find the address on the card you gave me."

CJ moved beside her and wrapped her arms around her. "I'm glad you did." She stroked the back of her head. "Please tell me what happened."

In between sobs, the girl explained how her stepfather had hit her and forced her to do *things*. Once he left her room, she climbed out of her window and rode her bike to the only place she would be safe. CJ switched from being sick to her stomach to being mad as hell.

"I don't wanna talk about it anymore."

"That's okay," CJ said. "We can talk later. Everything's gonna be fine. Once you eat, I'll take you to get checked out."

The child sniffed and wiped at her nose. "Do I have to?"

"I'll stay with you; it'll make me feel better if a doctor examines you."

They sat in silence before the girl lifted her eyes. "Is Ben your boyfriend?"

CJ shifted and cleared her throat. "Uh—yes."

"He's nice. He let me in, sat with me until you got back, and never pushed me for any answers."

She smiled. "Yes, he is."

The girl flinched when someone knocked on the door. "Who's that?"

"Silly Ben ... he doesn't have a key." CJ stood and headed to the door. "Wait here, and I'll let him in with our breakfast." Without peeping, she turned the knob and was knocked backward when the stocky Floyd Mason rushed past her.

He raced to Jolene and snatched her up by her arm. "You little bitch! What lies are you telling now? Didn't think I'd find you? Next time, clear your search off the computer."

CJ lunged, hit him broadside, and they both flipped over the arm of the couch. The nearby lamp crashed against the wall and broken glass shot across the floor. Terrified, the girl raced to the kitchen and hid behind the island.

Mason flung out his elbow and caught CJ on the bridge of her nose. Stars swirled before her, but she countered with a fist to his jaw and drove her knee into his stomach, causing him to let out a satisfying groan. She tried to grab his arms, but he twisted from underneath and pinned her to the floor.

He leaned in close and spat, "You meddling sl—"

Ben burst through the door and landed a wicked punch to the side of his head, sending Mason hard to the floor. Within seconds, he had both arms locked behind the man's back, and CJ tightened the cuffs on his wrists. "Floyd Mason, you piece of shit! You're under arrest."

Ben yanked the smaller man to his feet, dragged him out the door onto the landing, and slammed him against the wall. "Stay still!"

Over a string of profanities, CJ called for backup. Within minutes, two uniformed officers arrived and read Mason his rights.

"Whatta we charge the perp with, Detective?" one of them asked.

"Sexual misconduct with a minor, rape, and assault, for starters." She grabbed her cell phone and snapped a selfie. "I'll send you this. Add assaulting an officer and destroying private property since he busted my damn lamp."

The older of the two officers grinned. "You got it. Let's go, asshole."

Ben stood next to her in the doorway. Jolene squeezed in between them and they wrapped their arms around her as they watched her stepfather disappear into the back of a squad car on his way to jail.

EIGHTEEN

Monday, April 25
Downtown Charleston

"Oh, shit! What the hell happened to you?"

CJ dropped into a chair across from Captain Stan Meyers's desk and touched her nose with the tip of her finger. "I ran into Floyd Mason's elbow." She handed him a document. "Here's my report. It's all in there."

He stared at her. "Is your nose broken?"

"No, sir. The ER doc said I'm all good."

"Other than the two black eyes," he said.

"Yeah. Well, there's that."

He picked up the report. "How 'bout you give me the headlines?"

She told him how she'd gone to the Mason home, how Jolene had shown up at her apartment Sunday morning, and what the girl said happened. Then, she added how Floyd Mason arrived and attacked the girl before they got into a struggle, and she and Ben arrested him.

He leaned back in his chair. "So, you and Investigator Parrish subdued him?"

"Yes, sir." *Please don't ask me why Ben was at my house at the crack of dawn.*

"Is the asshole still in jail?"

"Yes, sir, and I want to keep him there. His wife and stepdaughter are terrified of him. And he's dangerous."

He nodded. "I'll make some calls, and perhaps we can set bail high enough to make that happen. How's the girl?"

She shrugged. "She's hanging in there. Ben and I took her to the emergency room … had a rape kit done."

"And?"

Chewing her bottom lip, she said, "The bastard raped her. The evidence supports her claim."

He flipped through the pages of the report. "Is she back at home?"

She shook her head. "No, sir. Her mother wanted her, but she wouldn't go. Cathy Mason knew what was happening and didn't stop it."

"What about her real father?"

"He died six years ago in a construction accident."

His eyes narrowed. "Did you take the girl to Social Services?"

"No, sir."

"School?"

She shook her head. "No, sir."

Leaning forward, he asked, "Are you gonna tell me where she is, or will we keep playing twenty questions?"

She cleared her throat. "She's gone fishing … with Harry."

Captain Meyers stood, went to the window, and stared at the Lockwood Drive traffic. "CJ, the hardest part about working sex crimes is not getting too attached to the victims."

"I know, but I couldn't *make* her go home, could I? She wanted to stay with me, so I let her."

He exhaled. "How's your uncle involved?"

"He dropped in to see how I was doing, and they got along well," she said. "Harry's great at helping victims. He was telling her about fishing and before I knew it, he'd told her he'd take her when she asked if she could go. So, he picked her up at seven this morning."

He turned around and pointed his finger at her. "What's done is done, but the girl goes home or to Social Services."

"I know. I'll call them."

He glanced at the clock. "It's almost time for roll call. After that, you make sure you do."

She stood and turned to leave before he stopped her.

"Lieutenant?" His lips curled. "Excellent job solving the case."

During the roll call, CJ gave her share of the briefing on the Ralston case and was asked why she appeared to have seen a few rounds in the ring. Of course, her fellow officers razzed her, but she was earning their respect.

Once they adjourned, she, Sam, and her two newest reports headed to her office. She needed some private time with Jackson, so she sent Sam with Janet to help get her squared away in her new job. Once the door closed, they were alone at the conference room table.

Holding up a folder, she said, "I ran across a cold case that mirrors the latest poisoning. You were the detective in charge, so I want to hear your thoughts."

Jackson took the file and opened it. "Oh, yeah. I remember this one. I'd only been a detective for a short time, and this was one of my first cases."

"According to the notes, you believed an intruder poisoned Wilson."

"Uh-huh."

She tapped her fingers on the table, waiting for more, which didn't come. "So ... how did you conclude that?"

"Hmm ... I don't remember. I suppose it made sense at the time."

"Really? Someone broke into the room and forced poison down the vic's throat?"

He shrugged. "Maybe."

She flipped open her notebook and read the highlights from her file review. Nothing supported a random break-in of the room, or an intruder. Jackson sat and stared at her.

"I'm having a hard time wrapping my head around how you handled this," she said.

"Maybe so, but it's easy to be a Monday morning quarterback," he said. "I had little to go on and—"

"What did Ricardson say when you interviewed him?"

"Who?"

"Percy Winston Ricardson III, the owner of the Duncan House at the time. He's Simpson's attorney now."

Vincent squirmed and lowered his eyes. "He told me he thought someone broke into Wilson's room and forced him to drink poison."

"And you bought that bullshit?"

"As I said, it's easy to second-guess someone," he mumbled.

She sighed. "I'll tell you what. I'd like you to work with me to solve this case, but that would be a mistake. Detective Janet Wallace's fresh eyes make more sense."

He crossed his arms and gave her a stiff smile. "You're the boss. You can do whatever the hell you want."

She was silent and gave him a chance to fight for the assignment, but he didn't. CJ collected herself and decided to throw out some things she didn't believe. She wanted to scream, yet she needed to get work out of him. "Okay. You're a good detective." *A lie.* "But you're overloaded with cases." *Another lie.* "I'll ask Detective Wallace to help us with this one. Does that make sense?"

"Well … yes. I could solve it, but my huge workload is a problem." He closed his notebook and stood. "If that's all, I'll get to work."

She nodded, and he left. She walked to the window and stared out at a brilliant Charleston day. The Ashley River sparkled under a crystal-clear blue sky, and a light breeze kicked up whitecaps. Several boats left their tracks on the river's surface.

I wonder how the fishing's going.

She turned when the door rattled open. Sam and Janet entered the room—all smiles.

"Are you all set?" CJ asked.

Janet raised one shoulder. "Kinda. I completed my paperwork, but it'll take another day or two to get my gun and vehicle issued. The chief's gonna swear me in tomorrow." She moved to the table. "I'm ready to work. Tell me what you need, and I'll make it happen."

CJ smiled at her eagerness, a welcome contrast to what she'd experienced with Jackson. *One lazy detective is more than enough.* "Sounds good to me." She pointed to the two whiteboards. "Grab a chair, and I'll bring you up to speed on two cases we can work together."

Sam hustled to her desk and back to her research.

The two detectives reviewed their evidence until noon. Janet declined to go to lunch. "If it's okay with you, I'd rather keep going."

It was almost three o'clock when CJ's cell phone buzzed. "Hey, Eddie."

"We identified the prints in Ralston's vehicle, including the lipstick. They belong to Rebecca Jennings, whose nickname is Sunshine."

"Nickname?"

"Yep. She's a prostitute. Started out with high-end clients, got into drugs, and lowered her standards. We've arrested her several times, so we have her in the system."

"What's on her rap sheet?"

"Besides prostitution, a couple counts of petty theft and a case of assault. She got into a fistfight on Market Street with the wife of one of her johns. I'll email you my info, including her last known address."

"Thanks. I'll have her picked up and brought in for questioning. Is she capable of murder?"

"Hmm ... I don't know. Maybe."

CJ stared at an item on the board with an asterisk. "By the way, while I have you, I need a favor. We have a pair of men's boxers with a stain collected from a ten-year-old cold case. Can you examine them and determine if we can run DNA?"

"Sure. I'll send a tech over to pick them up. Have they been tested before?"

"No," she said. "Nothing in the file to show that."

"Who had the case?" he asked.

"Jackson."

He exhaled. "Figures. Someone will be there within the hour." He chuckled. "You work cold cases now?"

"I guess so. It may be linked to the Ralston case. I'm not sure yet."

CJ hung up and went to her computer. Eddie's email popped up, and she printed the attachment and asked Sam to dig up anything else in the records on Sunshine. Turning to Janet, she said, "Do you know where the Rainbow Apartments on Dorchester Road are?"

"Sure," she said. "That's a sketchy area."

"We have a person we need to pick up." CJ handed her the address.

"This is North Charleston's jurisdiction, but I can have her here within an hour." Janet picked up her cell phone. "Assuming, of course, they can find her."

CJ added a fourth name to her suspect list. She stepped back and frowned. *Here I go again, adding suspects and not subtracting.*

NINETEEN

Monday, April 25
North Charleston, South Carolina

Rebecca Jennings peeped between the crack in the dingy living room curtains at the patrol car that had pulled up in front of her apartment complex. Her breathing escalated when she saw two North Charleston police officers climb out of the vehicle. They stared at the numbers on the buildings, then one of them pointed in her direction.

"Oh, fuck," she whispered.

Frantically, she ran to her bedroom and hid in the closet. Her fingers fumbled with the cell phone before she could hit the speed dial. *Pick up, dammit!* Her heart raced and her face burned. She'd have to jump from the second-floor balcony if she went out the back. It wouldn't have been hard if her stupid neighbor hadn't put that wrought-iron fence around her patio with those spikey things. There was no way she could get arrested again—she'd be off to jail and die without her fixes. *I knew this was a bad idea. Money always has strings attached.*

A loud knock on her front door interrupted her concentration on the phone ringing. She made herself as tiny as possible, hoping they'd give up, go away, and leave her alone. She rocked back and forth.

"Rebecca Jennings! This is the North Charleston police. We need to speak to you."

Panic consumed her, and she bolted from her hiding spot, crashed through the sliding glass door screen, and jumped. Her landing was unforgiving.

A few miles south of where Sunshine's blood now dripped onto the gray pavement, icy hazel eyes stared at the screen until the red button was pressed to decline the call. After wiping the cell phone down, it was tossed in a dumpster behind MUSC.

———

Rebecca Jennings's one-bedroom apartment was a cracker box with water-stained ceilings, grimy windows, and a tattered brown shag carpet. The paper-thin walls provided a serenade of crying babies, loud TVs, and neighbors arguing. The stench of alcohol mixed with leftovers in containers strewn around the place was so intense one could taste it.

CJ walked to the balcony railing and stared at the blood-stained sheet covering the body of their person of interest, Rebecca Jennings. When the woman jumped, she hadn't cleared the neighbor's fence, impaling herself on the pointed fence posts, and bled to death before help arrived.

A North Charleston officer held up a cell phone. "Detective, we found this by the body. I assume it's hers."

"Can we tell who she last called?"

He shook his head. "I doubt it. I think it's a burner. I'll get it to the tech guys. Maybe they can tell us what number was last dialed. Don't be surprised if it's a black hole."

CJ turned when Janet called her name.

"Lieutenant, the CSIs still have work to do, but one told me he found a credit card. It was Charles Ralston's." Janet held up a photo she'd snapped on her cell phone.

"Let's track it and see if she used it," CJ said. "We find anything else?"

"They found what appears to be cocaine taped underneath a bathroom sink and crystal meth in her sock drawer." Janet thumbed through more photos to show her.

CJ motioned to the North Charleston detective; a forty-year-old man built like a bowling pin. His gray sport coat couldn't contain his belly.

"What can I do for you, Detective O'Hara?" he asked.

She smiled. "Would you be willing to share your report and findings with us? We've got a case in Charleston where that might be helpful."

He grinned at her. "Certainly. I told Janet we'd be happy to help you guys."

"Oh. Do you know Janet?" CJ asked.

"I sure do. She's a good one."

"We're excited she's joined us." CJ extended her hand to him and they shook. "We'll get out of your hair, but here's my card. I look forward to your report and to what you find."

"By the way, if you don't mind me asking, how'd you get the black eyes?"

"From an unruly child molester who preferred not to go quietly."

He raised his eyebrows. "You nail his ass?"

She nodded. "He's locked away, neat and tidy, and a judge said he'll make sure he stays that way."

———

A little after 7:00 p.m., CJ dropped Janet off at the LEC and headed home. She pulled in, parked by Harry's Jeep, and plodded up the stairs. Harry and Jolene were curled up on the couch, eating ice cream.

CJ smiled. "I hope that's not all you fed her, Uncle Harry."

"Oh, no. We had pizza and a salad. This is our dessert."

"How was fishing, Jolene?"

A faint smile crossed her lips. "It was so much fun. Uncle Harry showed me how to bait a hook. He said we'll go far out into the ocean next time."

Uh-oh. "I'm glad you had a nice time." She sat next to the girl. "Listen, I know you didn't want to return home yesterday when we talked. Is that still the case?"

"Yeah. I don't wanna do that. I'm mad at my mom, and … I'm not safe at my house."

CJ glanced up at a frowning Harry. "I understand how you feel, but—"

"I wanna stay here with you." She turned to Harry. "And you too."

CJ exhaled. "As much as we enjoy having you, that may not be possible. So, if you don't go home, I'm supposed to find you a place to …" She sniffed. "A place to live until we can find you a family."

Tears erupted from the girl as she scooted over against Harry. "Uncle Harry can keep me. He told me how he raised you, and I won't cause any trouble."

A sharp pain stabbed CJ in the heart as she stared into the girl's pleading brown eyes. "Honey, I … I don't think that's the same thing."

Jolene's face became desperate, and she twisted her eyes up to him. "Uncle Harry, don't you want me with you?"

He took her hand and squeezed. "Sweetheart, if possible, I would let you live with me." He put his arm around her. "How 'bout CJ and I find you a great place to live, and you can visit us?"

Her little head slowly bobbed as tears ran down her cheeks. "Can I at least stay here tonight?" she asked as her voice cracked.

"Sure," CJ said. "You can stay here tonight."

"Uncle Harry too?"

"Sure. He can stay too."

Two hours later, CJ tucked Jolene into the pallet she'd made on the floor next to her bed. She kissed the little girl's forehead and closed the door to the bedroom.

"She asleep?" Harry whispered.

"She should be soon. The day on the water exhausted her."

"She's a doll. How someone could abuse her, and her mother wouldn't protect her, is beyond me. I always despised these types of cases."

"Yeah, I know. It breaks my heart."

He took her hand. "So, what are you going to do?"

She sighed. "I have no choice. She has to go to Social Services. Even if she wanted to go home, I'm not sure the mother is fit to take care of her."

She filled him in on the day's activities before she headed to bed and he stretched out on the couch. She tossed and turned, trying to make sense of where things stood. New questions kept coming up.

How did Sunshine get Ralston's credit card?

Who were you trying to call, Sunshine?

The little girl on the floor stirred and whimpered. CJ froze and listened for several minutes, but all was quiet. *How can I be sure this sweet little girl finds a loving home?*

TWENTY

Tuesday, April 26
Downtown Charleston

CJ stood outside the doorway of Stan's office, waiting. It was eight thirty in the morning, so she knew he was around somewhere. Minutes later, he rounded the corner and headed straight toward her. She gave him a weak smile. "You have a minute, sir?" She swallowed hard. "I need to update you on the Mason case."

He motioned her into his office. "Sure. Come on in." He slipped into his chair while she remained standing. "You can sit if you'd like," he said.

"I'm good." She sniffed. "I wanted to let you know Jolene Mason was dropped off at Social Services this morning. I got a caseworker on the phone last night and set it up."

He nodded. "That's good … well, not good, but necessary. How'd the girl take it?"

She exhaled, fighting back her tears. "Okay, I guess. The poor thing bawled." *So did I.*

"That's to be expected. So, how are you handling it?"

"About the same. She wanted to stay with Harry or me."

"They had fun fishing, I guess," he said, smiling.

"Yes. You could say that. When I got home last night, I found them curled up on the couch eating ice cream." She hesitated. "I knew I shouldn't, but I let her stay with me one more night."

"I know these situations are hard. I've been attached more than once, but the sooner we find a suitable home for her, the better. It'll be more stable for her."

"I guess." She cleared her throat. "On the Ralston case, we found his vehicle and the woman who had it."

His eyes widened. "Really? What did she say?"

"Nothing. The woman jumped off her balcony and killed herself. We're unsure if it was intentional, but either way, she's dead."

She gave him a run-down of what they found in her apartment, informed him the North Charleston PD was cooperating, and excused herself. "I need to head over to meet with Percy Ricardson. I wanna ask him questions about the Wilkins poisoning at the Duncan House ten years ago."

CJ signed in with the guard in the Market Street building lobby that housed the Ricardson Law Offices. He told her to take the elevator to the third floor.

The metal box squeaked as it rose, and there was a faint odor of men's cologne. After a *ding*, the door slid open, and she faced a twenty-something-year-old woman with bright red hair behind the reception desk. She provided her name, and the shapely woman in an expensive gray skirt suit took her to a conference room.

The room reminded her of the Duncan House with gold carpet, a dark cherry twelve-seat table with black leather high-back chairs, and a speakerphone in the center. One wall was all glass, providing an impressive view down Market Street. A glass-top bar sat in the corner with bottles of high-dollar liquor.

Frustration mounted the longer she sat. Finally, after twenty minutes, Percy Ricardson opened the door and entered.

"Sorry to keep you waiting, but my call ran long." He took a seat across from her and folded his hands. "I only have a few minutes. What's on your mind?"

CJ cleared her throat. "First, didn't you think it might be pertinent to tell me you owned the Duncan House before Simpson?"

He shrugged. "Not important, and to be honest, none of your business. Next question."

She glared at him. "What can you tell me about the death of Thurmond Wilkins ten years ago?"

"He died," he said.

"He was poisoned with deadly nightshade," she said, "the same thing that killed Charles Ralston. Don't you think it might be important to my current case?"

"A mere coincidence, and it has nothing to do with you." He flipped the back of his hand. "As you said, it was ten years ago."

She pinched her lips together. "I can see we have differences in what we think is important. Maybe you can tell me why you suggested to Detective Jackson he note that an intruder poisoned Wilkins in his report?"

His nostrils flared, and redness crossed his face. "Be careful, Detective." He jabbed his finger at her. "Spreading lies will cost you." He jumped up. "We're done here."

"Last question. How long have you been a member of the Palmetto Men's Society?"

He froze, his hand on the doorknob, and without turning back declared, "I have no clue what the hell you're talking about." With that, he stormed down the hall.

She had no proof he was in the men's club, but she'd wanted to see how he reacted. *He's clearly hiding something.*

CJ returned to where she'd parked her truck and reviewed her notes. She hit the green circle on her phone when Eddie called. "What's up?"

"I've sent the stained boxers to Columbia. We can get a sample and run a DNA analysis, but it's best if one of our experts handles it. The better the extraction, the better the result."

She frowned. "That's great news, but the report will take several weeks or months. I know the lab—"

"The expert who has it told me he'd have an answer within a few days. He loves to help solve cold cases."

"Oh, wow! I'll owe him. I just left a shitty meeting with Ricardson. Do you have any more positive news?"

He laughed. "Well, as a matter of fact, I do. I expect to have the DNA results for the Ralston case within a week."

Her eyes bulged. "No shit?"

"Nope. I'll call you ASAP once I get the info. Let's keep our fingers crossed that whoever's DNA we find is in the system."

She added to her notebook and texted Sam and Janet before pulling out, *Headed back. Need to see you two.*

Her cell phone chimed in less than two minutes with the response, *We'll be ready.*

Percy closed the door to his office and stared out the window. The sky looked heavy—a storm was coming. He moved to his desk, picked up his phone, and punched in a number. A woman's voice answered.

"O'Hara's getting to be a royal pain in the ass," he said. "If the bitch keeps digging, she's gonna cause trouble."

The woman laughed. "Poor Percy. Can't you dissuade her?"

"She's determined. I'm not sure it'll be easy to knock her off course."

"Give her a pile of cash."

He shook his head. "She can't be bought."

"You've got people," she said. "Call one of them for help."

Percy exhaled. "It's not that easy. I have to—"

"Grow some balls! What's your damn problem? Your father never had these kinds of issues."

"He never dealt with someone like O'Hara," he growled.

"Boo-hoo. What's the problem with her?"

"She's damn smart, perceptive, and … she ain't from here."

"Why does not being from here matter?" she asked.

"She doesn't know how the game is played," he mumbled. "She goes right down the middle, making waves be damned."

"Well, you better figure something out. Shut her fucking ass down! I swear, men are worthless."

Percy listened to a dial tone as thunder rumbled in the distance.

TWENTY-ONE

Tuesday, April 26
Downtown Charleston

CJ opened the door to her office to find Janet and Sam at the conference table. She joined them and spun her chair around to the board for the Ralston case. She pointed to the names she'd listed on it.

"Sam, you told me you had made progress on the requested background information of these people, and I wanna go through it. I'd also like to add the same request for Percy Ricardson and Richie Pickett."

"The two attorneys?" Sam asked.

"Yes. Find out everything you can about them."

Janet spoke up. "Should we add Jennings to the research list?"

"Good catch," CJ said. "Yes, let's add her as well."

Sam nodded and jotted down the three new names.

Once she'd finished, CJ pointed to her. "The floor is yours."

The young woman cleared her throat. "Okay. I'm compiling a report for each person and adding information as I find it." She paused and bit her lip. "I'm not as far along as I'd hoped. It's taking me a lot of time … I'm sorry."

"No problem. Let's discuss what you have now and cover any new information as you find it."

Sam nodded and started with Charles Ralston. She noted when and where he was born, his parents, schools, business endeavors, and outside interests. The most noteworthy items were that he was born and raised in Charleston and came from money. He had built a successful real estate development business and participated in all the high society events.

"Charles married Ava eight years ago," she added.

"Wait," CJ said. "Sophie is ten."

"That's right. Charles isn't her father. Ava had her before she married him."

"Any connections to the Palmetto Men's Society?"

"No. Not that I could find so far. I'm still digging."

CJ nodded for her to continue.

"The biggest gap is who might be his business investors or partners. It isn't easy based on the way he sets his businesses up. So I've asked for help from a guy specializing in analyzing financial and business interests. I know Charles has a net worth of over thirty million dollars."

Janet whistled. "Holy smokes!"

"I assume Ava is his beneficiary?" CJ asked.

Sam nodded. "That's what it looks like."

CJ stood and added *$30M* to the Ralston board. "Continue, please."

"I haven't gotten as far along on Ava. She's thirty-five and was born in Beaufort. She studied nursing at the College of Charleston, but there isn't much information on her early days. There are lots of gaps in what I could find so far. I'll keep digging and—"

There was a knock at the door, and Janet jumped up and answered it.

Captain Meyers stuck his head in the room. "Sorry to bother you, ladies, but I'd like to see CJ for a minute."

CJ left the table and followed him outside the room. "What's up, Cap?"

"Umm … I'm not sure. I just got an interesting phone call."

Her brow furrowed. "From who? If it was Ricardson, I—"

"No. It was from Mayor Sellers."

"Oh." She exhaled. "She made it crystal clear on Friday she expected me to get the Ralston case solved."

Stan frowned. "That's the thing. She wasn't raising hell about our progress. I can't put my finger on it exactly."

"I'm not sure I understand."

"It was strange. The mayor didn't come right out and say it, but she alluded to the conclusion the North Charleston woman must have been the one who poisoned our vic."

CJ pinched her eyebrows together. "First, how does she know about that? Second, since when does the mayor investigate cases?"

He shook his head and chuckled. "The mayor's an interesting lady, that's for sure."

"So, what are you telling me? I should chalk the murder up to Rebecca Jennings and close the case?"

He raised his palms. "Hell, no. I'm not giving you any such direction. On the contrary, I fully support you in going where the evidence leads." He put his hand on her shoulder. "Nothing more, nothing less. I just wanted you to know about the call."

CJ watched him walk away. She returned to the room and asked Sam to continue.

"Like Charles, Larry Simpson was born and raised in Charleston," Sam said. "He earned a business degree from Charleston Southern and has had numerous management positions. After serving as the manager for ten years, he bought the Duncan House a little over two years ago."

"So he managed the place when Ricardson owned it?" CJ asked.

Sam nodded.

"Son of a bitch!" CJ rubbed her eyes. "Yet another unmentioned fact." She flipped through her notebook. "Where did he live while he managed the Duncan House?"

Sam scanned her sheets. "He had an apartment a few blocks away."

"Where did he get the money to buy the Duncan House?" Janet asked. "Did he come from money too?"

Sam shrugged. "I don't know where he got the money. But unlike Charles, he didn't come from money."

"Add that to your research list, please," CJ said. "I'm not sure what he paid, but it wasn't cheap."

They spent another thirty minutes discussing what they knew about the three people. It had become clear crucial things below the surface needed to be uncovered.

"Mary Beth," CJ muttered.

Sam squinted her eyes. "Excuse me. Who's she?"

"Maybe no one important. I met her at the Duncan House when I went to interview Simpson. She may know nothing, but it appeared she wanted to talk."

Janet spoke up. "You said she works up front. How 'bout I swing by and see if she's around? No one knows me there, and I'm in the market for a venue to hold my annual meeting." She grinned. "I may be able to get a brochure and a number where you can reach her."

CJ smiled. "That's a good idea." *I like this girl.*

Janet left for the Duncan House, leaving CJ staring at the notes she'd jotted down from Sam's briefing. She circled an item.

"Sam, didn't Johnny say he got a degree in criminal justice from Charleston Southern?" CJ asked.

"Yes," she said, "he did."

"Do it quietly, but find out where Jackson got his degree, if he has one."

"Easy peasy." Sam stood, went to her desk, and tapped on her computer keys. "Vincent Jackson has a degree in criminal justice from there. Does that mean anything?"

CJ shrugged. "I don't know. I'm sure lots of people in the department went there." *Does Jackson know Simpson?*

"Listen, Sam. I need to take care of something. I'll text Janet to call me if she finds out anything, and you can call me if needed."

"Sure. Let me know if you need my help. In the meantime, I'll go back to digging."

CJ turned onto Calhoun Street and parked in front of the Department of Social Services. She followed the signs to Child Well-Being and smiled at the heavyset middle-aged woman behind the glass. "Excuse me. I'm Detective CJ O'Hara, and I brought a young girl in this morning and wanted to check on her." She held up her badge.

The lady nodded. "What's the girl's name?"

"Jolene Mason."

She waited while the woman scanned her computer screen. "I can give you the caseworker's name, and she can help you."

"I have her name … I guess all I want to know is that Jolene is safe. You see, I, well … I—"

"According to the records, we placed the girl with a foster family earlier today." She winked. "I'm not supposed to divulge any details, but I can tell you, she's in wonderful hands."

CJ wiped her eyes. "Thank you. That's all I need to know. Her caseworker has my cell number, and I'm sure she'll reach out if there are any issues." She turned to leave.

"Detective," the woman called her back.

"Yes, ma'am."

"Funny thing. You're the second Detective O'Hara who's been here today to check on the girl. Well, the other gentleman told me he was a retired detective."

CJ smiled. "Thank you." She returned to her truck and punched the speed dial on her cell phone. "Uncle Harry, I'd like your opinion on something," she said when he answered.

"Shoot."

She cleared her throat. "I was thinking I might check into keeping Jolene. I can't explain it, but this little girl—"

"That's a big step, sweetheart, and not a good one. I know you two connected, but—"

"That's it? You just cut it off without even considering it or listening to what I have to say?"

"CJ, it's just—"

"Never mind. There's no need to say anything else. I'm just surprised you won't even listen after you took me in at her age. I'll talk to you later."

TWENTY-TWO

Tuesday, April 26
The Boroughs

Janet opened the dark cherry front door of the Duncan House and smiled at the young blonde-haired woman behind the front desk.

The young woman popped up from her seat. "Welcome to the Duncan House. Can I help you?"

"I hope so," Janet said. "I'm visiting Charleston and hoping to nail down a place to hold an executive team meeting."

The young woman strolled across the room and offered her hand. "Wonderful. I'm Cynthia, and I'll do my best to take care of you." She motioned to a two-seat walnut table by the fireplace. "How about we sit over here? And you are?"

"Oh, sorry. I'm Janet."

The two women moved to the table.

"I'm happy to see the place in person," Janet said. I spoke to a young woman on the phone. "Her name was—uh—Mary …"

"Mary Beth?"

She snapped her fingers. "Yes! She was quite helpful. I offered to come take a look."

"Yeah, she was great, but she no longer works here."

"Oh, no. I looked forward to meeting her in person. Did she find a new job?"

"No. She had to move out of town. The owner said she had a family emergency. I'm upset I didn't get to tell her goodbye." Cynthia sighed and opened a planner. "Okay, how many rooms will you need?"

Janet went through the exercise of counting on her fingers. "I think there will be eight of us in total. Assuming everyone on my team comes."

"Okay, we can certainly accommodate that many."

The incognito detective glanced around. "How many rooms do you have?"

Cynthia pointed toward the stairs on the opposite wall. "Our guests stay on the second and third floors. We have three rooms and a suite on each level." She beamed. "Your group will fit perfectly."

"That's great. I'd prefer to hold our meeting in a quaint spot, and hotels don't offer a homey feel." Janet rolled her eyes. "God knows we all stay in our share of bland locations." Her brow furrowed. "Do you have a room where we could hold our meetings?"

"Absolutely. What others have done in the past is use our dining room. We would serve breakfast, clear the tables, and arrange it to fit your needs."

Janet rubbed her chin. "I suppose that would work."

Cynthia jotted notes. "How many days are you planning for the meeting?"

"Two days. We'd need to stay three nights due to travel."

The young woman scribbled more notes. "The critical item is when do you want to hold the meeting? Since you'd take over the place, availability will be key."

"Well, we can be flexible. I'm aiming at late summer, early fall."

"Hmm … that's our busiest time." She started flipping through the calendar.

"Let me do this," Janet said. "I'll talk to my folks and give you some potential dates. Then you can let us know what works."

"Or, if you give me your email, I could send you some open dates, if that would help?"

"It's better if I sort it out on my end," she said. "Do you have a brochure and card with your email?"

"Yes. Hang on." The young woman went to her desk and returned with a folder. "Here's information on us and an email where you can reach me. I included our rate sheet, but for a larger group, we may be able to provide a discount."

"This is perfect." Janet stood, shook Cynthia's hand, and turned for the door. She stopped and turned back. "By the way, we should have only eight, but if we had nine, would you be able to handle us?"

Cynthia's face twisted. "I'd need to check with the manager. He's also the owner. We do have one more room. We converted our Carriage House into a suite, but he holds that for some of our frequent guests. Often, they show up at the last minute." She turned. "Let me get him."

"Oh, no. Don't do that." Janet held up a palm. "It's premature, and eight rooms should do it. We can always talk about it if we need the extra room."

Cynthia nodded. "Okay. Sounds like a plan. I look forward to your email with potential dates. Oh, wait!" Her hand went to her mouth. "Silly me. I forgot to ask you the name of your group."

"No problem. You can put down the Janet Wilson Group." She stood while the young woman made one last note.

"Got it. Thanks for coming by, and we'll talk soon."

Janet climbed back into her Toyota Camry, her personal vehicle. It was less suspicious than the department-issued truck she'd have the next day. She pulled out and found a spot across from the museum to call CJ. She told her what she'd discovered, and she hadn't gotten a number to reach Mary Beth.

"Interesting that she suddenly moved away," CJ said.

"I thought about asking for a phone number to reach her, but that might have raised too many eyebrows."

"No. You did well. I'll see if Sam can find her."

"What do you need me to work on next?" Janet asked.

"We can regroup tomorrow morning and sort it out. It's late, but you can check on the North Charleston PD's investigation status."

"I'm on it. I'll call you back if I get anything significant."

Scarlett sat at a round wrought-iron table and opened the container of food she'd bought for an early dinner—a mixed green salad with baked chicken. She always enjoyed sitting outside under the shadows of the massive Magnolia trees, a break from the stale, antiseptic air of the hospital. She forced her worries out of her mind.

I'm sure everything's fine.

As she chewed, her eyes focused on a young girl, maybe eight, who took a spot across from her with her mother. The two of them chatted as they consumed their meal. Scarlett couldn't hear what they said and wondered if their conversation was like those she'd had when she was that age. Her hazel eyes squeezed shut.

The first thing to remember is men are worthless. You can only count on them for two things—riches and breeding. So you must learn how to control them.

Scarlett opened her eyes and shoved another bite into her mouth. The mother and child laughed and kept talking as she continued to replay the past in her mind.

To gain control, use your body. Make men want you so badly they'll do anything you want. Learn how to flirt, charm, and tease them, when to withhold what they desire, and when to let them have it. Always make them want more, but be careful. Men don't hear "no" and only think with their dicks.

But some men are nice, and I—

Don't be a fool! Men are pieces of shit. They only wanna get in your pants.

How do I learn what to do?

I'll teach you how ... and how to discard a man when you're through with him.

TWENTY-THREE

Wednesday, April 27
Downtown Charleston

CJ was up, dressed, and out the door before the rooster crowed. Traffic was sparse, and she made it to the LEC in less than fifteen minutes. She wanted Sal's to be open, but it was five thirty in the morning—too early even for her Italian workaholic friend. She waved without stopping as she passed a handful of officers loitering around the coffee pot.

Unlocking the door to the conference room, she turned on the overhead lights, listening to the hum of the bulbs. The row of fluorescents above the table refused to wake up, so she dragged the work surface against the wall where there was light. A chill went down her spine.

This room gives me the creeps when I'm alone.

There were three items on her agenda for the day. First, where had Ava Ralston gone on the Friday evening her husband was at the Duncan House? The woman had clearly lied to her about being home with her daughter.

Second, she needed to talk to Thomas again about the autopsies of the two victims. Understanding more about how deadly nightshade worked was essential to the timelines of the crimes. So she texted him, asking him to call her when he got to his office.

Shit! It's only six o'clock in the morning.

Third, she wanted Janet's update on the status of the North Charleston case and anything else from her Duncan House visit. She decided she and Janet might need to take another drive north. She needed to know sooner rather than later if Jennings was a legit suspect, especially after the mayor's call to her captain.

Maybe I should have been more forceful about how the investigation was conducted.

It was a few minutes after seven when Sam entered the room. She smiled and held up a Tupperware container. "Good morning. I brought homemade cinnamon rolls. Have you eaten?"

"Uh—not yet," CJ said. "Sal's wasn't open when I came in."

Sam frowned. "You need to eat. You can't lose yourself in a case. It's important that—"

"I'm fine." She stood, approached the younger woman, and took the container. "Here, give me one of those." She returned to her chair, held up a roll, and gobbled a bite. "Yummy."

"That's right." Sam rolled her eyes. "Make a show of it. I swear I have to watch you." She set her bag on the desk. "Why's the table over there?"

CJ continued chewing as she pointed a sticky finger upward.

Sam grunted, went to her desk, grabbed her phone, and called maintenance. "They'll come up shortly and we'll be back bright as day."

"Have we heard from your guy who was researching the cameras?" CJ asked.

"I'm supposed to call him at eight. He told me he expected to find Ava's car on one of the bridge cameras if she entered the city. Did you give any more thought to going back and talking to the gardener?"

"I can," CJ said. "I won't be surprised if I have to get a subpoena." She took another bite and added, "I'm certain Ava's attorney will simply say he's wrong."

"He said, she said."

"Exactly. A video would be much more effective." CJ glanced at the clock. "What time is Janet coming in?"

"She told me it'd be after nine. She's meeting with the detective working the North Charleston case so she has a new update for you." Sam's eyes scanned her email. "I expect to get some information on the Palmetto Men's Society. I have a friend who's helping me dig." She huffed and reported, "There's nothing in yet." She stood, went to the corner, and began making coffee.

"Who is this friend?"

Sam froze and then cleared her throat. "It's better I don't say. They asked me to keep their name out of it."

CJ's eyes narrowed. "Why?"

"I think it's because the society can be trouble if you cross them." She returned to her desk. "I'm calling about the cameras."

Ten minutes later, Sam hung up her call and joined CJ at the table. She told her Ava Ralston's jet-black BMW 335i had crossed the Arthur Ravenel Jr. Bridge into Charleston at 6:05 p.m. on Friday night, April 15. Her contact told her he'd send the video, but the license plate was hers, and you could see her face.

So she did lie to me, CJ thought.

"Interesting thing. A young girl was with her."

Her head snapped up. "Sophie was in the car?"

"That's what he said. Well, a young girl was with her. You'll have to see if it's her daughter."

"That probably rules her out as a suspect." CJ pursed her lips. "She wouldn't take her daughter to poison her husband." She stared at the board, at the names of her suspects, and sighed.

"Why would she lie?" Sam asked.

"No clue," CJ replied. "It seems stupid to do that. All she had to do was tell me where she and her daughter went." Her eyes dropped to her cell phone when it buzzed. *Thomas.* She answered immediately, and said, "Sorry I texted you so early. I'd already hit send when I realized what time it was."

"No problem," he said. "I get up at five every day and take my golden retriever for a walk. How can I help you?"

"I'd like to swing by and discuss how deadly nightshade works. Are you available?"

"Sure. I've got to finish an autopsy on a man found dead by the Cooper River County Park, but I should be free by ten."

"Murdered?" she asked.

"No. Looks like a self-inflicted drug overdose."

"Okay. I'll see you soon." She hung up and stared at the photo Sam handed her. It showed Ava Ralston and her daughter entering Charleston.

Janet called as CJ was parking in the Ashley-Rutledge Garage at MUSC. She said the North Charleston PD expected the DNA results for Rebecca Jennings early next week. They'd also recovered Ralston's wallet and cell phone from the bottom drawer in her bedroom closet.

"Did they find any towels from the bathroom?" CJ asked.

"No. Only the personal effects."

"Anything else of note?"

"No. The only fingerprints they lifted were Rebecca's. As expected, the woman's last phone call was to a burner, so we can't trace it."

"Thanks for the update. I'm walking in to see Thomas and get more information on deadly nightshade."

"Sounds good. I'll see you back at the LEC. I'm gonna see if Sam can help us track down Mary Beth."

CJ hung up and pushed through the Medical and Forensic Autopsy Section door. The tech she'd seen last time sent her back to the conference room to meet Thomas, who smiled when she entered.

"Perfect timing. I've finished my autopsy and pulled some details together for you." He motioned to a chair. "Have a seat."

She slid into a chair and glanced at the screen with a picture of a bush with purple, bell-shaped flowers and round, blackish berries. She pointed at the plant. "Is that Atropa belladonna?"

"That's it," he said. "It's a pretty plant, but extremely dangerous." He clicked on a second photo. "Here is what it looks like before the berries ripen. It's essentially all green."

"The berries are shiny when they're ripe."

He nodded. "They also have a sweet taste."

"What parts are poisonous?"

"All of it. The roots are the most toxic, but consuming the leaves or berries can kill a person."

"How would you poison someone?"

"Someone could make tea from the roots or crush the berries and use their juice." Then, rubbing his chin, he said, "I suppose you could chop up the leaves and add them to a salad."

She frowned. "Can you ascertain how the victims in our two cases consumed it?"

He tilted his head. "Well … maybe the roots were cut up, made into a tea, and added to the wine. But the berries could have been used, so I'm only guessing. They don't get ripe until the fall, but the green berries are more toxic." He sighed. "Either way, the result would be fatal because of the atropine and solanine."

She scribbled some notes. "Where do you think the killer found it?"

"That's a tough one. It's not native to the US. They grow it in parts of the Northeast and Pacific Northwest for medicinal purposes. Maybe they bought it somehow."

"How easy is it to grow?"

"You grow it using the seeds from the ripened berries, assuming you are careful. The bush typically grows to three or four feet tall but can get taller."

She added a note: *Where did the nightshade come from?* "I'll see if Sam has any luck finding out if someone bought it and had it shipped here." She scanned her notes. "You told me before that death would be fast, but not painless. Can you give me more details?"

He explained that within a few hours of ingesting the poison, a person would most likely experience symptoms such as a dry mouth, blurred vision, stomach pain, increased heart rate, slowed breathing, elevated temperature, hallucinations, and vomiting. Death would occur once the heart stopped, but it might take a few hours.

"Oh, shit!"

He nodded. "That's why I told you no one would use this to commit suicide. Of course, it could have been accidental, but where would our victims encounter it, and if so, why would they eat the unripened berries?"

CJ jotted down a few more items, and before she left, Thomas gave her photocopies of the deadly nightshade photos. She folded the sheets and slipped them into her notebook.

TWENTY-FOUR

Wednesday, April 27
Downtown Charleston

It was nearing noon when CJ returned to the conference room. Sam sat tapping on her computer keys while Janet stood beside her. Both gazed at the screen.

"Any luck running down Mary Beth?" CJ asked.

"We found her last name and address from an employment record," Janet said. "Now we need to find out where she moved. We found her emergency contact, so we can try that."

"Great. I'm unsure if she'll be any help, but I would like to talk to her," CJ said.

They spent the next hour reviewing what Thomas had provided, and Sam searched for possible places to purchase deadly nightshade. At one thirty, CJ called the number for Mary Beth's emergency contact. No one answered.

"I'm surprised I didn't get a recording to leave a message," she said. "I'll try again tonight. Maybe she's at work." She stood and picked up her notebook. "I'm going to revisit Ava Ralston and find out why she lied to me."

"Wow. I can't believe she agreed to meet you," Janet said. "I figured she'd only let you talk to her attorney from now on."

"Well, I told her I had her husband's personal items." CJ winked.

"Sneaky." Janet chuckled. "I love it."

"How 'bout you ride along?"

"I wouldn't miss it."

"CJ, do you have a couple of minutes before you go?" Sam asked.

"Sure," she said, and went to the younger woman's desk. "What do you need?"

Sam held up an eight-by-ten yellow envelope. "I just got this. There's something interesting inside."

CJ peered in, pulled out a sheet of paper, and scanned the black-and-white image. It was a copy of a photograph of three impeccably dressed men standing together—all smiles. Her brow furrowed. "What is this?"

"Check out the bottom," Sam said.

CJ's eyes locked on the bold note.

Palmetto Men's Society Annual Meeting–1976

"Oh, shit!"

"Yep. It has better information on the back," Sam added.

CJ flipped the sheet over. Three handwritten names were scrawled at the bottom.

Ralph Randolph

Percy Winston Ricardson Jr.

Eugene Gibbs

"Is this what I think it is?" CJ asked.

"Yep. Three members of the Palmetto Men's Society."

"How did you … never mind, not important."

Sam turned her computer monitor and CJ leaned down. "*Your* Ricardson is the son of the one listed. He died fifteen years ago, and it appears that's when his son inherited the Duncan House. Gibbs supposedly died of a heart attack a year after this photo was taken."

"And how about Randolph?" CJ asked.

"He's alive," Sam said. "He lives in the South of Broad. And the best part—he's willing to speak to you."

Her eyes went wide. "Do you think he'll tell me about this society?"

"He will. He left it years ago. His only condition is he will only meet with you, no recordings or note-taking, and you never mention his name to anyone."

"How do I reach him?"

"You don't. He'll give my friend a date, time, and place, and you show up."

"Jesus. This guy is rattled."

Sam nodded. "He doesn't want anyone in the society to find out he talked to you."

CJ pulled into the driveway of the Ralston home and made her way through the immaculate landscaping. She scanned everywhere, but there was no sign of Reggie. "I hope the witch didn't fire him," she mumbled.

"Fire who?" Janet asked.

"Oh, sorry. I was saying I hoped the lady of the manor didn't fire her full-time landscaper, Reggie. He's a wonderful guy, but she was unhappy he talked to me last time I was here."

Janet pointed to a young girl on the same rope swing CJ had seen her on before. "Is she the daughter?"

"Yes. That's Sophie."

CJ waved to the girl, but once again, she got no acknowledgment.

"She's not friendly," Janet said.

"Who knows what her mother said about me?" CJ put the truck into park. "I'm not sure how to explain it, but the little thing gives me a bad vibe."

The two women climbed out of the truck and went to the front door. Ava Ralston opened it as they approached and motioned for them to enter. She wore a yellow dress with brightly colored flowers—and an overabundance of makeup. Her dangling earrings reminded CJ of one of Harry's fishing lures.

"Come in. We can meet in the den," Ava said.

The two detectives took seats in black leather chairs while Ava dropped onto the sofa across from them.

CJ pointed to her companion. "This is Detective Janet Wilson. We work together."

Ava nodded. "It's nice the Charleston PD is hiring more women. But I have to say, I'm surprised."

"Why's that?" CJ asked.

She shrugged. "No reason. Do you have Charlie's belongings?"

Janet stood and offered her an envelope. "It's in there. His credit card is in a plastic bag. We found it separately and had to fingerprint it."

Ava tossed the package on the sofa beside her. "I guess that bitch Jennings got what she deserved for stealing my husband's things. She must have entered the room after he died from his heart attack."

CJ's jaw hurt from her clenched teeth and she fought to calm herself before responding. "We won't find out until next week if she was in the room."

Ava's eyes blinked rapidly. "How's that?"

"We were able to collect samples and expect to have DNA," she said. "Hopefully, it'll help us solve who killed your husband."

The woman flinched and narrowed her eyes, but stayed silent.

"I guess we've done what we came to do." CJ stood. "Oh. I have one more thing." She pulled the photo from her notebook and held it up before Ava's glaring eyes. "Why did you lie to me about being home on the Friday night your husband was at the Duncan House?"

Ava smirked. "Did I say that? I guess in my state of horrific grief, I got confused."

Liar. "So, where did you go?"

"I'm not sure I remember." She held her palms up. "Perhaps my daughter and I were just taking a drive." She popped up from the sofa and started toward the door. "If I remember, I'll be sure to call you. But if you ladies wouldn't mind, I need to go lie down."

CJ and Janet exited, walked past the brightly colored shrubs and flowers, and climbed into the truck.

"Jeez. That woman's a piece of work," Janet said.

"Yeah. She's clinging to her story and telling everyone poor ole Charles had a heart attack."

Janet giggled. "I loved her reactions to the news of the DNA and the photo. Do you think she had anything to do with her husband's death?"

"Well … I'm not certain, but she's keeping something to herself." CJ blew out a long breath and said, "She remains on our list." Then she stretched her arms and asked, "You wanna grab an early bite? After all, we missed lunch."

"Absolutely. It's your call where we go."

"I have just the place," CJ said, smiling.

CHAPTER

TWENTY-FIVE

Wednesday, April 27
Downtown Charleston

Thirty minutes later, CJ was pulling into a parking spot in the lot behind the downtown Charleston restaurant she wanted to go to. Taking the sidewalk on Anson Street, they rounded the corner and entered Henry's on the Market, a Charleston dining establishment with a long history. CJ suggested they go up to the roof.

They were lucky and found a two-seater table with a nice view across the city along the black wrought-iron railing.

Janet stretched her arms, and her cocoa-brown eyes danced. "I think I may love this place. I've heard of it but never been here."

"This was one of the first places I came to when I moved here a year ago," CJ said. "I'm not sure you've met him yet, but Ben Parrish brought me here and talked me into eating gator bites."

"Ooh, those are delicious. We should order some."

"Fine by me. My all-time favorite here in Charleston is the hushpuppies. I'm not sure they're on the rooftop menu, but maybe they'll sneak us some from downstairs."

A skinny young man with curly black hair approached. "How can I help you, ladies?"

"Can we order gator bites and a double order of hushpuppies, please? I'll take sweet tea to drink." She pointed to Janet. "You're welcome to have a drink."

"Uh … let me have a Palmetto Amber Ale to support our local brewers."

The young man jotted down their order and winked at CJ. "I'll need to grab the food from the downstairs menu, but I can do that."

For the next two hours, they chatted as they ate. They shared their backgrounds and got to know each other. Both learned they were single and had never married.

"Our jobs make it difficult to have a relationship," Janet said. "I've been seeing someone, and so far, he understands the chaotic nature of my job. How 'bout you?"

There was a tingle in CJ's chest. "Well … I'm in the same boat. So far, so good."

"Do you have a large family?"

CJ grimaced. "Uh—no. It's basically my two uncles and me. I lost my parents and older sister to a drunk driver twenty-two years ago."

"I'm so sorry." Janet stared down at her beer.

"It's okay. It was awful at first, but I'm doing fine now." *A lie.*

They sat silent for several minutes before their conversation turned to work.

"So the captain wants us to pursue the Wilkins case?" Janet asked. "Don't we have detectives to cover cold cases?"

"We do, but since this may be tied to our latest poisoning, Cap wants us to work on them both."

"Since Detective Jackson had the case originally, do you think he'd be helpful?"

CJ exhaled. "He could be, but I want fresh eyes on it. Besides, he's got a heavy workload now." *Another lie.*

Janet nodded. "Suits me. It gives me a chance to work with you." She leaned in closer. "I wasn't bullshitting you when we met. It's an honor to work with you. Your capture of the most notorious serial killer in South Carolina history, and the guy the press called the Heart Thief, were amazing."

CJ's face went pink. "Thank you. Lots of people were involved. It wasn't just me." She smiled. "By the way, I hadn't heard Elias Lewis referred to as the Heart Thief. I thought he was the Hoodoo Man. Where do people come up with these names?"

"Hell, if I know." Janet chuckled. "The press can be assholes."

CJ picked up the check. "Wanna head out? I'll take you back to pick up your truck."

Janet nodded. "Ready when you are."

CJ paid the tab and dropped Janet off at the LEC. She returned Janet's wave from the top of the stairs. *She's a keeper. I guess one out of two reports ain't bad.*

———

It was 7:10 p.m. when CJ unlocked her apartment door. She dropped her keys on the counter and stood at the picture window staring at the dim evening sky—a few stray black clouds floated over the harbor. Then she grabbed her notebook and cell phone, slipped onto the couch, and punched in a number. After five rings, a quiet voice answered at the end of the line.

"Hello?"

"Yes. Hello. Is Mary Beth at home?" CJ asked.

"Uh ... can I ask who's calling?"

"This is Detective CJ O'Hara from Charleston. I met her a few days ago and wanted to talk to her."

There was a muffled noise, as if the person had put their hand over the phone. A mysterious voice was heard in the background.

"Uh ... Mary Beth isn't here right now, and I'm not sure when she'll be back."

"Listen, I need to talk to her," she said. "Are you sure she's not available?"

Voices were muffled, then another person spoke.

"Hello, Detective. This is Mary Beth."

"It's wonderful to speak to you again. I hope you're doing well."

"I'm fine."

"I understand you moved and left the Duncan House. That's too bad. I was hoping to see you again."

"Yeah, I needed to be with my family."

CJ paused, waiting for her to expand—all she got was stone silence. "Look, Mary Beth. You wanted to tell me something before your former boss shut you down. You mentioned Charles Ralston."

The young woman only commented that what happened to him was terrible.

CJ cleared her throat. "I believe there's more to the story. It's okay if you tell me."

The young woman sniffed. "I have nothing else to say."

"I don't believe you." CJ lowered her voice. "Please tell me."

"I can't." Her voice was shaky, and her crying grew louder.

"Please. I don't have to tell anyone we spoke. I need your help, and you'll feel better if you get this off your chest."

"Okay," Mary Beth whispered. "But you can't let them find out, or they'll kill me."

CJ listened for ten minutes as the young woman spilled her secrets. She had been so excited when she took the job at the Duncan House. The owner treated her well, and she loved meeting all the new guests. However, her life changed when it was "demanded" she provide special treatment to a guest in the Carriage House suite. She initially refused and threatened to quit, but she feared for her little girl, so she agreed.

"Does *special treatment* mean what I think it does?"

"I had to have … sex." Mary Beth's voice caught.

"Who threatened you?"

"I'm not gonna say, but they gave me no choice."

CJ tried to convince the young woman to give up the name, but she stood steadfast. "What happened next?" CJ asked.

"Fortunately, it wasn't a routine thing. Most of the time, I did my shift and went home. I only had one person I had to meet unless …"

"Unless, what?"

"If someone else wasn't available, I'd have to fill in."

Heat flushed through CJ, and her heart pounded. *Son of a bitch.* She struggled to control her breathing and asked, "Then what happened?"

"After you came by and the owner saw us talking, they forced me to quit and leave town."

"Who are they?"

Again, Mary Beth refused to give her a name. Finally, she would only tell her they gave her a bonus, and she and her daughter left town.

"I'm sorry this happened to you. I will find whoever did this to you and make them pay."

Mary Beth burst into tears again and begged her not to tell anyone they'd spoken. If it got back to *them*, she'd pay.

CJ promised she wouldn't tell anyone about their conversation, and the call ended. She stood and returned to the window—the sky had turned pitch-black. *I have to figure out how to keep my promise.*

TWENTY-SIX

Thursday, April 28
Downtown Charleston

CJ turned left on Duncan Street and pulled into a parking space in front of the Duncan House. She hadn't made an appointment with Larry Simpson, but hoped he'd meet with her without his attorney. As she stared at the front door, an older couple meandered down the steps. She waited until they passed her before she hopped out and headed to the entrance.

Okay, CJ … be charming.

The lobby was empty when she entered, so she called out, and within seconds, a young blonde-haired woman appeared from a side door. Her pale blue eyes dropped to the gold badge on CJ's hip.

"May I help you?"

"I'd like to talk with Mr. Simpson, please."

The younger woman eyed her cautiously. "Can I let Mr. Simpson know who's asking for him?"

She added as much enthusiasm as she could muster to her smile. "I'm Detective CJ O'Hara."

"Wait here." The woman turned and pushed through the door behind the desk.

I wonder if she provides special treatment to the VIPs.

As she killed time, CJ wandered over and stared at the pictures on the wall. Each was a scene from downtown Charleston—City Hall, Circular Church, Calhoun Monument, Huguenot Church, and the Pineapple Fountain. The largest painting was of Fort Sumter, which sat in the Charleston harbor.

"He's not available."

She turned, and the young woman stood scrutinizing her—her decorated red lips pursed. She offered a stiff smile. "You'll have to come back."

"It's unfortunate he can't meet with me." She sighed. "I suppose I could obtain a warrant, but I was hoping—"

"What do you want now?" Both women turned to the glaring Larry Simpson standing in the doorway. "I've already said I won't meet with you without my attorney, yet here you are unannounced," he snarled.

"I'm sorry to bother you," she said. "I had a few questions, and you've been helpful before." CJ smiled. "I'm only trying to do my job."

He squinted and huffed. "You mean trying to pin a murder on me?" His eyes cut to the young woman. "Hold my calls."

CJ raised her eyebrows when he motioned her through the door. "I'll give you a few minutes, and I reserve the right to call my attorney."

"Understood." She followed him to his office. Once they got to his office, he pointed at a leather chair across from his desk. "Sit there." Simpson plopped into the brown leather high-back chair behind his desk and blew out a long breath—his lips made a puttering sound. "Ask your damn questions."

"Before I do that, I'd like to apologize."

His eyebrows squished together. "Uh ... for what?" She shrugged a shoulder. "We got off on the wrong foot the night Mr. Ralston's body was found, and I could have handled myself better when we talked. I'm sorry."

He tugged at an ear with a slack expression. "Well, I guess I should have done better too. But as you might expect, finding a dead man in one of my rooms was quite a shock."

CJ smiled. "How 'bout we start over?"
"Okay." He slowly nodded, his eyes wary. "That sounds fine to me."

She pointed to a painting of a Civil War battlefield behind him. "That's an interesting scene. It's so realistic."

He twisted around. "Yeah. That's one of my favorites."
"Did the same person paint that one and those in the lobby?"

"I'm not sure," he said. "They're all signed, but honestly, I've never checked."

"Well, I should see what questions I have so I can get out of your hair, as I'm sure you're busy."

She continued with her general questions and chitchat approach as his features relaxed. They talked about the history of the Duncan House, his background, and how Charleston had changed over the years. He proudly told her several things she already knew—he was born and raised here and got a business degree from Charleston Southern.

"Your turn. Tell me about you."

For the next ten minutes, CJ rambled on about herself—growing up in Boston, her time in law enforcement, and her move to Charleston.

"Do you like it here?" he asked.

"I do. It reminds me of Boston with all the history and water, but it's much smaller and more friendly."

He leaned forward, putting his elbows on the desk. "Ever been married?"

Okay. Guess we're gonna be personal. "No." She shook her head. "I haven't found the right guy yet."

"I find that hard to believe." He winked. "An exquisite woman like yourself surely has lots of men pounding on your door."

Is this asshole hitting on me? She chuckled. "Not as many as one might think."

As he leered at her, she shifted her gaze to her lap and notebook, opened it, and returned her attention to him.

"Let me ask what few questions I have left, and I'll be on my way."

She patiently asked him what she wanted, and surprisingly, he answered without asking for his attorney. He told her he worked at Charleston Southern for almost five years and never hesitated to give her the years. She wrote *at a business function* when she asked where he met Percy Ricardson.

"How did you wind up purchasing the Duncan House?"

"It was a tremendous business opportunity, so I took out a loan and bought it."

She tapped her pen on her notebook. "I think that's about all I have. Oh, wait! There's one more thing. Who called it in when Thurmond Wilkins died here ten years ago?"

He squinted. "I'm not sure we need to discuss that incident."

CJ leaned forward and touched his hand. "Come on, help me out. My boss asked me, and I couldn't answer him." Her eyes locked on his. "Pleeeease."

"I guess it would be okay." He cleared his throat. "Percy called it in, but he and I were both here."

"Was anyone with Mr. Wilkins?"

"Uh … not that I remember," he stammered.

She patted his hand and winked at him. "See how easy that was?"

He beamed. "It wasn't too bad."

She jumped up from her chair and turned to go. "Thanks again. I can show myself out."

There was no way to confirm it, but she swore his eyes burned a hole in her butt as she left. She smiled and waved as she passed the young woman in the lobby. She went to her truck, climbed in, and rubbed her eyes. Her skin crawled as she reflected on Simpson's leering gaze. "He makes me wanna puke," she mumbled. She took a couple of deep, satisfying breaths and congratulated herself on controlling the urge to slap him for Mary Beth.

Before starting her truck, she opened her notebook and added asterisks to the items she needed to check.

———

Cynthia peered out the window and watched CJ leave. She pushed open the door and knocked on the doorframe. Simpson glanced up from the papers he was reviewing. She smiled. "I'm gonna take a quick break."

Once she was safely out of earshot, she punched a number into her cell phone. A man's voice answered. "What's going on?"

"I wanted you to know the detective was here again."

"O'Hara, or the other one you didn't know was a detective?"

She flinched. "O'Hara. She talked with Larry in his office for several minutes, and the door was closed, so I couldn't hear them."

"That dumbass! I told him more than once to keep his damn mouth shut."

"Uh ... that's all I had."

"Thanks for letting me know. I'll deal with Larry." He paused. "You'll meet me at nine, right?"

"I'll be there," she said.

"I'll be ready. Cynthia, one more thing."

"Yes?"

"Wear the red lace tonight. And be there on time."

TWENTY-SEVEN

Thursday, April 28
Downtown Charleston

Scarlett sat on the cold examination table, trying to keep the gown around herself. Every time she took a breath, the damn paper underneath her erupted with a crinkling noise. She wished the doctor would get her ass in here. She despised waiting.

There was a light tap on the door and a middle-aged woman with straight black hair entered the room. "I'm Doctor Dunn. Sorry to keep you waiting, but it's been a crazy day." She opened the folder and scanned the information inside. "Okay, how about you tell me what you've been experiencing?" She reached behind her, pulled a round stool in front of the young woman, and sat.

"Well, I'm pregnant, but I've been bleeding for a few days. It can't be my period, so I'm worried about my baby."

The doctor glanced at the paperwork again and furrowed her brow. "When was your pregnancy test?"

Scarlett shook her head. "I didn't have one."

"You haven't seen a doctor?"

"No."

"Did you take an at-home test?"

"No."

The doctor stared at her. "Are you sure you're pregnant?"

"Absolutely. I didn't have my period last month, and I've been nauseous, plus my breasts are tender. My belly is a little swollen too." She leaned forward and whispered, "I felt the baby move."

The older woman pursed her lips. "How long have you been pregnant?"

"Hmm ... about two months."

Doctor Dunn nodded and smiled. "Okay, let's check you out and see what's happening."

"That's all I'm asking. I wanna be sure my baby girl is okay."

The older woman opened her mouth but stayed silent. For the next several minutes, she examined her. After she finished her pelvic exam, she called a technician and performed an abdominal ultrasound. Her brow wrinkled as she watched the screen. "Hmm ..."

The tech left, and the doctor asked Scarlett for a urine sample. "I'd like to check one more thing, but the good news is, we can run the test quickly and discuss everything at once." She reached for the doorknob. "You can get dressed, take your sample, and leave it with the nurse. I'll meet you back here."

Scarlett stared out the window, exhaled, and checked the time on her cell phone. Her head pounded and her eyes stung. *Where's the damn doctor?*

Ten minutes later, the doctor returned and asked her to have a seat. She pulled the round stool back over in front of Scarlett and took her hands.

"Doctor Dunn, did you find out anything from the tests?"

"I did."

"Well, is my baby okay?"

The older woman cleared her throat. "I'm sorry, but you're not pregnant."

Scarlett's hazel eyes went wide. "That's impossible." She shook her head.

"I'm afraid it's the truth. I think—"

Scarlett's face went bright red. "You're wrong!"

"Please calm down and listen to me."

The younger woman jumped to her feet and paced back and forth. "You're an idiot. I can't believe I've come to you for help and you can't tell me what's wrong."

Doctor Dunn stood, wrapped her arm around her, and guided her back to her chair. She opened the file, pulled out the urine test results, and held them up.

Scarlett's eyes watered, and she wiped them with the back of her hand. "I ... I don't understand."

"It's my medical opinion you have a false pregnancy. The clinical term is pseudocyesis. I found nothing to indicate you're pregnant."

"What? No. That doesn't make any sense."

The older woman leaned over and hugged her. "I'm so sorry. I'd like you to meet with a counselor. I believe it would—"

Scarlett shoved her away and leaped up, crashing the chair against the wall. "You're wrong!" She raced out the office door, slamming it in her wake. She sprinted across the parking lot and jumped into her BMW. Wetness covered her face as she slammed her fists on the dash. Her eyes stared into the rearview mirror and her chest grew tight. If the doctor was right, she'd need to find another target ... and soon.

———

CJ scampered up the stairs, two steps at a time, and through the door into the LEC. She avoided the eyes of fellow officers in the bullpen, slipped her key in the lock, and swung the conference room door open.

"How'd it go?" Sam asked.

She opened her notebook as she approached the younger woman's desk. "Actually, it went well. I tried a little sugar, and it caught me a fly," she chuckled. "I need my research wizard to help me with some items."

"Someone's walking on air," Sam said. "Whatcha need me to do?"

CJ flipped to her notes from her meeting with Larry Simpson and found the five items she'd asterisked. She started with the first one, the years Simpson had worked at Charleston Southern. She wanted to know if these years matched when Vincent attended school there.

Sam's fingers went to work on the keyboard, and within minutes, she pointed to her computer screen. Two of the years overlapped. Both men were there at the same time and, based on the location where Simpson said he'd worked, the Whitfield Center, they were often in the same building.

The next item was the business function where Simpson said he met Ricardson. He hadn't provided the event's name but mentioned it was at the Palm House in July. Based on the number of years Simpson indicated he had known his attorney, they agreed on a five-year period Sam would research for meeting information.

"The next one may be difficult," CJ said. "Simpson told me he got a bank loan to buy the Duncan House. Would you be able to find anything on it?"

Sam nibbled on her thumb. "Did he mention the bank?"

"No."

"I'll see what I can do. I can probably find some information on the sale, but the actual financial records are difficult." She glanced up at her. "What's next?"

"Simpson told me Ricardson called in Wilkins's death. See if you can find any record of the 911 call to confirm this."

The younger woman scribbled a note. "That's number four on my list. Anything else?"

CJ held her notebook down to Sam. "I managed to read the young woman's name at the desk on her planner. Her name's Cynthia Marks. Let's add her to the background checklist."

"Got it," Sam said. "Is that all you need?""

CJ closed her notebook and scratched her chin. "I need to run an errand, but there's one other thing. Is there any way you can find information about escorts in Charleston?"

Sam's mouth dropped open. "You mean prostitutes?"

"Yes."

"Uh ... I'm not sure. People used the Adult Services section on Craigslist until the company shut it down last year due to pressure from numerous state attorneys. I remember reading about it in the *Post & Courier*. Of course, there's still the Personal Services section, but it's not as open for prostitution." Her forehead wrinkled. "Perhaps there are other websites, but I'll need to search."

CJ shook her head. "I doubt high-end escorts would use Craigslist. My guess is these girls would be too expensive for those looking for sex there."

"I'll see what I can find." Sam spun her chair back to her computer terminal and giggled. "I never thought I'd be searching for a high-dollar hooker, and I hope the IT folks don't get the idea I'm moonlighting."

"Thanks. I'll call you later." CJ turned to go before stopping. "By the way, where's Janet?"

"Oh. She had to go to the range to re-up her firearm qualifications. I don't expect her back today, but she said to call her if we need her."

TWENTY-EIGHT

Friday, April 29
The French Quarter

CJ's emerald-green eyes peered into her bathroom mirror. She pinched her lips together and pulled her auburn hair up. For today's appointment in court, she wanted her appearance to be proper. She exhaled and let the strands fall back to her shoulders.

After she decided to wear her hair down, she moved to her closet. She needed to be professional, but not rival the attorneys who'd be there. Her usual attire of jeans, a blouse, and boots wouldn't work, but she couldn't handle a dress today.

She pulled on a pair of black slacks, twisted her body, and checked the fit in the full-length mirror on her closet door. The pants were acceptable, so she added a white blouse and a matching black jacket. Her shoe options were slim— sneakers were in, but she chose a pair of black loafers.

After she pulled on her shoes, she picked up the notes from the last afternoon's meeting with Jolene's caseworker and sat on the corner of her bed. Her eyes scanned them, and then she reviewed her notes from the involvement with the young girl. Finally, she exhaled and went to do one last task.

She removed a walnut box from the top drawer of her dresser, opened it, and peeked inside. She owned little jewelry, but one piece was priceless—her mother's white pearls. She added them as the final touch, examined her face in the mirror one last time, and headed out the door.

The Judicial Center, where the family court was held, was close to her apartment. She took the short drive north up East Bay Street, turned left on Queen Street, and proceeded until she pulled into the Charleston County Parking Garage.

After a short walk, she entered the building where the courtrooms were housed. She was screened, took the stairs to the second floor, and an officer directed her to where she'd find the Honorable Judge Amos White. Thirty minutes before the nine o'clock hearing for Jolene Mason's custody, she parked herself on a bench in the hallway.

As people of various shapes and sizes passed her, she recalled her last time in family court, when Harry officially became her guardian. Then, like now, her stomach fluttered, her mouth was bone-dry, and her heart raced. She looked down. The piece of paper with the court information was damp and crushed in her hand.

Am I freaking out because of my memories or for the little girl?

CJ glanced at her cell phone—8:40 a.m. She stood and paced back and forth before she couldn't wait any longer and went to the courtroom door. She eased it open, tiptoed in, and slid into the back row pew. The judge wrapped up a custody dispute and exited the courtroom, as did the others involved. She was alone, and her thumping heart was all that broke the silence.

A few minutes later, the judge returned, and Cathy Mason entered with her attorney. The woman never looked her way as she passed. The door creaked as a man and woman in their mid-thirties entered. Each of them held a hand of the petite Jolene Mason. The little girl wore a pale blue dress with white flowers, and her hair was pulled back with a matching scrunchie. Her face lit up when she saw CJ.

The proceedings began, and the attorneys from both sides presented their case to the judge—a Black man with kind, brown eyes. After they'd finished, he asked Cathy Mason why he should rule that she take Jolene back home. With a shaky voice, she pleaded with him to return her daughter, whom she said she loved more than life itself.

The foster parents were allowed to explain why she should remain in their care. Wetness ran down the foster mother's face as she described how Jolene was doing in their home. She offered pictures of the room the three had decorated and the yard littered with children's toys. She also informed the judge she was unable to have children of her own, but there was nothing she wanted more in the world than to be the girl's mother.

The judge's eyes found CJ. "You must be Detective O'Hara?"

CJ stood. "Yes, Your Honor. I am."

His long fingers beckoned her to the bench. "I want to hear what you have to say."

She drifted to the front and described how she was involved, the nature of the sexual assault, her time in the Mason home, and the encounter with Floyd Mason.

The judge leaned forward, and his eyes bored into her. "When you visited the home, what was your sense?"

"Excuse me, Your Honor. I'm not sure I understand your question."

"Did you fear for the girl's safety?"

"I did," she said. "I …"

"Go on. Tell me."

"I feared for the safety of both the mother and the child. There were signs of physical abuse on both."

"Was Cathy Mason protecting Jolene from the stepfather?"

CJ swallowed hard and licked her lips. "Not in my opinion." Cries from the chair on her right shook her before she regained herself. "I wanted to remove the girl that day, but as you know, the law doesn't allow me to act without the proper evidence. Unfortunately, at the time, neither of the victims would tell me what was happening."

The judge folded his fingers into a tent. "Is it true the little one came to your apartment and refused to return home?"

"Yes, Your Honor. That's true."

"How did she know where you lived?"

She bit her lip. "Well … I snuck her my card with my address before I left her home."

"What did you do when she didn't want to leave your home?"

"I let her stay. She spent the night with my uncle and me before taking her to Social Services in the morning."

His right eye twitched and his lip curled. "Do you usually invite victims to stay with you?"

"Not as a habit, but she was terrified, and I …"

"Go on."

She exhaled. "I wanted to protect her any way I could. I couldn't forcibly take her from her home, but if she came to my house of her own accord, I could keep her safe."

He stared down at his notes before lifting his eyes. "If you were me, how would you rule?"

Her eyes widened, and her mouth dropped open. "Uh—I'm not sure I'm qualified to answer. I'm not a professional in these types of situations."

"I've got an expert's report, but I spoke to your chief, and he says you have the best instincts he's been around in a long time. Walter and I go way back, so I trust him." He smiled. "Let me get at this another way. What do your instincts tell you?"

CJ glanced to her right at Cathy Mason and her pleading eyes, then she turned to the hopeful couple on her left. Jolene rested her head on the woman's chest and her face was relaxed for the first time CJ had seen.

"Your Honor. My heart tells me Jolene should remain where she is now. She deserves two people who will love and protect her."

"Thank you, Detective. If you have nothing further, you can return to your seat."

The attorney for Mrs. Mason jumped up and tried to interject, but the stern hand from the bench caused him to drop back down.

The judge stood. "Miss Jolene, can I talk to you over here?" He pointed to the corner of the room.

Everyone's eyes were glued to the two of them as they stepped aside. The judge bent down, so he was at eye level with the girl. He spoke in a whisper, so CJ didn't know what he said. Jolene answered whatever he asked her, and when they were finished, both returned to their seats.

The Honorable Judge Amos White cleared his throat. "These cases are always messy and there are pros and cons, no matter how you rule. My only concern is for the well-being of this angel. As such, I rule she remains where she is for the next one hundred and eighty days, at which time I will entertain a motion to adopt should the parties desire it."

Cathy Mason screamed and collapsed against her attorney. The foster parents cried for a different reason. While the judge covered the last formalities, CJ exited. On her way out, she stopped to drink from a water fountain.

"Miss CJ!"

She turned to find Jolene. Her transformation after only a few days was nothing short of amazing. She returned the little girl's hug and smiled at the couple, who stood a few feet away. The woman mouthed, "Thank you."

"I got permission from my new parents to go fishing with Uncle Harry," the little girl said. "Can you tell him for me? We're gonna go way out next time. Here's my new phone number."

"I will," she said as she accepted the paper.

Jolene hugged her once more, took the hands of the couple, and took the steps out the door. CJ waited until they'd gone and headed for her truck. Once settled in her seat, she rested her forehead on the wheel and cried.

Harry rubbed his aching arm. It had bothered him all morning and tingled every time he cast his fishing rod. He rubbed his eyes and yawned. Sleep had avoided him last night, and he was dragging today.

"Enough of this. I need to lie down," he mumbled.

He packed up his rod and tackle, jumped in the seat, and fired up the motor. He sat for a couple of minutes, working to catch his breath. Lately, even the slightest activity left him exhausted. Fortunately, he wasn't far from home.

Harry pulled into his dock, left everything in his boat, and trudged up the steps on his deck, where he dropped into a lounge chair. His chest was tight, and he fought to catch his breath. He squeezed his eyes shut and massaged his burning chest.

TWENTY-NINE

Friday, April 29
The French Quarter

Sam wrinkled her brow and sighed. She had spent over three hours searching for the information on the bank loan she'd been asked to find. Progress was tedious. She stretched her arms over her head and refocused.

"Where are you hiding?" she whispered. Her head snapped up from her computer screen when her boss entered the office at ten thirty. "Wow! You look nice today. What's up?"

"Yeah, an uncomfortable step up from my usual attire. I had to go before a judge at nine this morning and figured I better present myself as a professional."

"A judge?" Sam grinned. "What did you do?"

CJ chuckled. "It wasn't anything I did ... well, not really. I attended Jolene Mason's custody hearing. Her mother filed a motion in family court to have her returned from the foster family who's been caring for the girl."

"Uh-huh." The younger woman pursed her lips. "Did you volunteer, or were you asked to go?"

"I didn't insert myself, if that's what you mean," CJ said. "The judge invited me since I was the one who brought the little girl to Social Services. I got a call from the clerk and was told to attend."

Sam nodded, still eyeing her suspiciously. "How was the hearing?"

"In the end, it worked out for the best. The foster family will keep the girl for now." She dropped into a chair beside Sam's desk. "It was painful for the mother, as could be expected, but her daughter doesn't want to stay with her. Jolene blames her for not protecting her from her stepfather."

"Is she right?"

CJ pinched the bridge of her nose. "Sadly, she is. The mother knew what was happening and didn't stop it." She exhaled. "At least this way, the poor girl has a chance at a normal life, and the couple who has her are wonderful."

Sam leaned forward. "I bet you checked them out?"

"You're damn right I did," she said. "The little girl's a sweetheart, and I want to be sure she's in good hands. Why the interrogation?"

"I don't want you to get too attached."

CJ glanced at the computer screen and pointed. "How's the digging coming along?"

"To be honest, painfully slow," Sam said. "I make progress and then hit a brick wall. I've never had this many strange stumbling blocks in finding stuff. But I do have most of the information for you." She grabbed her yellow pad.

Opening her notebook, CJ stared at her. "Ready when you are."

"Okay. You gave me five new items to research. We already covered the first one. The dates Jackson and Simpson overlapped at Charleston Southern. For the second one, the meeting where Simpson met Ricardson, I found a Charleston Men's Club event held at the Palm House in July twenty-five years ago."

"Hmm ... any idea who booked it?"

"No. I didn't find any details except it was held in the basement. I can't confirm the group is the same as the Palmetto Men's Society, but there's no such thing as the Charleston Men's Club." Sam frowned. "I've been to several events at the Palm House, but this is the first time I've heard of a basement."

"We may need to go check it out," CJ said. "What's next?"

"The bank loan Simpson said he took to buy the Duncan House. I've had no luck so far in finding anything. I haven't found a purchase and sale agreement between Ricardson and Simpson. But I've called a friend, and I'll find something. What are you most interested in?"

"I want to confirm the purchase and if partners are involved. It's hard to believe Simpson had the money to swing this deal."

"Okay. Got it. On to number four." She leaned over and picked up a sheet of paper. "I was able to grab a copy of the log for the 911 call the night Wilkins was found." She handed it to CJ.

The detective scanned it. "Not much information here. No record of who made the call except the *owner of the Duncan House*."

"Can we assume that's Ricardson since Simpson hadn't purchased it yet?" Sam asked.

"Probably. I'd like to have confirmation, but either way, it's not a big deal. I have Simpson's statement now—he and Ricardson were both at the scene."

Sam picked up a file and scanned it. "On the woman you met at the Duncan House, Cynthia Marks. I didn't find much on her, but she was born in Beaufort twenty-five years ago. She moved here six years ago to attend the College of Charleston, but she only lasted a year and a half. She had three waitressing jobs before she started working at the Duncan House two years ago."

CJ flipped through the folder Sam handed her. "Can you hand me the updated background information for the others you've compiled?"

Sam passed more files to her. "Not much stands out in any of these, either."

"Ava Ralston was born in Beaufort, but she's ten years older than Marks, so I doubt they'd know each other," CJ said. "Hmm ... this shows Ava's maiden name was Gibbs. Not much in any of these to point us in the right direction. There have to be some connections."

I wonder if Eugene Gibbs from the photo is connected to Ava? She handed the folders back to Sam. "Anything else?"

"Let's talk escorts." Sam laughed and turned her monitor so both had a good view. "There are a couple of shady websites where *companionship* is offered." Her fingers tapped on the keys and a website appeared. "You can scroll through and find various women available for a *date*. However, if you look closely, most of them are listed as inactive. I'm sure Craigslist's shutdown of this type of listing has hampered their business."

"Shit! Most of these chicks are scary." CJ pointed at the screen. "A high-end escort wouldn't advertise this way. These companions scream cheap."

They spent the next thirty minutes scrolling through the websites and agreed there was no way these women would be the type to wind up in the Duncan House. Sam had one site she found with a listing for escorts, and photos of the women were classy, but the contact number no longer worked. The Special Victims Unit had provided her some information, but they were focused on human trafficking and women they agreed wouldn't fit as escorts.

CJ leaned back in her chair and rubbed her forehead. "Well, Ralston was either having an affair with whoever was with him, or there's an underground means of obtaining an escort."

"Why do you think it might be a pay-for-play girl?" Sam asked.

"To be honest, I don't know." CJ shook her head. "Maybe I'm off base, but my gut tells me it's not an affair with another man's wife type." She shrugged. "I'm probably wrong."

"Well, if you're finished with these sites, I'm deleting them off my computer," Sam said. "I also need to go home and shower." Both laughed. Her cell phone dinged, and Sam stared at the text. "You have a meeting with Ralph Randolph on Sunday morning at seven. He'll meet you at the Pineapple Fountain."

"Should be easy enough," CJ said. "I can walk there from my apartment, and I doubt many folks will be wandering around so early in the morning. You know what he looks like?"

"No, but Randolph's ninety years old, so he can't be hard to miss."

They quietly sat as CJ thumbed through the information they'd covered.

After a few minutes, Sam spoke up. "Do you mind if I take off a little early today? I have what I hope is my last dress fitting. I tried to move it to—"

"Sure," CJ said. "Go. Get out of here. You've earned it this week." She smiled. "How's the wedding planning going?"

"Well … you've met my mom. She's all over it with a group of friends she's organized into a wedding task force." Sam laughed. "All Will and I need to do is show up. His suggestion of eloping to Vegas is sounding better by the minute."

"You can't do that. You're an only child, and your parents would die. I can only imagine the fun your mom's having. How's Will handling the planning?"

"He's been wonderful." Sam grinned. "He rolls with the punches and is smart in asking, 'What do you think?' before he weighs in on anything. My mom thinks he hung the moon, and my dad is thrilled with how he treats me."

"How many are you inviting to the wedding?" CJ asked.

"We got the list down to three hundred," Sam chuckled. "At one point, we were close to four fifty."

"Yikes! I cannot fathom knowing so many people. I'm sure your parents are inviting lots of their friends."

"Yep. Most of the list are people I don't know. Poor Will's list is shorter than the wedding party. Speaking of that, did you give my mom your size for the bridesmaid dress?"

"I most certainly did," CJ said, laughing. "She called me the day after you asked me."

They chatted for a few more minutes, and Sam took off.

———

CJ sat alone in the conference room, staring at the two boards littered with notes. Her eyes scanned what evidence they had so far. "A whole lot of nothing," she mumbled.

She scanned the list of names, and none of her possible suspects could be ruled out—the wife, the owner, or the visitor. In fact, she was beginning to think Ricardson was involved somehow. *Could Ralston have crossed him or someone else? Where does Jennings fit? Was she the mystery woman in the room that night? The list is getting longer, not shorter.*

It was nearing four o'clock. She wanted to call Ben and invite him to dinner, but … her insides quivered and her stomach churned. They already had plans for tomorrow night. *Am I getting too deep, too fast?*

She rubbed her face with both hands. It was time to get out of this room and go to her apartment. She piled some files into a banker's box, stood, and walked to the window. A flock of seagulls floated over the Ashley River Memorial Bridge and the increasing Friday afternoon traffic. As she left, she eyed the one word on the board she hoped would solve her two cases. *DNA.*

———

CJ answered the knock on the door. "Hey, Ben."

"I'm glad you called. Is it okay if I come in?"

She stepped back. "Sure." They dropped on the couch and chatted for the next couple of hours. Since the week before, when Ben had told her his secret, they'd seen each other several times and were finally beginning to relax. They sat silently, watching an old movie and eating buttered popcorn until the credits rolled.

She stood. "I'll be right back." She disappeared into the bedroom and went into the bathroom. Her heart raced as she gazed at herself in the mirror. *Am I ready for this?*

"Would it be okay if we went to bed?" she called to Ben.

He rounded the corner and froze at seeing her standing barefoot, wearing nothing but a white T-shirt. "Uh … yeah. I'm sure you're beat from your long day." His eyes went wide when she pulled the only clothing she had on off over her head.

"I'm not tired, but I wanna go to bed."

THIRTY

Sunday, May 1
The French Quarter

CJ slid off the side of the bed and crept in the dark to her bathroom. For the second night in a row, she hadn't slept alone.

Ben snored softly and never stirred. She closed the door, flipped on the light, washed her face, and brushed her teeth. She slipped on her jeans, pulled a Charleston RiverDogs sweatshirt over her head, and laced her boots. A flip of the switch returned her to darkness.

"I don't get a goodbye kiss?" Ben twisted the knob, and the room lit up.

"I was trying to not wake you, but since I failed, pucker up." She pressed her lips to his and melted against him as he wrapped his arms around her.

He winked at her. "You know. If you have a few minutes ..."

"Sadly, I don't." She kissed him again and pushed herself up. "If this doesn't take long, and you're still here when I get back, I'm sure something could be arranged." She returned his wink.

"Oh, I'll be here, no matter how long it takes. We can conserve water and shower together. Besides, you owe me brunch."

She gave him one more peck, grabbed her raincoat, and scampered down the stairs.

CJ arrived at the Pineapple Fountain at 6:50 a.m. As she expected, people were scarce, with just a few joggers and people walking their dogs. Her eyes scanned the area, but there was no sign of an elderly man. She found a bench under a group of palms and sat. *I hope Randolph isn't a no-show.*

As she waited, she gazed out at the harbor. An early morning mist hung over the water and the sun's rays hinted at a rainbow. She fidgeted and checked her cell phone—7:05 a.m. *Shit! Where are you?*

She was staring at a woman in her sixties walking a scruffy-looking terrier when a voice from behind startled her.

"Miss O'Hara?"

CJ turned to find a man standing with his arms behind his back. He had a wiry build and wore tan khakis, a yellow raincoat, and a pair of Nike walking shoes. His eyes, the color of steel, were sharp, and his hair was white as snow.

"I'm Ralph Randolph." He gave her a sly smile and pointed down the walkway. "How 'bout we chat while I get my morning walk in?"

She stood and offered her hand, which he accepted with a handshake. "It's nice to meet you, and I appreciate you agreeing to talk to me."

Randolph turned and strolled down the walk as she fell in beside him. "Normally, I wouldn't have, but I was impressed with your work catching that nasty serial killer. I watched all the press conferences and have to say you're a damn impressive young lady—tough, smart, and beautiful." Stopping, he turned to face her. "You agree to my terms, correct? No hidden recorders and no notes."

"Yes, sir. I do." She pulled her cell phone from her pocket and held it up as she turned it off.

He nodded and continued his path. "How do you like the Holy City?"

"I'm happy here. It's a unique place, and the people are so friendly."

"Ben especially," he said.

What the hell! "Uh … can I ask how you—"

"I know many things about the people in the city," he said, chuckling. "I did a little research on you, so I knew who I was meeting."

They strolled another fifty yards in silence before he stopped and pointed across the water. "Fort Sumter's sparkling this morning. I love how the sun hits it when it's clear."

"Yes, it is," she said, nodding.

"You have a nice view of it from your apartment," he said as he resumed walking.

What doesn't this guy know about me?

They ambled along for several minutes as he told her about Charleston and she worked to control her building frustration. Learning more about her new home was great, but she preferred her tours with Harry. She nodded, smiled, and gave him a few oh wows while he prattled.

As they neared White Point Gardens, he turned around and began retracing their steps. "How 'bout you ask your questions? You've indulged an old man's ramblings long enough."

"I've enjoyed listening to you. You have a wealth of information, and it's all quite interesting."

He stopped and eyed her. "No need to bullshit me. Ask what you came here for."

She sheepishly smiled and nodded. "Fair enough. What can you tell me about the Palmetto Men's Society?"

He resumed his stroll and spoke in a low tone. "The group was formed after the Civil War to rebuild Charleston. It was made up of powerful people tied to major businesses and old money. The purpose was legit."

"Was it as secretive as it is now?"

He shook his head. "No. It was out in the open. There wasn't a need to stay out of sight."

"How could someone join?"

"At first, anyone could apply, but it took a majority vote of existing members to get accepted."

"When did you join?"

His forehead wrinkled. "Let's see. It was almost fifty years ago, when I was only forty years old."

"How many members make up the group?"

"Used to be around four dozen, but it's much less now. I'm not sure since I'm no longer involved."

"Uh … when did you leave the group?" she asked as her eyes followed a flock of seagulls sailing over them.

"I finally quit ten years ago, after Wilkins was killed."

"I thought he died of a heart attack?"

He stopped and glared at her. "Don't play with me. We both know he was poisoned at the damn Duncan House."

Her cheeks burned. "Yeah, I know. That was stupid of me. How much do you know about that night?"

He resumed his stroll, picking up the pace. "More than I'm willing to tell you. I tried to get it through his thick skull he was headed for trouble." He pointed back to where they started. "I'll talk till we hit the fountain, and then I'm done."

"Okay. What kind of trouble?"

He glanced sideways at her. "I'm not going into the details, but that was it for me. A group of men I no longer wanted to be associated with consumed the society. My departure had been a long time coming."

She frowned. "I'm not sure what you mean."

"Ten to fifteen years after I joined, an incident started us down a dark path. I hung around hoping we'd get straight, but we only went further off track."

"What happened?"

He exhaled. "I ain't saying, 'cept some members started thinking with their little head instead of the one on their shoulders. Add in less than ethical business practices, and it ruined all the good the society had done over the years."

"Are you saying certain men were into prostitution?"

His pace slowed, and he smirked. "You could call it that. Damn unsavory women, man-haters, bitches that took full advantage."

"So, you're saying—"

He waved her off. "Nothing more on the topic. It all turned to shit when Wilkins died, and I ended my relationship with the society once and for all. Hell, I'd almost stopped attending the meetings, anyway."

CJ glanced ahead. They were almost at the fountain, and her time would be up. "Speaking of meetings. Where were they held?"

"By the time I joined, we always met at the Palm House."

"In the basement?"

His head snapped around and he nodded approvingly. "You've done some homework."

The fountain was less than fifty yards away, so she slowed, hoping for more time. "There were two other men in the photo with you, Gibbs, and Ricardson. How did Gibbs die?"

He shook his head and remained silent.

"Whose side was Ricardson on?"

The old man jammed on the brakes. "This is where we part ways. I wish you all the best, Miss O'Hara."

"Please answer my question," she said, touching his arm.

He stared at the ground. "I like you, and you're even smarter than I thought, so I'll answer and give you one last bit of advice." He leaned over and whispered in her ear, "Ricardson was the ringleader." He turned to her, and his eyes were icy. "Stay away from his son. He's worse than his father and far more dangerous."

She stood rigid as he plodded across East Bay Street and disappeared.

THIRTY-ONE

Sunday, May 1
The French Quarter

Ava rolled over and peeped at the clock on her night-stand—8:14 a.m. She sat up in her king-size bed and squinted at the light from under the bathroom door. The loud, disgusting noise of last night's bedmate blowing his nose made her skin crawl. Why did she put herself through this? He was such a pig.

Richie Pickett swung the door open and danced back toward her. His nude body was flabby, pale, and splotchy. "Good morning, sexy." He climbed in beside her, pulled her against him, and nuzzled her ear. "How'd you sleep? I slept like a baby. You wore me out last night," he said as he snickered.

She fought the urge to gag. "Me too, baby," she said as she twisted away and slid off the mattress. "I need to go to the little girl's room." Before he could drag her back, she scampered away.

"Don't be too long." He leered at her naked body. "I'd like to go again before I go home to my bitch of a wife."

Ava closed the door and stared into the mirror. "Dammit," she whispered. Her neck was bright red from his unshaven stubble. She'd never understand why he thought it made him more appealing. It worked on some men, but made this fool look dirty and lazy.

She washed her face, added some cream to the whisker burn, brushed her teeth and gargled, hoping to get his taste out of her mouth. Spending time with him was necessary, but at the bottom of the list of things she enjoyed. Sure, he spent lots of money on her, but she didn't need his cash. She was the sole beneficiary of her late husband's estate.

"I'm gonna grab a quick shower, darling," she called to him. "I won't be long, promise." She turned the knob, and the spray erupted.

"You want me to join you and wash your back?"

"No. It'll be faster if I'm alone." She stuck her head out the door and gave him her best *I want you* smile. "That way, I'll be back in bed sooner."

"Ooh … I'll be ready," he said, grinning.

She turned back, exhaled, and hopped into the shower. The hot water pounded her skin, and she scrubbed. But she'd need more than a few minutes to rid herself of his stench. *I can't do much more of this.*

The door opened, and he stuck his head in. "Honey, are you about finished? I gotta leave soon, so hurry if you want a morning romp."

She rolled her eyes. "Almost. Go back to bed. I'll be there soon." She rinsed one more time, stepped out, and dried herself. Her eyes peered in the mirror. "I look like shit," she mumbled. She dried her hair, sprayed on his favorite scent, and opened the door. Standing in the doorway, she offered him a lustful grin. "Whaddaya think?"

He patted the spot beside him. "Come over here, and I'll show you."

She did what she had to do.

Propped up on a pillow afterwards, Richie let out a long and ridiculous *aah*.

She forced a giggle. "I assume that met your desires?"

"Oh, yeah," he said, as his fingers caressed his potbelly. "You always do."

"Wonderful. I want to please you." She slipped from his grasp, walked to her closet, and pulled on her pink, knee-length robe. "What do you think of O'Hara?"

He was busy trying to button his pants around his plump waist. It would have been easier if he'd gone to a bigger size instead of insisting he wore the same as in college. "Huh?"

"O'Hara? She seems smart and determined."

Richie finally squeezed himself into his pants and fumbled with the buttons on his shirt. "I don't know. She's okay, I suppose."

Ava sighed. "She's more capable than you think, and may figure everything out. I'm certain she caught my slip when the three of us met here. I almost called you honey."

"Now, now, sweetheart." He dropped to the edge of the bed and patted her arm. "Don't you worry. I can handle her." He pulled on his black socks. "Besides, I'm not the only one she has to contend with."

She moved to the floor, grabbed his black dress shoes, and pushed them on his feet. Lacing them, she grunted. "I'm depending on you to make all this go away." She made her eyes go moist as she eyed him. "You promise to protect me?"

Joining her on his knees, he wrapped his arms around her. "I will. There's no way she'll hurt you." He glanced at his watch. "Oh shit! I need to run, baby."

She nodded. "Yeah, I need to leave soon as well. I have over an hour's drive to Beaufort to pick up Sophie at her grandmother's."

Once he was dressed, she led him to the back door, gave him a long, slow kiss, and stared at him as he walked to his charcoal Mercedes. He unlocked it, blew her a kiss with both hands, and pulled away.

She raced back to the shower and the steaming hot water.

Harry felt like death warmed over for the third day in a row, and he had no energy. He was sprawled out on a lounge chair on his back deck, hoping the view and fresh air would help. A call to his doctor should have been made Friday. Maybe when he called, they'd have an opening sooner than later.

The wind caused the marsh grasses to rustle and make a low rattling noise. The pelican CJ liked to call hers was perched on the broken pole, his wings spread to dry. Usually, Harry enjoyed the smell of salty air and decaying plant matter, but today, it added to his nausea.

He hadn't felt himself for a few weeks, but the last three days were the worst. He couldn't explain it, but it was like a weight was on his chest, and sometimes his world swirled. His whole life, he'd been healthy—maybe he had the damn flu.

A soft ringing got his attention. He glanced at the number on the screen and answered his brother's call.

"Hey, Harry. How goes it?"

"I'm sitting out back, taking in nature. What are you up to?"

Craig provided an update on his latest charter and the overnighter he had the next day. Harry was uncharacteristically quiet.

"Hey, you wanna have dinner tonight before I head out again?" Craig asked. "We could meet somewhere, or I could bring some fresh fish over."

Harry rubbed his arm and cleared his throat. "Can I have a rain check? I'm beat after working on my boat all yesterday and this morning." *A lie.*

"Uh … sure. Are you feeling okay?"

Harry made his voice as chipper as possible. "Sure. You know how us old guys get tired sometimes."

"Would you tell me if you were sick or something was wrong?"

"Yeah. I'm not sick, and everything's okay." *Another lie.*

"Well, I'll let you go back to your nature, but you call if you need anything."

"I will."

They said their goodbyes and hung up.

———

CJ rubbed at the back of her neck and stared out her picture window as she listened to her uncle Craig's voicemail message.

"Hey, CJ, it's Uncle Craig. I'll be on a charter until Tuesday, but I'm worried about my brother. Can you go by and check on him when you get a chance? Bye, and hope you solve your cases."

She deleted the message. She wasn't ready to talk to Harry yet.

THIRTY-TWO

Monday, May 2
The French Quarter

Thunder rolled in the distance as a predawn storm passed. CJ had been awake for the last two hours, so she gave up on more sleep and hopped out of bed. Her mind was cluttered with how she'd present today's briefing to Stan. On the one hand, she had a bunch of clues, but on the other, she didn't have squat.

As the hot water rained down on her, she relived the conversation with Randolph. He'd given her solid information she didn't have, but it only added more questions. Unfortunately, he'd withheld as much information as he'd passed on. He'd been clear he'd provide nothing further, and her riddle was more confusing than ever.

After she finished her shower, dried her hair, and dressed in her jeans, pale pink blouse, and boots, she trekked down her dimly lit stairs and jumped in her truck. The positive thing about being up at four thirty in the morning was no traffic. Nobody in their right mind ventured out this early on a Monday.

Fifteen minutes later, she sat in the artificially lit conference room turned office. She'd pulled the blinds up, but only a dark sky looked back. The sun refused to get up at this ungodly hour. She tapped her foot as she waited for the coffee's final drip and filled her jumbo-sized travel mug. She regretted not staying in bed.

Her stomach rumbled, reminding her she hadn't eaten since brunch yesterday. The vending machine down the hall didn't appeal to her. Maybe her work mom would have a surprise for her. She stared at her pad. "This is as good as it gets," she mumbled. She flipped off the lights, rested her forehead on the table, and dozed off.

"What the hell! Did you sleep here?" Sam asked. The younger woman stood near the table, frowning at her.

"Uh—no. I got here early and was taking a break."

"You're doing it again."

"Doing what?"

"Letting a case overwhelm you. Last time, you almost—"

"I'm not doing what I did last time," CJ grumbled. "I went to bed early and wanted to get an early start. That's all." She pointed at the dish in Sam's hand. "What's that?"

"Sausage, egg, and cheese sandwiches." She lifted the foil on top. "I wanted something for the meeting." Her lips curled at the corners. "Why? Are you hungry?"

"No. I'm starved."

Sam stopped her scolding, grabbed some paper plates and napkins, and passed the container to her. "I made a few extras, so take one now."

"Mmm … these are out of this world. Will's a lucky man."

"Is that the summary of the meeting?" Sam asked, pointing to the yellow pad on the desktop.

Her mouth was stuffed, so CJ just nodded. Within minutes, the typed document was passed to her. She read it over, sighed, and asked Sam to make copies.

———

CJ sat reviewing the background files again until Janet arrived at seven thirty with Rebecca Jennings's DNA report. It was a break when DNA was available for the young woman after being collected during her arrest on drug charges a few months ago.

CJ attached the information to the board with a magnet. "So as soon as we get the lab work back for the samples from the two murder scenes, we can compare her DNA from the scene to that reported. She's too young to have been involved in Wilkins's death, but is a prime suspect for Ralston."

"When did Eddie tell you the other results would arrive from Columbia?" Janet asked.

"Early this week, so I've got my fingers crossed it's today or tomorrow." She nibbled at her thumbnail and paced as she stared at the board.

"Do you think it's Jennings?"

"Well." CJ stopped and dropped into a chair across from her. "Let's say I'm hopeful."

"You don't think it was her, do you?"

"No. My gut tells me it wasn't. She was in his vehicle and had his credit card, but wasn't at the Duncan House."

Janet furrowed her brow. "How did she get his stuff?"

"Someone gave it to her. A person who wanted us to believe she did it."

Their discussions were cut short by a knock on the door at eight thirty. Stan entered, and Chief Walter Williams trailed him. The chief's appearance wasn't expected.

"I hope you don't mind if I crash the briefing," he said. "As I'm sure you remember, the mayor's watching this closely."

"No, sir," CJ replied. "Come in, grab a seat. Sam brought us treats if you two are hungry."

Both men grabbed some food, refilled their coffee, and found a chair. Between bites, Stan let her know the floor was hers.

"We've got a handout of what's on the board. I'll talk from it." CJ passed copies of her summary to each of them, and for the next thirty minutes, she covered the details of the Ralston case and how the Wilkins cold case might be connected. Finally, she finished and stood waiting.

"Who was the detective in charge of the Wilkins case?" the chief asked.

"Detective Jackson, sir," she replied.

He grunted. "It figures. That explains why there was a shitty job done. I tried to tell Paul ..." He jabbed his finger at her. "He's your problem now, so get his ass straight, or else."

She nodded.

The chief stood and joined her at the board. "I'd like to focus on the latest case and not be reminded of what a fuck-up Jackson is." He stared at the bullets she'd written and repeated them one by one.

- *No witnesses*
- *Victim's fingerprints on wine bottle and glass*
- *Simpson's fingerprint on bathroom mirror*
- *Brown hair on victim's shirt, unknown person*
- *Odor on pillow beside victim, unknown person*
- *Victim's missing personal belongings – Jennings's apartment*
- *Missing bath linens – unknown*
- *Victim's vehicle – Jennings's fingerprints*
- *Residue in wine bottle and on bed (vomit stain), high levels of tropane alkaloids – (deadly nightshade)*
- *ME report – deadly nightshade in body*
- *Stain on bedsheet under victim – DNA pending*
- *Dried fluid on victim – DNA pending*
- *Jennings's DNA on file*

He turned to Stan. "If we get the pending DNA back and it matches Jennings's, do you agree this case will be wrapped up?"

"Hmm … I'd think so," he answered. "With our prime suspect dead, we can't interview her, but DNA at the scene would be significant."

CJ glanced at Janet, who was seated with Sam at her desk.

"I saw that," Walter said. "You don't agree, Lieutenant?"

Her heart rate ramped up, and she shifted her weight. "Based on this list, I'd say so, but ..."

"But what?"

She shook her head. "It doesn't feel right. Jennings doesn't fit the mold of one you'd expect to be in bed with our vic. There are many unanswered questions about Ava Ralston and Larry Simpson, and there's something about Percy Ricardson. I also can't—"

"Don't make a mountain out of a molehill," Walter said, glaring at her. "It's clear if the DNA matches Jennings, we have our murderer. So take the victory lap and move on. We've got too damn many unsolved cases to waste any time." With that, he marched out of the room.

Once the door closed, Stan asked, "What else were you going to say?"

She shrugged. "It's hard for me to believe a whacked-out druggie such as Jennings could get her hands on deadly nightshade, or understand how to use it if she did."

He smiled at her. "Keep doing your job. We'll chat after we get the DNA results and go from there. I'll support you." He started for the door, stopped, and turned back. "Your instincts have been right so far. Don't doubt yourself." He turned and left.

"How can I help?" Janet asked. She stood beside CJ, who'd been too lost in thought to notice.

She pointed to the board. "I'll tell you what; there's not much you can do on these murder cases until we hear from the lab." She stepped over to Sam's desk and grabbed three folders. "I had Jackson leave these so I could review them. He's on vacation for the next two weeks. How about you take a gander and see what you can do with 'em?"

Janet took the files. "Sure. I'll get to my desk, start immediately, and be prepared to brief you by tomorrow."

Sam spoke up from her desk. "I have the full files here as well." She pointed to a cabinet. "You have copies of the key documents, so feel free to write on them."

CJ smiled. "Thank you both." She turned and scanned the board again. "I'll be out of the office the rest of the day, but reachable if you need me. I'm going to go shake some trees and see what falls out."

THIRTY-THREE

Monday, May 2
The Business District

Market Street was bustling when CJ parked across from the building where the Ricardson Law Offices resided. She hadn't called ahead, but a surprise visit was more appropriate. She signed in and rode the clanky elevator to the third floor. The door slid open to the same twenty-something-year-old woman with flaming red hair she met on her first visit.

"Hello, Detective. Can I help you?"

She nodded and smiled. "Yes. I'd like to see Mr. Ricardson, please."

The younger woman's face twisted. "I'm sorry, he's not available."

"Here and unavailable or out of the office?" She leaned forward and pressed her hands on the reception desk.

"Uh—he's here but meeting with a client and asked not to be disturbed."

CJ flipped her hand. "No worries. I'll wait." She dropped into a high-back leather chair in the corner, pulled out her notebook, and reviewed the items she'd jotted down from Sam's background review on the attorney.

"It's gonna be awhile." The receptionist stood and glided over. "Maybe you should make an appointment and come back later."

"No. I'll wait."

She sat, eyes down, for twenty minutes, scanning her notes. She listened as the younger woman answered calls. For all but one, her voice was cheery and pleasant. However, she turned her back on one call and spoke in a low tone—too faint for CJ to eavesdrop.

At 10:35 a.m., the door to Ricardson's office opened and two men emerged, laughing and smiling. The face of the attorney went dark when he glanced up and saw her. He said his goodbyes to the other man and marched over. "I don't think you're on my schedule today," he hissed.

"I wasn't, but I was down the street and thought I'd enjoy seeing my favorite attorney." She hopped up, grinned, and spread her arms. "So, here I am."

His lips twitched. "What the hell do you want now? I answered all your questions last week." He leaned in close, his eyes glaring. "At least, all I'm going to answer."

She started for his office door.

"Hey, where do you think you're going?"

She wheeled around and eyed him. "I'm not leaving until we chat. It won't take long, but I have some follow-up items I need your help with."

Biting his lip, he turned to his keeper. "Hold my calls for ten minutes." He glared at CJ. "That's how much time I'll waste on you today."

The two crossed the gold carpet, and he motioned her to a black leather high-back across from his desk. He dropped into his chair and glared at her. "You don't wanna sit?"

"No. I'll stand."

"Suit yourself. What the hell do you want?"

"You lied to me."

"I most certainly did not," he said, as his face flushed.

Making a show of opening her notebook, she said, "When I asked you if you had ever been a member of the Palmetto Men's Society, you told me no." She locked eyes with him.

He blinked rapidly and dropped his eyes. "Well …"

"Well, what?"

"It's none of your damn business what clubs I belong to," he growled.

She clicked her pen and jotted. "I'll take that as a yes." She offered a sly smile. "I'll forgive you for misspeaking last week." She tapped her finger on her notebook. "Oh, here's another one. Are you still holding your meetings in the basement of the Palm House?"

"I—I have no clue—"

She lowered her voice. "Let's not keep lying, okay?"

He slammed his fist down on his desk, sending a stack of papers flying. "I demand to know who's spreading malicious gossip about me."

"The basement ... are the meetings held there?"

"I have no interest in telling you my whereabouts."

CJ pointed her finger upward. "Okay, I'll take that as another yes. But, hmm ... here's my favorite. Are you and your buddies involved with escorts? You know, prostitutes?"

"You bitch!" He jumped to his feet and pointed toward the door. "Get out!"

She shrugged and winked. "I'll assume that's also an affirmative." Then, as she started to turn for the door, she asked one last question. "Is your pal Pickett part of the ring of deviants?"

He threw a coffee cup at the wall, and glass shattered everywhere.

CJ waved to the wide-eyed receptionist standing outside the door as she left. "Your boss dropped his coffee."

Climbing in her truck, she blew out a long breath. She had the sneaking suspicion she'd be getting called on the carpet, but she had obtained her information. No words had been offered, but his reaction told her all she needed to know. Peering into the rearview, she mumbled, "One rat down, one to go."

The King Street law office of Richie Pickett was nearby, so CJ hopped out of her truck less than ten minutes later.

She'd know soon enough, but she bet he knew she was coming. She could picture a panicked Percy stabbing the numbers on his phone, giving her next target a heads-up.

Unlike Ricardson's sizable office space on a third floor with an expansive view, Pickett's office was small and street-side. She opened the glass door to yet another attractive twenty-something staring at her.

The blonde-haired young woman stood, her face pale. "Uh—Mr. Pickett's not accepting any new clients at this time."

"Oh, I don't need an attorney," she said, flashing her badge. "I only need a moment of his time." Pointing to the only office door in the lobby, she said, "Should I show myself in, or do you wanna announce me?"

"Well—I—I think you should leave. Mr. Pickett's not—"

"So go right in," CJ said as she plowed through the door.

"What the hell!" Pickett yelled. "Didn't my assistant tell you I was busy?" He jumped from his oversized mahogany desk and attempted to herd her out.

"I'd suggest you not try to manhandle me, Mr. Pickett. It won't end well for you."

He jerked back, and his fiery eyes tightened. "Are you threatening me?"

"Absolutely not!" She cocked her head. "I'm only advising you that assaulting an officer of the law is never a good move. We carry guns, and all that coffee makes us jittery as hell."

He wiped his face and exhaled. "Why are you here?"

She dropped into a gold chair. "Have a seat, and I'll tell you." Opening her notebook, she added, "It'll only take a couple of minutes, and I'll be out of your hair."

She questioned him for the next ten minutes while he squirmed, deflected, and sweated. He acted as though he'd never heard of the Palmetto Men's Society, didn't know Charleston had a Palm House, and was madly in love with his wife. His mouth flew open at the mere suggestion he'd have anything to do with an escort or cheat on the woman he married.

CJ pressed him on where Ava had gone the Friday night her husband was at the Duncan House, and he tried to tell her she was at home with Sophie. She corrected him, as Ava had admitted she had come downtown when confronted with the photo from the camera on the bridge. He offered that she had taken her daughter to a play at the Woolfe Street Playhouse.

"Well, I guess that's it." CJ stood and his face relaxed. "Oh, wait! I almost forgot. The day I met with you and Ava Ralston, she started to call you honey." She clicked her pen and opened her notebook. "How long have you two been having an affair?"

His whole body shook, his face went crimson, and a vein on his right temple poked out. "You have a lot of nerve, Detective." He pointed at her and his eyes squinted. "You're disgusting for accusing me of such an awful thing with a fine woman who recently buried her husband."

"Cremated."

"What?"

"She had her husband cremated."

"Get the fuck out of my office," he growled. As the glass door closed on her exit, he yelled, "I'll be calling your superiors!"

Good. You and Percy can hold a conference call.

⸺

CJ searched for the theater Pickett told her Ava had taken her daughter to on the Friday night in question. It was ahead, off King Street, and within minutes, she turned right on Woolfe Street and found the red brick-faced building. She parked in a large lot across the street and headed toward the structure.

The front door was locked, but she saw lights when she peered in. She knocked until a young man appeared with curly, dark brown hair and pure brown eyes.

He opened the door when she held up her badge. "Is there something I can do for you?" he asked.

She asked if she could look around, and after hesitating, he agreed. He led her into the gorgeous interior, much more elaborate than the exterior would suggest. Her escort explained the building had once been a meat-packing warehouse. It was renovated and used by a local repertory company as a theater offering music, comedy, and drama.

"Can you tell me what event was held on Friday night, April 15?" she asked.

"Let's go take a look." He pointed to a poster on the wall with a list. "Good. April is still up." His eyes scanned. "*The Taming of the Shrew* was performed at seven thirty."

"Okay, thanks."

"By the way, have you ever done any acting?" he asked.

She chuckled. "No. I played a tree in the third grade but wasn't very good. I had a hard time holding up the branches."

His puppy dog eyes stared at her and he nibbled his lip. "I'd think someone would've cast you in the lead."

She smiled, thanked him, and followed him to the front door. "Do you know if there are any records of who purchases tickets?"

"Oh, jeez. I doubt it. If someone paid by credit card, there might be a record."

She scribbled a note, shook his hand, and crossed the street to her truck. Standing in the lot, she scanned the roof-line and power poles until she saw something helpful—a video camera pointed directly at her. Someone would have been captured if they had taken her path to the front of the theater. She punched a number on her cell phone.

"Hey, Sam. I need you to find something for me."

THIRTY-FOUR

Monday, May 2
Downtown Charleston

Scarlett requested to work in the emergency room to keep her mind off her problems. The ER was always a zoo, and she'd be too consumed with her tasks to focus on her personal life. She'd already had a young boy puke on her shoes, a drunk slobber down her arm, and consoled a distraught wife who'd lost her husband.

She postponed another trip to the ladies' room when a gurney burst through the double glass doors carrying a young man with a knife wound in his lower abdomen. A paramedic ran alongside the metal cart, pressing his hand on a blood-soaked towel against the injured man's stomach. She waved him into a space divided by white curtains hanging from the hooks on the ceiling and screamed for the nearest ER doctor.

A gangly physician in wrinkled and stained green scrubs raced around the corner and took over from the paramedic. Scarlett's fingers worked feverishly, grabbing instruments, checking vitals, and being an extra pair of hands to him. After four years as a nurse, she'd seen almost everything, and often was as knowledgeable as the physician about what needed to be done to save a patient. Losing a patient crushed her. *He's losing too much blood. Rush him into surgery.*

"We've got him stabilized, but we need to take him into the operating room now!" the doctor barked. "Where the hell is an orderly?!"

She squeezed past him. "Watch out, I got him." Her legs driving hard, she wheeled the dying man through more glass doors, down a long hallway, and into an open room. A surgeon and two nurses immediately went to work. "You need me to stay and help?"

A masked face peered up, while his hands never stopped. "We got it. Thanks, Nurse."

Scarlett returned to the bleeps of monitors, hacking and coughing patients, and the chaos of the ER. The mixture of antiseptic, cleaning products, vomit, and body odor refilled her nostrils. She changed her surgical gloves and did her best to remove the red chunks of hot dog from her white shoes. "That's as good as it's gonna get," she mumbled.

Cracking the double doors, she scanned the waiting room, relieved it was thinning out. Her eyes stopped on a woman rocking a little girl of about five in a chair in the corner. She squeaked across the floor. "Excuse me. How long have you been waiting, ma'am?"

The woman's red, puffy eyes stared up at her. "I'm not sure. We've been here hours, and my daughter's so sick."

Scarlett dropped to a knee and touched the little girl's forehead. She was burning up with a fever. Motioning a sign-in clerk over, she asked, "Why is it taking so long to send this baby back so we can treat her?"

"Uh—well, I'm waiting on her insurance to approve—"

"It's approved," she said, glaring at her. She lifted the girl out of her mother's arms and hustled to the treatment area."

"Hey! You're supposed to wait …" The clerk closed her mouth as she disappeared.

Once the pre-midnight surge had dissipated, Scarlett took her long overdue breather and headed for the breakroom. The later arrivals typically meant another knife wound, a gunshot victim, or someone in a car crash. But on Mondays, people didn't stab, shoot, or wreck as often as on the weekends.

She drifted through the breakroom door and went to her assigned locker. Gazing around to ensure no one would notice, she pulled a box out of her bag and cupped it in her hand. Her heart rate escalated as she entered the bathroom and closed the stall.

Her eyes stayed glued to the plastic stick in her hand for five minutes—no plus sign came. She wasn't pregnant for the third time today and the twelfth time since leaving the doctor's office. Tears ran down her cheeks and dripped onto the tile floor. *Time is running out.*

THIRTY-FIVE

Tuesday, May 3
Downtown Charleston

"Thanks for calling as soon as you had the DNA reports back," CJ said.

Eddie smiled and offered her a seat beside his desk in the forensics lab. He moved stacks of manilla folders and papers to the floor and slid into his rolling chair. "You want some more coffee before we start?" he asked.

She shook her head. "No. I've had my fill for the day."

His eyes widened. "Have you cut back? It's only seven thirty in the morning."

"I haven't," she chuckled. "I helped Sal unlock the door to his place this morning at six."

"Well, let's get started," he said as he eyed her cautiously. "How familiar are you with DNA?"

Her brow furrowed. "I'm not sure what you mean. I've reviewed numerous reports and am aware no two people have the same DNA unless they're identical twins."

"Correct," he replied. "Before we examine the information from SLED, let's discuss the samples themselves."

She pinched her lips together as her chest grew tight. "Are you about to tell me we didn't get DNA? I understood we—"

"Don't worry. We got DNA from both scenes. I wanna discuss the samples and how the tests were conducted, so the results make more sense."

For the next thirty minutes, Eddie covered the basics of DNA, test methods, and interpretation of the results. She stifled her impatience the best she could. Finally, he got to what they had in her two cases and opened a yellow envelope.

"I'll cover the stain on the bedsheet under Ralston first." He placed the report on the edge of the desk so they could both view it. "The technician told me he was able to extract the sample from the cloth material and have a sufficient quantity to run the test twice."

CJ leaned in close and stared at the DNA fragment pattern. "Okay, so what does this mean?"

"We have the profile of two people, a man and a woman," he replied. "The male is Charles Ralston."

She exhaled. "Do we know who the female DNA belongs to?"

He shook his head. "No." He reached over and grabbed another report. "It's not Rebecca Jennings. We've run it through federal and state databases, and there's no match."

"So we have no clue who the woman was in bed with Ralston," she whispered.

"Not yet. I've called our friends at the FBI and requested they check it. Perhaps they'll be able to find a match." He stood and went to his whiteboard and added a bullet.

- *Stain on bedsheet – DNA from Ralston and unknown female*

CJ rubbed her chin. "Can you determine how old a person is from DNA?"

"No. We only know the sex of the person." He joined her at the desk and picked up the second report. "The dried fluid on his groin also produced two DNAs, a man and a woman. Like the first sample, the male is Ralston and the same unknown female." He stood again and added a second bullet to the board.

- *Stain on victim's groin – DNA from Ralston and unknown female*

"How about the Wilkins case?" she asked.

"The sample we had was degraded due to time, but our tech was able to get DNA using a method where shorter strands can be typed," Eddie said. "Again, we found male and female DNA." He handed her a copy of the report.

She scanned it and read the note at the bottom. "It says both are unknown persons."

He nodded. "We don't have Wilkins's DNA, so we can't confirm if he's the male, and there's no match in the system for the female DNA." He walked to the board and added a last note.

- *Stain on Wilkins case bedsheet – DNA from unknown male and female*

He returned to his chair. "There's one other item that's, well … weird."

She tilted her head. "What?"

"I'm no expert, but it appears the women in the Ralston and Wilkins samples are related."

"Holy shit! Can you do me a favor?"

"Sure."

"Have SLED share everything with the FBI." She opened her notebook and copied the contact information of the analyst who'd helped her in the past. "I'd like to have her dig into the family connection of the two female DNAs. It would be helpful to know how close these people are on the family tree."

"Will do. A specialist in this area may be able to help. Based on my understanding of what we have, the two people don't have the same father and mother."

She left his lab, walked to the front, and opened the door to sheets of rain blowing sideways. *Perfect. Can this day get any worse?*

CJ drove through the ponded rainwater on her way to the LEC. Every vehicle that passed tossed a wave across her windshield. Finally, she parked, waited until the rain slowed, and raced up the steps and through the door.

"Here you go, Lieutenant." The patrol officer, whose wife had recently had a baby, handed her a towel.

She thanked him and squished down the hall to an empty conference room. Sam had left her a note letting her know she had gone to pick up some information for Janet. She also needed to check her email for a copy of the video from Woolfe Street.

CJ went to her desk and booted up her computer. She leaned in close as she peered at the people walking across the street from the parking lot to the front door. At 7:19 p.m. on Friday, April 15, a woman and a young girl crossed the street hand in hand. She stopped the video and stared again.

"That's Sophie, but who the hell is with her?" she muttered. She jotted down the time and sent a note to the analyst who sent the video asking if she could obtain an enlarged photo.

She spent the rest of the afternoon reviewing the Ralston case files again. Even with the DNA, she was not much closer to solving the puzzle. *More we know, but not who.*

She called Stan and advised him of the new information. All she could definitively conclude was Jennings wasn't the person who'd poisoned their vic. So much for the mayor's theory.

Her cell phone buzzed as she updated the boards with the new information. She shook her head and answered. "Hey, Uncle Craig." There was a long pause. "Are you there?"

"You need to come to the ER at MUSC," he said, his voice shaky.

Her pulse shot up. "What's wrong?"

"It's Harry, and it's bad." She stood stunned as he cried, then raced out the door and down the hallway.

Her day had just gotten worse.

THIRTY-SIX

Tuesday, May 3
Downtown Charleston

CJ skidded to a stop in front of the entrance to the ER. She got a break when a beat-up black Chevy backed out and left an open parking spot. She pulled in, jumped out of her truck, and sprinted through the double glass doors. "Excuse me!"

A clerk glanced up from behind a glass partition. "Yes?"

"My uncle was brought in—Harry O'Hara. Can you help me find out what's happening?"

The woman pursed her lips. "And you are?"

"I'm his niece—CJ O'Hara."

"Hmm, he's not showing in the system," the clerk said, her eyebrows pinching together. "Are you sure he came to MUSC?"

Wiping her eyes, she nodded. "My other uncle, Craig, called me, so I'm sure he's here."

The clerk stood and pointed to the waiting room. "Is the man in the corner your uncle?"

CJ spun around and surveyed in the direction the woman pointed. Her eyes fixed on a figure slumped over with his head on his knees. His cap gave him away, and she raced to him. "Uncle Craig!"

His head popped up, and he ran to meet her, wrapping her in his arms. Her tears erupted and her body shook. "How is he?"

He whispered, "I'm not sure. He's been in the back for a while. I've been waiting for the doctor to give me an update." Fighting tears, he escorted her back to the corner. "A nurse came out a few minutes ago and told me they'd give me a status soon."

The two of them fidgeted in the cold metal chairs. As hard as they tried, the small talk didn't make the wait more bearable.

Forcing a chuckle, he said, "I'm a sight." He ran his hands down his tan fishing pants. "I got back from my charter and swung by Harry's on my way home, so I haven't changed." Lifting the sleeve of his shirt, he sniffed. "I stink like fish."

She nodded without comment. Her focus was on not bawling and trying to stay positive. "Did the nurse tell you anything?"

He exhaled. "The young lady told me it was his heart. Unfortunately, he has a severe blockage, so they're assessing how much damage ..."

She collapsed against his shoulder. "This is my fault. You left me a message to check on him Sunday, but I didn't. I—"

"This isn't your fault." He squeezed her. "You can't always put the blame on yourself for these things. You've carried the guilt for your parents' and sister's deaths for over twenty years. Now, and then, you're wrong."

"You don't understand," she said, peering up at him. "We got into a stupid spat last Tuesday and I haven't spoken to him since, even after he left me several messages. If he's not okay, I'll never forgive myself."

Before he could respond, the glass doors from the back slid open and a twenty-something-year-old nurse with delicate features and sharp brown eyes exited. They jumped to their feet as she approached.

"How is he?" Craig asked.

"He's going into surgery soon."

CJ lost it, and Craig had to hold her up.

The nurse leaned in and wrapped her arms around them. She whispered, "He's in skilled hands, and from what's in his chart, his health gives him a solid chance of recovering. I'll be with him and make sure he receives top-notch care. I'm Annie, by the way."

"Does he have much damage to his heart?" CJ asked.

"I'll have the doctor who will perform the surgery come talk to y'all soon while we get Harry ready." She patted their arms. "I'll be observing the surgery and won't leave him until he's in recovery."

She pulled out a piece of paper, jotted down her cell phone number, and handed it to Craig. "Here's my number. If I don't answer, it's because I'm in the operating room with one of the top heart surgeons in the Lowcountry." She hugged him and left.

Fifteen minutes passed as they sat quietly and CJ rocked. Finally, when the doors opened and a tall, gray-haired man in blue scrubs exited, they rocketed to their feet.

The man smiled and strode toward them. "Good evening. I'm Doctor Anson. I'll be performing Harry's surgery." He motioned them back to their chairs and squatted in front of them. "Hey, I know you. You're the detective who caught the serial killer, Bryan Parrish."

CJ nodded.

For several minutes, Doctor Anson described what he believed was the issue and how he hoped to correct it. It would require opening the chest cavity and performing a coronary artery bypass grafting, or CABG. He told them everyone called it "cabbage."

"I'm not gonna kid you. This is a major surgery. It does have a high success rate, and it's my specialty." He gave them the recovery process after he finished describing the steps in the procedure. "He'll be in the Intensive Care Unit for three days and, if all goes well, in a standard room for up to another week."

"So, Doc, in this grafting procedure, how many arteries will need to be fixed?" Craig asked.

"Based on what I've seen, I'd expect this to be a double bypass surgery, so two. There appears to be a minimal blockage on a third artery on the scan, but I won't determine if it has to be addressed until I perform the surgery." The doctor stood. "I assume y'all will wait here while I do my surgery?"

Both nodded.

He smiled. "Okay. I'll return and tell you how everything went once I'm finished. I'd guess it'll be in three hours or so." His eyes trailed up at the clock on the wall. "It's 8:15 p.m. now, so I should be back around midnight. Don't be surprised if Nurse Annie beats me out here. I agreed to let her observe, since she's taken a liking to our patient."

"Am I able to stay with him in the ICU?" CJ asked.

"Our normal visiting hours are 9:00 a.m. to 9:00 p.m., but we can provide special permission for overnight stays. I'd not recommend it for the ICU, but we'll have a nurse with him."

She sniffed and swiped at her eyes. "I want to stay with him …"

The doctor smiled and squeezed her hand. "We'll sort it out once we have him through surgery." He turned and scampered back through the glass doors.

At 8:30 p.m., Ben hustled through the door and ran to them. He wrapped his arms around CJ, and she burst into tears as he rubbed her back. Craig described the issue and what the doctor planned to do to correct it.

"Have you two eaten anything?" Ben asked.

Both shook their heads.

"You need to eat. I know there's no way in hell you'll leave, so I'll go grab something."

"I'm not hungry," she said.

"You can't help Harry if you let yourself get run-down. I'll be back soon."

"You two seem close," Craig said when Ben left.

"Yeah ... well, we've been seeing each other."

He nudged her with his shoulder. "It's about damn time. Guy's been gaga over you since you got here from what I've heard."

Sam, Janet, Thomas, and Eddie walked through the door minutes after Ben left. Craig repeated the doctor's story. No one wanted to go until after the surgery, so Eddie rounded up more chairs. Ben returned with food and coaxed CJ to eat part of it.

Everyone sat, stared at the clock for the next three hours, and waited for midnight.

Nurse Annie emerged at 12:09 a.m. and approached the group as they all stood. Her lips curled into a bright smile. "The doctor has finished, and our guy's doing well." She squeezed CJ's hand, who burst into tears, and then hugged Craig.

"Can I see him?" CJ asked.

"No. Not yet. We'll keep him in recovery for several hours, then move him to the ICU. Doctor Anson will advise us when you can visit, but I'd expect it to be some-time tomorrow."

"Uh—okay." CJ sighed. "I was hoping to see him—"

"He's sleeping now, and that's what's best for him." The young woman leaned in closer to her and whispered, "Tell you what. If the doctor says it's okay, I'll take you back and let you peep at him from the door."

"I'd like that."

After a bleary-eyed Doctor Anson gave them a post-op report, Nurse Annie took CJ back and allowed her to peer in at Harry. Her eyes filled with tears at all the gadgets and gizmos surrounding him, but she was thankful the surgery was a success, according to the surgeon.

"I'm so sorry, Uncle Harry," she whispered. As Nurse Annie escorted her back out, she said, "Thank you for at least letting me see him."

"Glad to do it. I'll see you tomorrow." She smiled. "I'll be taking care of Harry in the ICU."

THIRTY-SEVEN

Wednesday, May 4
Downtown Charleston

"Oh, shit," CJ mumbled. She was sore and stiff from the metal chair where she'd spent the night in the ER waiting room. Craig had tried to get her to go home, but she'd refused. Her head pounded, and she was groggy.

She stood, bent over, and touched her toes. A grimy-looking man with no front teeth smiled at her as her fingers punched in the number for the ICU. She got another, "He's doing fine," from the nurse. They had to be sick of hearing from her every hour. "When Harry wakes up, please tell him I'll return at nine."

CJ limped to her truck and went home to shower and change clothes. She planned to go to the LEC to see Stan before returning to stay with her uncle. The dawn traffic was sparse, and she got home in fifteen minutes.

She raced up the stairs, stripped off her clothes, and jumped into the shower. Toweling off, she switched on the hair dryer and then dressed as fast as possible. She flew back down the stairs and jumped into her truck at 7:05 a.m. As badly as she needed caffeine, she passed on Sal's.

Her fingers fumbled with her key card before she heard the beep and slipped into the LEC door. Several officers in the bullpen told her they wished the best for Harry as she hustled past.

Her captain glanced up from a file when she knocked. "How's your uncle?"

"According to the nurses, he's doing fine," she said. "I can get in to see him at nine."

He motioned her to a chair. "Make sure you let him know we're all praying for him." He stared at her. "No offense, Lieutenant, but you look like hell."

"Thanks. Every girl wants to hear that," she said with a weak smile. "Perils of getting smacked in the nose and sitting in a metal chair all night."

"Sorry." He chuckled. "Whatcha got for me?"

She opened her notebook. "We covered the DNA results, but I've asked the FBI to investigate the profiles and help with the family relation between the two unknown females. I'm still trying to wrap my head around it. I've got another item that has me puzzled." She handed him a photo. "The attorney for Ava Ralston told me she took her daughter to a play at the Woolfe Street Playhouse, but that's not her." She pointed to the older female. "This woman is much older."

Stan stared at the photo. "So, another lie."

"Yep," she said. "Based on the bridge video, Ava came into Charleston with Sophie, but apparently dropped her off with this woman."

"Have you ruled Jennings out as a suspect?" he asked.

She nodded. "Yes. Since her DNA wasn't at the scene, it makes sense." She stared at the notes. "Of course, we still don't know why her prints were in Charles Ralston's Range Rover and his wallet and cell phone were in her apartment."

"Could she have stolen them from the room?"

"I guess it's possible, but if she did, she left no forensics behind. Plus, I checked with the owner, and he confirmed the door was locked when he found the body." She exhaled. "If she was stupid enough to leave prints in the vic's truck, why not the room?"

CJ stretched her arms over her head. "Bottom line is, Jennings was involved, but I don't think she poisoned anyone."

"What's next?"

Her brow furrowed. "Well, there are three critical items besides the DNA and its connection. All we can do is wait for the FBI to solve this puzzle. So, I need to investigate who took Sophie to the play, run Ava's whereabouts to ground, and figure out how Jennings was involved." She stared at her notes on her meeting with Randolph and decided to keep that to herself. "I'll be in my office till eight forty, and reachable on my cell afterward." She thanked him and headed down the hall.

Sam jumped up from her desk and hugged CJ when she entered the office. "You look tired."

She eyed the younger woman, who was fresh as a daisy. "Jeez. I must look like shit, since everyone keeps commenting on my appearance."

"No, just tired. You stayed at MUSC all night, I bet."

"I did, and I'm returning to see Harry at nine, but wanted to finish some work."

"How can I help?" Sam grabbed a pad.

CJ went to the board, copied the bullets from Eddie, and pointed to the new information. "That's where we are on the DNA." She handed Sam the photo. "Can you find out who this woman is with Ralston's daughter?"

"I'll give it a try. What else?"

"See if you can find more cameras in the Woolfe Street area. I want to find Ava's car, if possible. Search the 6:00 to 8:00 p.m. time slot on Friday, April 15."

"Got it."

"For this last one, I'm not sure where to start. First, we need to work out how Rebecca Jennings was involved—why her prints were in Ralston's vehicle and how she got her hands on his wallet and cell phone."

Sam scratched her chin. "I'll search for her acquaintances. Perhaps we can find someone who knows something."

"That'll work." CJ stared at Sam. "Thanks so much for all you do for me."

The younger woman's face went pink, and she hugged her. "You're welcome."

"I need to leave soon for the hospital. Anything else?"

"Uh—it can wait, but Janet still wants to brief you."

"Oh, that's right! Ask her if she'll swing by MUSC later this afternoon, and we'll do it there."

Sam nodded. "I'll let her know as soon as she gets here."

CJ told her she could be reached on her cell phone and she'd keep her posted on Harry's recovery. "I know lots of folks want to visit, but it may be best if it's after he's out of the ICU." She grabbed her notebook and headed to her truck.

"Uncle Harry, I'm so sorry." CJ leaned down and kissed Harry's forehead. "I shouldn't have acted like I did. You were only trying to talk some sense into me. And not returning your calls ... please forgive me."

"You're forgiven, sweetheart," he said scratchily. "I love you."

"I love you too," she said, kissing his forehead again. "How do you feel?"

"I'm not ready to dance yet," he weakly smiled. "I'm sore as hell, and the meds they have me on keep me goofy."

She patted his arm and pulled his blanket up. "Is your pillow okay? I can go get—"

"Stop fussing over me. I'll be fine."

She gently hugged him, careful not to touch his chest. Moisture covered her face, and she wiped it away. "You scared me to death, and I've never seen Uncle Craig cry before."

"I'm sorry. I didn't realize I was that sick. I've been doing a bunch of work around the house, on my boat, and in the yard. Figured that's why I was so tired. My arm was painful, but I thought I pulled a muscle."

"Uncle Craig said your chest had been bothering you too." She eyed him.

He shrugged and grimaced.

"Stop that! You'll tear out your stitches."

"Listen to your niece." CJ turned to see a young nurse with brunette hair and hazel eyes behind her. She smiled. "I'm Cara. Your uncle here is a troublemaker," she said, grinning. "He's already wanting to go home." She busied herself checking monitors.

CJ sat with him until he dozed off, and then she snuck out to talk to Cara. The nurse told her the recovery was normal so far, and she reviewed what was expected for the next week. They'd have Harry get out of bed soon and move to minimize the risk of blood clots. The biggest thing to watch for was an infection.

When her cell phoned buzzed, CJ glanced down. *Janet.* She told Nurse Cara she was leaving but would be back soon. She found Janet in the waiting room, and they went outside. Janet briefed her on Jackson's three cases, the highs and the lows, and her planned next steps. She'd identified some new potential witnesses, and she and Officer Johnny Jones would meet with them. "I think I may be able to solve one of the cases by the end of the week."

"Really?" CJ said as her eyebrows raised. "That would be tremendous. Jackson has had them for over three months."

Janet smiled. "Let's keep our fingers crossed. I'll let you get back to your uncle. I'll keep you posted—and yell if you need anything."

When CJ returned to the hospital room, Nurse Annie was sitting on the edge of the bed, massaging Harry's forehead with her fingertips. "It helps him sleep," she whispered.

"When did you get here?" CJ whispered back.

The nurse motioned her to the hall and closed the door behind her. "I got here a few minutes ago. I'm working three to three, so I'll take over for Cara. Did she go over everything with you?"

"She did. I've got copies of what Harry's supposed to do when he gets home."

"It's important he moves around but not to overdo it. He strikes me as the type who could do more than he should. He's a bachelor, right?"

CJ nodded. "I can always stay with him, and his brother will help. He has his own home but can easily stay at Harry's, like me."

Nurse Annie left to check on two other patients, and she returned to the room.

While Harry slept, CJ reviewed her notebook until Craig came in and she shared what the nurses had given her. Harry woke up a little before six, had dinner, and drifted back to sleep soon after.

At 9:00 p.m., Nurse Annie asked them to come back into the hallway. She told them it would be best to go home, so Harry would rest better. "Don't worry, I'll be here and watch him closely. He's a sweetheart, and my only patient for the rest of my shift."

"I understand," Craig said.

Reluctantly, CJ agreed.

THIRTY-EIGHT

Thursday, May 5
Downtown Charleston

"That's her vehicle," CJ said as she peered at the video on Sam's computer screen. "The time stamp shows 7:05 p.m." She leaned back and rubbed the back of her neck. "Do you have the time when the bridge camera caught her handy?"

Sam tapped the keys. "An hour earlier, 6:10 p.m."

"Where was she for the hour in between?" CJ stood, went to the window, and stared at the heavy gray clouds.

"I've still got searches ongoing," Sam said. "I had the guys start with the Woolfe Street area." She pressed the play arrow and watched Ava Ralston's BMW as it pulled into the parking lot across from the Woolfe Street Playhouse. "Oh, look! An older woman."

CJ hustled back and joined her at the screen. A navy-blue Mercedes sedan with a clear view of a license plate was parked next to the BMW. "Can you zoom in?"

Sam huffed. "Crap! It won't let me." She grabbed her phone. "I can get it blown up." A few minutes later, she clicked on a link to a photo. "Here we go." She hit print and the image of the plate dropped into the printer tray.

MSA 212.

"We need to find who this is registered to," CJ said.

"I'm on it." Wheeling back in her chair, Sam grabbed her phone again and made another call. "They'll call me back shortly."

"Any luck finding anything on Jennings's acquaintances yet?"

"No." Sam sighed. "I'm still searching. If I can find where she worked, it'd be a start."

CJ dropped into a chair at the table. "This is solid progress. Finding the woman who took Sophie to the play helps us. I'll be able to interview her and determine if she knows anything about Ava's comings and goings."

The phone rang, and Sam grabbed it. After speaking to the person at the end of the line, she said, "The woman's name is Susanna Davis, and she lives in Beaufort." She stood and handed her a note with the name and address.

CJ added the information to her notebook. "I'll need to take a little drive. I'm not exactly sure when, since I don't want to be gone for half a day with Harry in the ICU."

"When are you going over to MUSC?"

"I'll leave here soon, so I'm there by nine. The doctor approved me staying overnight, and I plan to tonight."

Sam frowned. "I understand, but you can't run on no sleep."

"I know. I'll catnap in the recliner. It's sorta comfortable." She exhaled. "I may have to fight the nurse for it."

"Who?"

"Nurse Annie. She ran Craig and me out at nine last night. She told us she'd stay with Harry, but she's off today, so I'll be fine."

"Are you jealous of the nurse?" Sam asked, giggling.

"No. I wanna be with my uncle, and it's difficult when she's hovering over him."

"Is she cute?"

CJ shrugged. "I suppose. She's plain, doesn't wear makeup, and puts her hair in a bun. Plus, it's always hard to tell when someone's in scrubs." She stood. "I'm gonna swing by, update Stan, and head to the hospital. Call me on my cell if you find any more videos."

"Will do, boss."

"That's weird."

"What?"

"I think that's the first time I've been called boss." CJ laughed. "It makes me feel old."

As she exited, Sam called to her, "Be careful driving, old lady!"

CJ strode down the hallway to Stan's empty office. She stood in the doorway to wait. After several minutes passed, she thumbed at her cell phone—8:50 a.m. She needed to leave for the hospital, so she scribbled a note with her update and left it on the desk.

When she had parked in the Ashley-Rutledge parking lot, she called Craig. He told her he planned to see Harry later that afternoon and stay through dinner.

"Sounds good," she said. "They're not fond of both of us visiting at the same time, so I can sneak out and make some calls."

She hustled to the elevator bank and hit the button for the sixth floor. The odor of Mexican food almost choked her. After the *ding*, she exited left, dodging gurneys and wheelchairs as she made her way down the hall. The door to Harry's room was closed, so she asked the nurse at the desk if it was okay to go in.

"Yes," she replied. "Mr. O'Hara should be awake. Nurse Annie's with him."

"Isn't she off today?" CJ asked, frowning.

"She is, but she wanted to check on him."

CJ shrugged and headed to the door. Annie sat on the side of the bed, smiling at her uncle while he laughed at something she'd said. The young woman wore white shorts, a pale green top, and white sandals. Her face was different—she had tastefully added makeup, and her hair was down. She was quite attractive.

She eyed the off-duty nurse. "Hey, Annie. I'm surprised you're here on your day off."

"I wanted to check on my guy here," she said. "I'm leaving soon."

CJ squeezed past her and took Harry's hand. "How are you feeling today?"

"I'm doing better. The doctor has cut back on my meds, so I'm not constantly out of it."

Annie moved to the other side of the bed and stood, caressing his arm. "That doesn't mean you can move around a lot. We still have the bleeding issue."

"Bleeding issue?" CJ's eyes bulged. "What's that about?"

He waved his hand. "It's normal. I—"

"Blood shouldn't be seeping out of your wound after two days," Annie said.

"Uh … how long is normal?"

The younger woman nibbled her lip. "Usually no more than a few hours, a day at the latest."

Oh, God. CJ's heart rate bumped, and she tightened her fingers on his hand. "I need to speak to the doctor and find out what he thinks." She glanced up at the young nurse. "Will Doctor Anson be around today?"

"He'll probably come back later. I spoke to him on his seven o'clock rounds, and he's concerned about the seepage."

You got off at three, so why the hell were you here at seven?
"What if it doesn't stop?"

The young nurse pinched her eyebrows together. "The doctor would have to go back in and correct the problem."

"How can I reach the doctor?"

Annie removed her hand from Harry, went to a whiteboard on the wall, and leaned in close. She pointed to a phone number. "This is his cell phone number. I'd suggest you text him in case he's with a patient. I'm certain he'll call you back."

She returned to the bed, pressed her lips on Harry's cheek, and told him she was leaving. She added she'd be back tomorrow by 3:00 p.m. and would be with him for her twelve-hour shift.

Once the door closed, CJ turned to her uncle. "She's a friendly little thing."

He chuckled. "She's sweet. I think she treats all her patients this way."

She pursed her lips. "I'm not sure she goes around in her sexy little shorts and kisses all her patients."

He grinned. "Don't worry. You're still the only woman in my life."

"Since she got off at three this morning, I was surprised she was here."

"Oh. She stayed with me until six. I think the nurses were short-handed. She must have showered and changed here."

"Uh-huh."

CJ spent the rest of the day in his room, except for running to the cafeteria to eat a not-so-bad turkey sandwich. They swapped places when Craig arrived at 4:00 p.m., and he stayed while she went to the lobby. She called Sam, who told her she had found another video of Ava's vehicle on Coming Street in front of the Mace Brown Museum of Natural History at 6:49 p.m.

"She was right around the corner from the Duncan House thirty minutes before her husband checked in." CJ jotted down a note. "What else?"

"Your original search timeframe was six to eight that evening, but I've asked our people to keep searching until ten. Ava had to go somewhere after she dropped her daughter off."

"That's a good idea."

Before they hung up, Sam told her she found where Rebecca Jennings was employed. She worked as a stripper at Ricky's Cabaret on Pittsburg Avenue.

"Good work," she said. "I'm not looking forward to going to a strip club, but I may find someone who knows about her other profession—prostituting herself."

"You need to be careful when you go," Sam said. "It'd be best if you took someone with you. Perhaps Ben could ride—"

"I'm not taking Ben around half-nude women, or worse," she said with a grunt. "If I take someone, it'll be Janet. She'll pay attention and not be gawking at the girls every time they bend over."

They hung up, and she returned to Harry's room and her overnight in the worn, brown recliner. Between worrying about her uncle's continued bleeding from his wound and her case, she wouldn't sleep, anyway.

THIRTY-NINE

Friday, May 6
The Business District

Percy Ricardson III told his assistant to hold his calls and ushered Richie Pickett into his office. The two men dropped into black high-back leather chairs around a circular glass table. They made small talk until Percy suggested they have a drink.

"It's fucking ten o'clock in the morning," Richie said.

The older man flipped his hand. "So what? I'm not talking about power drinking, but I need something to take the edge off."

"Yeah. This bitch O'Hara is making life hell. Bourbon and water for me."

As he mixed the drinks, Percy told his guest he'd spoken to *her* and was uneasy. "She blew me off—told me to handle it."

"She doesn't have a clue about how bad this may get for us all."

Percy handed him his drink. "Agreed. How's Ava holding up?"

"Okay, I guess," he said, shaking his head. "O'Hara forced me to give her details of where Ava went on the evening of the fifteenth, and I lied and said she went to a play."

"She'll figure out you're full of shit," Percy said. "The woman is smart and determined, with damn good instincts." He laughed and said, "She does have a nice ass, though."

"She sure does. Too bad it's being wasted."

Percy leaned over. "Speaking of asses, how's Ava in bed?"

Richie burst out laughing. "I disgust her, but she's a phenomenal actress."

"She always was good at her job. Too bad she has no idea how bad you're actually screwing her."

They both downed their drinks and agreed a second round was warranted. Richie did the honors and returned with more brown liquor and less water in the glasses. "How's your client holding up?"

"Larry's all freaked out. I forced him to remove Mary Beth from the equation by sending her out of town. The only decent thing about his dumb ass is he follows orders."

"Why'd Mary Beth have to go?"

"Stupid girl almost tipped our hand to the detective. Nothing worse than a snitch."

Richie swirled his drink. "I sure did enjoy her."

"Yeah, me too. It's too bad she won't be around to fill in on occasion."

Their conversation turned to who provided information to O'Hara on the Palmetto Men's Society. They had some ideas but nothing solid.

"I'll kill whoever ran their fucking mouth," Percy growled.

After finishing their third mid-morning drink, they concluded the best thing for them would be some relaxation and de-stressing. Percy stood and went to his desk. He punched in a number and placed his order. When he'd finished, he motioned to Richie to do the same.

"The Carriage House suite is available, so you take it. Since I'm Simpson's attorney, it'll be easier to explain why I'm parked up front." Percy offered his hand, and they shook.

CJ turned into the Ralston driveway and its pristine landscaping. There were more flowers than on her last visit, and she wondered if Reggie had planted them. Bright colors ran the length of the front of the house—reds, yellows, oranges, and multiple shades in between. A freshly planted weeping willow stood not far from the flowering plants.

She climbed out of her truck and strolled up the walk, observing a man on his hands and knees near the side fence.

Stopping, she held her hand to shade her eyes and studied if this was the long-term gardener. He must have sensed her eyes on him as he turned and stood. He removed his straw hat, smiled, and waved.

Thank God she didn't fire you.

After returning his greeting, she zipped up the steps and rang the doorbell. She glanced at her cell phone at the time—3:35 p.m. Since she didn't have an appointment, it would be interesting to see if Ava would invite her in.

There was movement in the door's sidelight; the lock tumbler rattled, and she faced Sophie.

"Hello." CJ leaned over so she was eye-to-eye with the young girl. "Is your mom home?"

Her little head bobbed. "She's on the back deck, sitting in the shade with him."

"Uh—who's *him*?"

"The short, red-nosed fat guy who always comes here." She leaned in closer and whispered, "He's always staring at me. He wants to get in my pants."

CJ's mouth fell open. "Uh … tell you what," she said as she handed the child her card. "If he tries to do anything, you call me."

Her light brown eyes focused on the card, and she nodded. "Will you shoot him?"

"I'm not sure, but I'll arrest him if he touches you."

Satisfied, Sophie told her to follow, and she'd take her to her mother. The two traipsed down a long hallway with family photos taken from various places adorning the walls—London, Paris, Rome, and locales across the US.

Bright smiles were the common denominator in all of them.

Ava, who wore tan shorts and a pale blue bikini top, jumped to her feet as she approached. Pickett, her attorney, sat with his back to CJ, but snapped his head around and leaped up. As she stepped onto the deck, he moved between the two women.

"What are you doing here?" he demanded, and jabbed his finger at her. "I don't recall arranging a meeting. This constant harassment had better stop."

CJ smiled. "It's nice to see you too, and I'm glad you're both here. It saves me a trip."

"I asked why you're here," he said as the nostrils on his beet-red nose flared.

She held up an envelope. "I have a few questions for your client." She wagged her finger. "Now that I think about it, I have a couple for you, too."

"Make her leave, Richie," Ava moaned from behind him.

"Oh, I will." He moved closer to CJ, and the stench of alcohol on his breath made her eyes water. "We're not answering any questions today." He dramatically pointed at the steps to the walkway. "Leave now or—"

"Or what? You'll call the police?" She winked and curtsied. "I'm already here and at your service."

"You fucking bitch! I'll have your badge if you don't leave." His hands clenched into fists and he breathed heavily.

"Okay. I'll go … for now." Her fingers pulled a photo out of the envelope and dropped it on the glass table. His eyes cut to it, as did Ava's, who now leaned around him. "I'll come back with a warrant, then you can answer why you lied to me." She shifted her eyes to the half-hidden woman. "And you can tell me who the woman is with your daughter and where you went after you dropped her off."

"Richie," Ava whined.

His fists relaxed as his face twitched. "No judge in this town will issue a warrant for such bullshit."

CJ leaned into him, hoping not to gag from his breath, and said, "Try me. I'm sure you're familiar with the Honorable Judge Amos White. He's a friend of mine and doesn't care for you."

His hand went to his mouth and rubbed his lips. "You're bluffing. He's a family court judge."

She pulled out her cell phone, scrolled through her contacts, and held it up. "Should I hit the speed dial and we'll find out?" Her thumb gently rested on the button.

"Wait!" Pickett turned and whispered in Ava's ear.

She shook her head, and he pulled her to the side of the deck. The two talked back and forth in a tone too soft for CJ to make out, but she knew what would happen. The short, stocky man with the beet-red nose plodded back over.

"Look. I told you Ava took Sophie to a play, but ... the fact is, she was with me." He rubbed at the back of his neck. "We were at the Regency Charleston Waterfront. I'm not proud of it, but we've been seeing each other for over three years."

CJ opened her notebook, jotted down the hotel name, and said, "I'll confirm this, so you better not be lying to me again."

His head hung and he said, "I'm not. I've got a credit card receipt to prove it, and I'm sure the clerk at the desk will remember. She—uh ... always makes sure we get our usual room."

CJ shoved her notebook at him. "How 'bout you write down her name for me?"

Sighing, he scribbled a name.

"Now. Who's the woman with Sophie?"

He turned, motioned Ava to his side, and put his arm around her.

She shifted her weight, stared at the floor, and said, "She's a friend—"

"You're lying," CJ said.

The woman covered her face with both hands and exhaled. "Okay, okay. She's Sophie's grandmother. Her name is—"

"Susanna Davis, and she lives in Beaufort," CJ answered for her.

Ava's head snapped up. "How did you know?"

She smiled, closed her notebook, and turned to go. "Because I'm damn good at my job." She started down the back stairs and called to them, "Thanks so much for your hospitality. Have a wonderful evening!"

As she rounded the corner of the house, the two stunned figures stood frozen, watching her leave.

After settling in her truck, she listened to Janet's message and called her. Janet said she'd tracked down the witness they'd discussed at a no-name bar on Dorchester Road. After some coaxing, he'd given up his friend, a suspect in a murder last year. The man was with the guy when a fight broke out over a game of pool.

Janet said the witness was willing to testify, and the nail in the coffin was a video he took on his cell phone—clear footage of when the suspect pulled a weapon and fired three shots into the victim. Janet was ready to make an arrest.

"That is excellent work," CJ said. "Have Sam help you with the warrant. She knows who to contact. Then call SWAT and have them run point. If the guy was willing to shoot someone over a game of eight-ball, he'd have no issue doing it again."

"Assuming I obtain the warrant this afternoon, when should we arrest him?"

"Let's defer to SWAT, but tonight would make the most sense to me. We need to surprise him."

"Makes sense," Janet said. "Uh—can you go, or should I take an officer with me? I'm fine alone and know you're trying to stay with Harry."

She rubbed her chin. "Shoot me a text once you have a time, and I'll plan to go with you. Unless the news at the hospital is bad."

"You got it. Thanks, and tell your uncle hello."

CJ ended the call and immediately dialed Sam. She asked her to have her contact search for any videos of the Regency Charleston Waterfront hotel entrance after Ava dropped her daughter off.

"Have them search from 7:00 to 8:30 p.m., and maybe we'll catch Richie and Ava entering."

"By the way, how was last night in the recliner?" Sam asked.

"Uncomfortable, but I slept a little."

"Are you staying again tonight?"

"I'm planning on it. The only break I may take is to go with Janet and SWAT to make an arrest. She'll fill you in and ask you to help with the warrant, since she's new to the department." Starting her truck, she said, "I'm heading back to the hospital to meet with the doctor and sort out what's happening with Harry. He's still bleeding from his wound."

FORTY

Friday, May 6
Downtown Charleston

CJ hustled down the hallway to the ICU nurses' station. She wanted to confirm when the doctor would arrive to discuss his plan to stop the continued bleeding from Harry's chest. The nurse indicated she could expect him within the hour.

She pushed the door open to her uncle's room and crept in. He was sound asleep. She slumped into the worn brown recliner and rubbed her burning eyes. The wear and tear of the last few days was taking its toll. The juggle of being at the hospital and working her cases was crushing her.

Harry stirred awake, and she jumped up to his side. He told her his mouth was dry, so she helped him drink water.

Her eyes grew wet as she stared at the man who had raised her lying painfully before her. His wound had prohibited him from much movement, and the nurses were concerned about bedsores.

She bent down and kissed his forehead. "Uncle Harry, you're gonna be better soon. The doctor is coming to discuss getting you back on your feet."

He moaned. "I'm fine, sweetheart. They'll have me out of here in a few days. Can I have some more water?"

"Sure." She refilled the plastic cup and tipped it to his mouth, biting the inside of her cheek as she fought her tears. He weakly waved to signal he'd had enough. "Do you want me to put some ointment on your lips? It might help with the cracking."

She was sitting on the edge of his bed when the doctor tapped on the door and entered. He smiled at her, grabbed the chart off the table, and flipped through it. Then he picked up the controller and adjusted the headrest so Harry was more upright. "How're you feeling, young man?"

"I've been better, Doc. When can I go home?"

Dr. Anson chuckled. "Not today. We'll get you out of here as soon as we can." He pulled the gown back to examine his chest. "Your incision appears slightly better, but we still have seepage."

"How can you stop it, Doctor?" CJ asked.

He stood and sighed. "I'm not sure until I go back in."

She wiped her eyes. "You mean another surgery?"

He nodded. "Yes. Unfortunately, it's the only way to correct the issue."

"When?" Harry croaked.

"Depends on the availability of the OR, but sometime tomorrow. I'll let you know as soon as I find a slot. The good news is, it'll be a Saturday, so I'll have more options." The doctor picked the chart up again and scribbled a note. "I'll give you something to help you rest better tonight."

CJ followed him out of the room. When they were in the hall, she asked, "Does a second surgery happen often?"

"Hmm, not really." He put his hand on her shoulder. "I should be able to get Harry back on his feet. He's a strong man." As he left, he told her she shouldn't spend the night, so her uncle would rest better.

She nodded. "Okay. I'll leave when visiting hours are over and return first thing tomorrow." Her eyes trailed him, as he went to the nurses' station, and the young woman tapped the keys on her keyboard.

He nodded and motioned her over. "We're set for the procedure at seven tomorrow morning, so we'll take your uncle down around six thirty for prep."

"I'll be here," she said. Once he left, she returned to Harry and told him when the surgery was scheduled. They discussed her cases until he drifted off to sleep. She moved back to the chair and reviewed her notebook.

While he ate a light dinner at six, she called Uncle Craig and told him about the plan. He told her he'd join her there. She called Ben and Sam, who said they'd also come. Cara, the nurse she'd met on Wednesday, gave Harry the doctor's prescribed meds. CJ gazed at the young woman as she caressed his forehead with her fingertips until he fell asleep.

Maybe he's right. All the nurses here are overly sweet.

Her cell phone buzzed, and she left the room to answer a call from Janet. She told CJ they were all set to make the arrest at 1:00 a.m.

"Text me the address and I'll join you," CJ said.

Despite the other woman urging her to get some sleep for the early morning return to the hospital, CJ insisted she would come.

She kissed her uncle's forehead at nine o'clock and whispered that she loved him. Annie's brown eyes and bright smile met her as she exited. The young nurse appeared the same way they had first met—no makeup and hair in a bun.

The two chatted for a few minutes, and Annie told her she'd stay the night with Harry and be there when she returned. CJ's emotions overcame her, and she burst into tears. Wrapping her arms around her, the nurse whispered in her ear that everything would be fine.

CJ wiped her eyes and nodded. "Thank you for being so kind to my uncle. He means the world to me."

———

CJ pulled her truck in behind Janet, hopped out, and joined her in her vehicle. Janet said SWAT should arrive soon, so they had thirty minutes to prepare.

"I've had an officer staking out his house since 8:00 p.m. Let me call him and get the status." She dialed a number, spoke with him, and frowned.

"What's up?" CJ asked as she slipped on her bullet-proof vest.

"He told me the suspect left around 9:15 p.m. and hasn't returned." She glanced at her cell phone. "It's twelve thirty now."

"Okay. Have the SWAT guys wait out of sight until our target appears."

Janet called the team leader and relayed the instructions. "He'll hold his team around the corner. It's a dead end, so our guy shouldn't come home that way. They have a visual on the front door."

CJ's eyes scanned the dark house. "There's no garage, so he can only park in the driveway."

"How's your uncle?"

She sighed. "Under the circumstances, he's okay, I guess. I hope the procedure tomorrow will do the trick. How 'bout you have the SWAT crew position themselves outside the house if they can stay hidden?"

Janet nodded and made the call. "They're good with that. Said it's easier and safer to take him down before he enters his house."

At 1:35 a.m. a beat-up, maroon Ford Crown Victoria crawled up the street and passed where they sat. It slowed and turned into the driveway.

"There he is," Janet whispered as she grabbed her door handle.

CJ touched her arm. "Wait. Let SWAT handle him. If we get out, he may see our inside light and bolt."

The door creaked as he opened it, and a dark-haired man climbed out of the car. He stood, stretched his arms over his head, and spat on the ground. He dropped his keys when he tried to lock his car door.

"What the hell is he doing?" Janet asked.

"I think he's drunk. He's probably been at the bar drinking all this time. Can you see any movement by our guys?"

She shook her head. "No. It's too dark."

CJ pointed to tall shrubs at the corner of the house opposite the driveway. "I bet they're hidden there. It's less than five yards from his door."

"Dammit! The idiot's still crawling around searching for his keys."

The man stood and went back to fumbling with his car door.

"Will your man who's staked out waiting be able to cut him off with his vehicle if he runs?"

Janet shook her head. "I doubt it. He's on the street past the house."

Their suspect messed around with his car for what seemed like an eternity. He got in at one point but exited soon after. They thought he was about to leave when he staggered toward his front door. When he was within about twenty feet, he abruptly stopped and peered at the bushes where SWAT was hidden.

"Uh-oh," CJ said. "He's suspicious. Get ready to start your truck and block the road. It's his only escape."

Janet slid her key into the ignition. "Ready."

"If he takes off on foot, I'll jump out and help keep up with him. He can't get far as drunk as— Oh, shit! There he goes."

The man took off running away from the house, back the way he'd come. SWAT burst through the bushes in hot pursuit. Their suspect made a sharp right, running up the street where the detectives sat. Within fifteen feet of their position, CJ drew her Glock, swung the door open, and jumped out.

"Stop! Charleston PD!" she screamed.

"Fuck you!"

He tried to swerve and run past her, but he miscalculated how quick she was as she slammed into him broadside and drove him face-first to the pavement.

She spun her body, landed with a thud on top of him, and yanked his arm behind him. "I told you to stop! Hold your ass still."

"You bitch! You're breaking my arm!"

Within seconds, two burly officers jerked him up and off his feet. "The lieutenant gave you an order," one said. The man kicked, twisted, and squirmed as they held him until the van pulled around, and he was hauled off.

The team leader approached her. "You okay, ma'am?"

CJ rubbed her shoulder and laughed. "Yeah. I'm fine. I used him to break my fall."

"We'll take him to the station and book him. You wanna interview his sorry ass tonight or let him sleep it off first?"

"Actually, my partner will handle him." She turned to Janet, who stood with her mouth open and eyes wide from watching CJ take down the suspect. "The scumbag is all yours, Detective." She pulled off her vest, climbed in her truck, and headed for her apartment—she'd grab a shower and return to the hospital.

CHAPTER

FORTY-ONE

Saturday, May 7
Downtown Charleston

CJ rushed home after the early morning arrest, took a short, fitful nap, and prepared herself for Harry's second time in the surgeon's hands in less than a week.

As the steamy water from the nozzle rained down on her, her tears mixed with the spray. Her whole body shook—she was dizzy, her stomach churned, and her chest tightened. She raced for her truck at 5:15 a.m.

Her uncle was in good spirits despite the pending procedure. She held his hand and did her best to be upbeat. Nurse Annie busied herself tending to Harry and calming CJ. The young nurse kissed him on the cheek as the attendants wheeled him into surgery, then wrapped her arms around CJ and softly rubbed her back.

Uncle Craig joined her, and they followed the rolling gurney as far as possible. Their fingers squeezed the sick man's hands one last time before he entered the OR area. They stood frozen in the hallway for several minutes before meandering to the waiting room, where they met Ben, Will, and Sam.

For the next two hours, the group reminisced about all the times they'd had with the man they loved. Sam attempted to persuade CJ to eat some of the food she'd brought, but she took only three bites. Everyone jumped to their feet when Nurse Annie appeared in the doorway.

"Harry's out of surgery, and Dr. Anson told me it went well." She motioned to CJ and Craig. "If you two want to return to the room, the doctor will brief you soon."

Nodding, they followed her.

The surgeon entered the room fifteen minutes later and advised them the repair was successful. One graft hadn't held, but he'd corrected it and stopped the seepage. He'd keep a close eye on it for the next twenty-four hours, but he anticipated no more issues.

"So, if all goes well, what happens?" CJ asked.

"We'll bring your uncle back here for three days, then move him out of the ICU into another room. After that, I guess he'll need another week before we can discharge him." He stepped toward the door. "I suggest you go home after he returns from recovery. Grab some sleep tonight. Nurse

Cara will stay with him until seven, and Nurse Annie will return for an overnight shift. You can call them to check his status and visit tomorrow at 9:00 a.m."

CJ exited the Ashley-Rutledge Parking Garage, turning left on Ashley Avenue. She never noticed the black Cadillac Escalade pull from the curb as she turned right on Bee Street.

Ava passed the Marine Corps Air Station as she neared Beaufort. The drive had been slow and the unusually heavy Saturday traffic was murder. Stopping twice for Sophie to pee had only added to her foul mood. She sighed and flipped the visor down to shield her eyes from the bright sunshine. Her destination was less than ten minutes away.

The Davis home, where she grew up, was over one hundred years old. It was a white, three-story structure with spectacular round columns running from the ground to the second floor. Black shutters, pale sky-blue trim, and wrought-iron railing added eye-pleasing contrasts.

Massive magnolias blocked the view of the house until she reached the end of the long driveway. As always, the landscaping was immaculate. Before putting her BMW into park, her daughter bounded from her seat and raced across the deep green grass. Yelling at her was a waste of time.

"Come on, Mommy! I wanna see Grandma!" Without waiting, the little girl bolted through the front door.

Ava cut the engine, exhaled, and rubbed the back of her neck. Her insides quivered. No matter how long she was away, the same old feeling engulfed her—soul-crushing dread. She gathered herself, stepped out, and drifted to the open entrance. Rounding the corner, Ava found herself in the expansive sitting room.

Her mother sat on the gold couch, brushing Sophie's brown strands. Without glancing up, she said, "It's 'bout time you arrived. I thought you'd wrecked."

"The traffic was terrible, and we had to make a couple of stops," she said.

"Your problem is, you never plan," the older woman said. "If you had gotten gas before leaving Charleston, no stops would have been needed."

Ava opened her mouth but remained silent. It was no use trying to argue. Even when the facts were on her side, she'd lose. She crossed the deep red area rug with gold embroidery and plopped into a side chair across from the other two.

Susanna Davis finished her granddaughter's hair. At sixty, she was remarkably beautiful, with brunette hair only starting to gray, and hazel eyes. No matter the day, she always wore makeup and was well-dressed. Today's attire was a flowing white dress tailored to fit her slender, five-foot-eight frame. She never missed a chance to point out her daughter barely resembled her. Even when Ava had dyed her hair brunette in her early twenties all she got was a laugh.

"Go pour Grandma some sweet tea, little one." When Sophie scampered to the kitchen, Susanna immediately turned to Ava. "Now that your piece of shit husband is dead, what happens?"

"Uh … I'm not sure what you mean."

"Are you gonna shake your little ass and land another one?"

Ava grunted. "You're really something. Fucking unbelievable."

Susanna's hazel eyes twinkled. "It's much easier the other way. You could always—"

"I married Charlie, hoping for a normal life," she spat. "Just because you—"

Susanna's eyes flashed. "Don't you sass me. I provided everything for you. Everything!" She jumped up from the couch. "I'll be on the back porch with my little angel. How she's your child, God only knows."

Ava was left alone in the room she hated most, where the meet-and-greet parties were held. Their only invited guests were powerful men with lots of money and an eye for gorgeous things. She had once been one of those.

After several minutes, she exited the front door and strolled around the house to the back garden. The perfectly shaped shrubs and brightly colored flowers were always where she went to hide. She wove along the rock paths, and the sweet odors and singing birds began to calm her.

Her breath caught when she viewed the glasshouse at the end of the last walkway. She froze as a figure busily worked. She struggled to slow her pulse, wheeled around, and returned to the house.

FORTY-TWO

Sunday, May 8
Downtown Charleston

CJ left the hospital after she'd spent the morning with Harry. She was relieved the wound on his chest was no longer bleeding. As soon as he dozed off after his lunch, she headed to the LEC. While she lacked physical and mental energy, she had to work on her cases.

She sat at the conference table, staring at the two boards, when her cell phone buzzed. She glanced at the number. *Jimmy from the Cold Case Evidence Room.* She answered, and he told her he'd like her to come down, as he had something for her.

"You are aware it's Sunday, right?"

"I am," he said, "but you're parked across from me in the lot. So, like you, I'm here working."

CJ hung up and trudged to the door. *Why can't he tell me what he has over the phone?* She rode the elevator to the basement and knocked on the Cold Case room door.

Jimmy swung the door open and waved her in. "Thanks for coming down. I'm so sorry to hear about your uncle. How's he doing?"

"I went to visit him this morning. He's much better, and the doctor expects him to go home in a week or so."

He smiled. "That'd be wonderful. It's been a difficult time for you." He stared at the floor and poked at the corner of a loose tile.

"So, what did you need to tell me?" she asked.

He exhaled. "It's best if I show you." He motioned for her to follow. "On Friday, I received the last of the old files from the warehouse where we had them stored and have been logging everything all weekend." He pointed at the table by his desk. "That's when I found this."

She peered at a battered, yellowed box labeled *Eugene Gibbs Case*. "What's this?" she asked, furrowing her brow.

"It's another victim who was poisoned with deadly nightshade. Thirty-five years ago."

Her eyes went wide. She slipped on a pair of surgical gloves and opened the lid. The contents didn't fill the box—the only items inside were a sealed paper bag and three manilla folders. "Are you sure?"

Removing the paper bag and setting it aside, he handed her the first folder. "Read the summary sheet."

Her eyes scanned the typewritten page.

A fifty-four-year-old man was found in a guest room on the first floor of the Duncan House. Based on the lab's analysis, the victim died from poison—deadly nightshade.

She leaned back in disbelief. *Just like the other two.*

She pulled all the information out and spread it across the table. "Have you reviewed this?"

He nodded. "Yes. Well, enough to determine the MO matches the Ralston and Wilkins cases. That's why I called you."

She dropped into the metal chair, stretching her head to relieve the knot in her neck. "Let me review what we have, and we'll copy everything tomorrow."

She held up the paper bag. It was labeled with a handwritten note, *Gibbs Bedsheet with Stain.* "Can you help me with this? This appears to be our only forensic evidence, and I'd like to see it."

"Sure." He moved everything off the table and slipped on surgical gloves as she pulled the bedsheet from the bag. He took one end of the white cloth, and she carefully unfolded it.

"There's the stain," she said, pointing to the center of the linen.

"According to a note in the file, the stain was under the victim. I didn't find any mention of testing, but as you know, DNA wasn't a thing that long ago."

She slowly nodded. "Okay. Let's fold it back up, and I'll have the CSU guys examine it. Maybe they can do something with it. But we'll need some luck since it's been so many years, and the sample may be degraded."

Once the bedsheet was back in its original packaging, she picked up her cell phone and called Eddie, who was on call for the weekend. He picked up right away and asked about Harry. Then, niceties out of the way, she asked him for another favor.

"I have a stained sheet from an old case. I'd like you to examine it and determine if we can get a DNA analysis sample."

"Is this more evidence from the cold case from ten years ago? I thought we had—"

"No. This is a different one. Twenty-five years prior. The summary report indicates the vic died from nightshade poisoning."

"Oh, shit! So now we have another one?"

"It looks that way. I haven't reviewed the files yet, but I'd like this stain processed ASAP."

"What's it in?"

"A paper bag. And it was sealed and labeled."

"Okay, good. I'll send a tech over now to pick it up. We'll push it as fast as we can. A heads-up, though … we may have a budget problem. Where are you?"

"I'm here with Jimmy in the basement. I'll be here reviewing the other information."

"You are aware it's Sunday, right?" he asked.

"I am."

He chuckled. "Tech's on his way."

She hit the red button on her phone and flipped through the paperwork until she found the responding officer's report.

The nude body of a man was found lying face-up on a bed in the first-floor room of the Duncan House by a housekeeper. The body had no apparent signs of wounds, and the establishment's owner stated he believed the man had a heart attack. Two empty wine bottles were on the glass table near the couch. The sheet from the bed had a stain underneath the man's midsection. The body was picked up by the coroner and transported to the morgue for an autopsy.

"There's no mention of who the owner of the Duncan House was at the time," she growled. "You'd think the officer would have listed that somewhere." She turned to Jimmy. "Are you sure this is the only box?"

He nodded. "I only received ten boxes, and I checked them all. I confirmed there's nothing left in the old storage area, and I'm embarrassed we're just finding this stuff after all these years."

"Okay. I'll keep searching. Maybe there are witness statements in here somewhere." She held up the report. "Can I copy this?"

"Sure. Let me have it. I'll do it for you."

She passed him the information and continued her review. There was an additional document from the detective's investigation, but no actual leads or suspects. One note stood out: *A guest said a woman left the room through the back door around midnight.*

"That's it?" she whispered. "No follow-up. Who writes a report and doesn't list the damn name of a witness?"

She found the ME's report and read it. The cause of death was poison that disrupted the nervous system, causing the man's heart and breathing to stop. It was identical to what had happened to Ralston and Wilkins. *Sudden cardiac arrest.*

She rubbed her eyes and her chest tightened. *Does this have anything to do with the other cases?*

"Can you copy this as well, please?" she asked, handing Jimmy the ME's report.

Twenty minutes later, Jimmy answered the knock on the door and a young technician entered. He placed the paper bag in a case and obtained her signature authorizing the removal for testing.

CJ picked up the copied paperwork and told Jimmy that Sam would get the rest.

"I'm sorry I'm bringing more bad news," he said. "It's never a good time for a surprise, but with all you have on your plate … this sucks."

She blew out a long breath, feebly smiled, and headed back upstairs. She debated it but called Sam. "Listen, I have something for you first thing tomorrow morning."

"No problem. I'll come in early. What do you need?"

She walked to the window, gazing at the dark clouds rolling toward the city. "Jimmy called me to the Cold Case room. He found another deadly nightshade poisoning case—we have three to solve now."

For the next hour, she surveyed the sky as sheets of rain obstructed the Ashley River Memorial Bridge. Her day had started on a high note but had gone south. She grabbed her notebook, slipped on her raincoat, and plodded out the door. Sitting in her truck, she texted Ben.

Checking on Harry. Wanna have a sleepover?

PART THREE

FAMILY TRADITION

FORTY-THREE

Monday, May 9
The Business District

Ava hummed along with the radio as she traveled down King Street. If her meeting with her attorney didn't run too long, she'd grab a bite at the Palmetto Café. She might even invite a few friends to join, and they could sip champagne and celebrate. After all, it was not every day someone took complete control of over thirty million dollars.

At Horlbeck Alley, she took a left and pulled into a parking spot in front of the Pickney Law Offices. She peered in the mirror and admired herself. No matter what her sorry-ass mother tried to tell her, she was one damn fine-looking woman. At thirty-five, she had many years to attract men's lustful gazes.

She hopped out of her BMW and strolled through the front door. A woman in her late forties greeted her with a smile and escorted her into a cozy meeting room. "Can I bring you something to drink?"

"You know what I'm in the mood for? A mimosa."

The older woman raised her eyebrows. "Uh—okay. I have fresh orange juice, and the boss keeps champagne around for when we win a big case." She hurried out the door and, within minutes, returned with a flute.

Ava sat, enjoyed her late-morning treat, called a couple of girlfriends, and invited them to meet her for lunch. She'd need to arrange to sell her husband's development company soon. She had no interest in being involved. She would turn her proceeds over to her investment advisors and let the money make her more.

The door opened and the sixty-five-year-old Franklin Pickney glided in. "Good morning, Mrs. Ralston. How are you today?"

"I'm wonderful, and I'm sure you're about to make me fantastic," she said, her honey-brown eyes twinkling.

"I'll do my best." He slid into a brown leather chair across from her and placed a red, three-inch ring binder on the table.

The two made small talk for a few minutes before she told him she had lunch plans and would like to cover everything so she wouldn't be late. He nodded, opened the binder, and described how the assets would transfer, considering her husband's death.

Midway through his discussion, she stopped him. "Nothing's changed. I know it all goes to me, and when I'm no longer around, it all goes to Sophie."

He scratched his cheek. "Um ... yes."

"Good. Let's go through what I have and skip all the formalities."

He nodded and began going through the assets in the Ralston Family Trust. "First, let's talk about the two residential properties. We have the home in Dunes West and the condo in Vail. You, of course, own those."

"I think I'll sell the condo," she said. "That was Charlie's thing, and I hate the snow."

He shrugged. "Totally up to you." He returned to the list. "Next, we have the investment portfolio last valued at over four million dollars. In addition, there are some other personal items, such as the boat at the Isle of Palms Marina." He passed her the sheet, showing various assets.

"Hmm ... I'll keep the boat, since Sophie loves it. Some of these smaller things I'll sell."

"Again, that's up to you."

"How much is all this worth?" she asked.

He flipped through pages and pursed his lips. "I don't have the latest estimates, but I'd say seven million dollars."

She let out a low whistle and raised her glass.

"Of course, that doesn't factor in the second mortgage on the Dunes West property. I'd need to—"

"My home is paid for," she blurted out. "Charlie paid for it in full when we built it eight years ago."

He rubbed his chin and went back to his notebook. "That was true, but he took out a home equity loan two years ago."

She crossed her arms and frowned. "How did he do that? I never signed anything."

Pickney flipped through the sheets and turned the binder to her. "The loan was for two million dollars." He pointed to the bottom of the document. "Both you and Charles signed for it, and it was notarized."

Her cheeks turned red, and she clenched her teeth. "I never did such a thing," she said, pinching the bridge of her nose. "This must be a mistake. My husband couldn't just do whatever he wanted." She jabbed a finger at the lawyer. "Our trust wouldn't allow it ... unless you fucked up!"

"You're correct. Your husband couldn't act alone. However, you agreed to it when you signed the paperwork."

Her chest pounding, she asked, "When did I allegedly sign this document?"

His eyes trailed down the page. "July 8, 2009."

"That was Sophie's eighth birthday, and we had a big party for her at the house in the backyard. There's no damn way ..." Her heart tightened, and she whispered, "Charlie had me sign some paperwork, but he said it was routine stuff."

"Did you review it?"

"Uh—well—no. I was so busy preparing everything for the party, I simply signed it."

"Did someone notarize it?"

Oh, God. "I think so. There was some young woman …
I don't recall her name …"

He studied the agreement again. "Does Meredith
Powers ring a bell?"

Dizziness surrounded her. "Yes. She works for my other
attorney, Richie Pickett."

He shook his head. "I'm sorry. You can challenge it, but
there's a legal loan against the house now."

"I'll need to sort this out," she said in a shaky voice.

"I guess there's good news in all this," he smiled. "You
have a considerable sum in the investment account, so you
can pay off the loan." He closed the binder and stood. "Let
me know when you want to revise the trust."

"Wait!" She slapped her hand down on the table. "Sit
down so we can review how much the business is worth. I
need to know so I can plan for its sale."

His eyebrows squished together. "Mrs. Ralston, you
don't own the business."

She bolted upright, and her high-pitched voice asked
what he was talking about. She was the only person the
business could go to based on the trust.

"That would be true if your husband still owned the
business," he said. "He transferred ownership to his partner
two years ago. You signed a document for that on the same
date as the loan."

She collapsed back in the chair and burst into tears.

He stood silent, staring at her before speaking. "I'm
sorry, but it's all legal."

Her fiery eyes glared at him. "Who in the fuck did my husband give the business to?"

"It was transferred into an LLC called the Sawgrass Development."

"Who in the hell owns that?!"

"I'm not at liberty to say. You'll need to—"

She leaped to her feet, knocking her glass across the table and crashing it to the floor. "You damn well better tell me what thief stole what is mine!"

He exhaled. "Richie Pickett owns the LLC."

Her whole body went rigid as a flash of heat swept over her and she collapsed back into the chair. Pickney mumbled he was sorry for the confusion and left her alone in the now cramped room. She managed to get to her feet, plodded out the door, unlocked her car, and climbed in. She rested her forehead on the steering wheel and sobbed. *How could these two men do this to me?*

She hadn't been faithful to Charlie, but had kept a lovely home and appearances. And that bastard, Richie. She knew he was a snake, but never imagined he could pull anything like this off. She hadn't realized he even knew her husband that well, much less was in business with him.

She tried to convince herself she still had loads of money. But she couldn't shake it was only a fraction of what she expected by the time she repaid the loan. She wiped away her tears, repaired her makeup, and jerked her car into reverse. She pushed the gearshift into drive, and her tires squealed as she took off toward King Street.

Within minutes, she skidded to a stop before Pickett's ground-floor law office and burst through the front door. "You little bitch!" she screamed at the wide-eyed young woman behind the front desk. "You're a thief, and I'm gonna sue you."

"I'm not sure what you're talking about," the young, blonde-haired woman said.

"You know damn well what," she said. "You came to my house and had me sign away my husband's business."

She coyly smiled. "Oh, that. I'm certain I explained it all to you in detail before we executed the documents."

Ava snatched the office door open and faced her attorney, who sat on the edge of his desk, arms folded. "Hello, sweetheart." His mouth curved into a smile. "What a pleasant surprise."

She stood rigid as her heart pounded. "How could you do this to me?!"

He spread his arms. "Honey, it was just business."

"Why would my husband transfer his company to you and lose control?"

"I was doing him a favor." He smirked. "He was gonna divorce you and wanted to protect his company."

She lunged and slapped him. "This'll never hold up in court!"

He caressed his cheek. "Sadly for you, it will. You signed the papers after my assistant, a notary, explained everything to you." He gave her a loathsome grin. "She told me all about it last night—while we were in bed together."

She slammed a chair against the wall and stormed out.

"Honey, do you still want me to come by tonight for a roll in the hay?" he called as he erupted into laughter that followed her to her car.

FORTY-FOUR

Monday, May 9
Downtown Charleston

After spending the morning with Harry, CJ drove to the LEC. She was anxious to learn what Eddie would tell her about the latest sample sent to SLED in Columbia for analysis, and he'd agreed to meet in her office.

It was amazing how a couple of days could turn things around. Her uncle was drastically improved and would be moved out of ICU tomorrow, her relationship with Ben now scared her less, and the weather contributed a bright, sunny day with a crystal-clear blue sky. Having three un-solved cases didn't seem to weigh as much.

"How's Harry?" Sam asked when she came through the door.

"So much better. Dr. Anson told me he's never seen a quicker turnaround."

The young woman crossed the room and hugged her. "I'm so relieved." She eyed her. "For both of you."

"Eddie's swinging by to discuss our newest case." CJ slid into a chair at the table. "Did you get everything copied?"

"Sure did. Jimmy had me bring up the originals for cases two and three, and I locked them in the file drawer. I wanna protect them if we decide they don't connect to Ralston and need to return to the basement."

"That's a good idea, although Stan told me he wants them solved, so they're not returning," CJ said.

"Fair enough. I'm running out to grab lunch. Any requests?"

"Surprise me."

Shortly after Sam left, there was a knock, and she opened the door to find Eddie. He joined her at the table and told her the sample was in SLED's hands. The analyst who ran the samples for the other cases would handle them, and he'd agreed to sneak them up in priority.

"Why's he being so helpful?"

Eddie grinned. "He's my cousin, so we're getting the family discount on timing." He added this would be the last special favor for a while, as a large batch of samples had come in from a high-profile murder case in Greenville.

"Has he examined the sample yet?"

He nodded and told her his cousin agreed with him. The sample was old, but whoever collected it appeared to have done so correctly, and putting it in its own paper bag inside a cardboard box was a huge break. That, and the fact the warehouse where it had sat for all those years was climate controlled, should help provide a solid result.

"I know we send our samples to Columbia, but what happens if I need one run for a suspect if they're backlogged?"

He shrugged. "You have to wait, unless the department has the money to use a private lab. They're more expensive, of course."

She exhaled. "Stan's been clear how tight our budget is, so we'll cross that bridge when we get to it."

"Have you come up with an angle to get Ava Ralston's DNA yet?" he asked.

"No. We need probable cause. She's not gonna volunteer it. Same for Larry Simpson, although he's not a female, and I'm certain it's a woman we're searching for."

They said their goodbyes, and she returned to her files. Suddenly, it hit her. What about Mary Beth as a possible match for the DNA sample? The young woman had been helpful, but had also rushed out of town. Was it because of Simpson, or could she be the mystery woman? CJ added her name to the board.

She and Sam spent the rest of the day reviewing each case again. It was after six when she ran across a note of something she'd agreed to do—visit the ballroom at the Regency Charleston Waterfront for Sam and Will's wedding reception.

CJ held up the note. "I'm sorry I haven't gotten around to this. It's been so crazy."

"I know." Sam sighed. "Let's pass on you taking the time. Two of my other bridesmaids have seen the plans for the room, and we all know how picky my mom is. I like what's planned, so you don't need to go over."

She shook her head. "No. I'm going. In fact, I'll go now."

"Are you sure?"

"Yep." She stood, grabbed her notebook, and headed for the door. "I'll call you and let you know what I think."

"Wait. I can go with you." The young woman headed for her desk. "I need to call Will and tell him dinner's off."

CJ chuckled. "What? And disappoint the poor man. No way."

———

The hotel was close, so she walked over and got some fresh air. The sky had dimmed, and the yellows and pinks hanging over the horizon would soon go dark. She entered the impressive lobby with its white tile flooring, off-white walls, and black desks. She asked a desk clerk for the manager, who happily agreed to show her the ballroom. It was no surprise she was a friend of the Ravenels.

The woman was about her age and took her to an expansive ballroom with mauve carpeting with multi-colored swirls. She explained they planned to hang sheer curtains from the ceiling, cover the tables with matching tablecloths, and add candles and crystal centerpieces.

"So what do you think?" the woman asked.

CJ scanned the room once more. "I think it'll be beautiful, and there's certainly enough room."

The woman clapped her hands. "I think we're all set. You were the last person on my list to give it your blessing."

"I approve," CJ said. She thanked her and headed back toward the lobby. Exiting the ballroom door, she recognized two young women leaving the lounge—the nurses caring for Harry. They wore classy but sexy dresses. One was a shimmering white, the other peach colored.

"Hey, ladies," she said.

Their faces lit up, and they joined her and chatted about her uncle and his pending move out of the ICU. Both young women told her they'd still care for him, as they often worked in other parts of the hospital and followed patients until they were released.

Annie's lips curled upward. "And since we love Harry, we made sure we went with him." Her brown eyes flashed. "I'm not sure he's told you, but I've offered to stay with him at his home until he's back on his feet."

"I'd also volunteer," Cara added with a smile.

"Uh—no," CJ said. "He hasn't mentioned it, but we'll be fine between Uncle Craig and me helping out. We plan to take turns staying at the house."

"Well, think about it and let me know," Annie said.

"I will. By the way, what brings you girls here looking so gorgeous on a Monday night?"

"We had the night off, so we came over for drinks," Annie said. "We were thinking about stopping by the hospital." She did a little twirl, and the overhead chandeliers made her dress sparkle. "Maybe let Harry see us out of our work clothes."

"Uh … okay," CJ said. "Well, it's terrific to see you girls, and thanks so much for all you've done for my uncle."

They both leaned in, hugged her, and said their good-byes. Her eyes trailed after them as they strolled through the glass doors and hopped into a white BMW the valet had pulled around.

CJ sniffed the air and gasped—there was an unusual scent. *Oh, shit!* She raced back to the LEC to her truck and drove to the hospital as fast as she could. She parked in the loading and unloading lane in front of the hospital doors and scampered to the elevator. As soon as the door chimed and opened, she jumped in, hit the sixth floor and *close door* buttons.

When she pushed open Harry's door, he was asleep. She found the nurse on duty, a woman in her mid-forties named Bethany. She told CJ that Craig had stopped by, but he had been the only person other than her. CJ slipped into the room and sat there until 9:00 p.m. As she left, she asked Bethany to call her if anyone else visited.

"Sure. Since visiting hours are over, I don't expect any-one else. We don't let non-hospital personnel in without a doctor's approval."

CJ thanked her and headed for the elevator. *It's the hospital personnel I'm worried about.*

FORTY-FIVE

Tuesday, May 10
Downtown Charleston

CJ jerked herself awake. She'd tossed and turned most of the night as her mind raced about the scent she'd recognized in the hotel lobby the night before—a sweet, minty vanilla aroma ... the same one she'd smelled at the Ralston crime scene. She couldn't shake it. Which one of the young women wore it?

Sliding out of bed, she roamed to the window and opened the blinds. The half-moon hung over the harbor, and stars flickered faintly against the dark sky. She glanced at the glowing digits on her bedside clock—5:10 a.m. She rubbed her eyes and strode to the shower.

As the hot water doused her, she worked to determine her plan for resolving her latest dilemma. *Who wore the perfume?* She was frustrated she hadn't noticed sooner and asked about it. That would have been innocent enough. *I could have said, 'Wow! What a great fragrance. What is it?'*

"Dammit!"

Once she'd washed the conditioner from her hair, she twisted the knob, stopped the shower, and stepped out to dry herself. She gazed in the mirror at her puffy, red eyes. *At least they're not black anymore.* She dried her hair and dressed—black jeans, a tan blouse, and her usual lace-up boots.

She grabbed her notebook, credentials, and gun, and hustled down the stairs to Sal's. Maybe if she found a quiet spot while she had her coffee, she'd devise a plan. Her stomach was empty, but she had no appetite.

Sal was sweeping the sidewalk in front of his shop as she approached. He dropped his straw broom and spread his arms when he noticed her. "*Ciao, mia bella signorina,*" he said as he winked.

She offered him a warm smile. "I'm not sure about the beautiful lady today. I didn't get much sleep last night."

His forehead wrinkled, and he ushered her through the door. "I'll grab you something delicious and your usual coffee."

"I'm not hungry, but the coffee will help."

He wagged his finger at her. "You must eat." Then he playfully smiled. "You're too skinny, and I like my women with meat on their bones."

Mission accomplished. She laughed. "Okay. I'll try."

Her coffee appeared on the counter first, followed by a pastry. She greedily sipped the black liquid. "Mmm ... nice and hot." She pointed to the light brown crescent roll. "What do we have here?"

He grinned. "It's something brand new—a blueberry croissant. Don't tell the French."

Nodding, she picked it up and took a bite. "Holy smokes, Sal. This is wonderful."

"I have your napkins." He pushed through the swinging door and guided her out the door to a two-seater wrought-iron table under a massive live oak. After brushing leaves from the cushion, he held the chair for her to sit. "Enjoy."

She didn't want food, but couldn't stop shoving pieces of Sal's latest creation in her mouth. Crumbs bounced on the stone patio, only to be fought over by a growing group of pigeons. The largest of them dominated, grabbing the morsels, so she pinched off a piece and tossed it to the littlest one in the back.

Once she'd wiped her fingers clean, she opened her notebook. As she tapped her pen on a blank page, her mind wrestled with how she'd get to the bottom of the mystery scent. She'd missed her chance to inquire naturally which young woman wore it, so she'd have to devise another way.

Her eyes cut to her buzzing cell phone on the table beside her notebook, and she saw Ben's face on the screen. "Hey," she answered.

"Good morning. How'd you sleep?" he asked.

She sighed. "Not well. I had a hard time with everything going on."

"Well, if I'd known that, I'd have come over. We could snuggle instead of me throwing a soggy tennis ball into the waves for Jake."

They spent several minutes discussing Harry's progress and his move from the ICU. She explained her latest situation on her Ralston case and asked if he had any ideas. He offered some, but they agreed none worked. She heard a dog barking wildly in the background.

"I guess I need to go. My crazy dog's chasing seagulls since I'm not doing my part in this fetch thing. Have fun celebrating with Harry today."

She froze. "Wait. Say that again."

"Uh … have fun celebrating—"

"That's it! Thanks, Ben. You're a genius."

"Okaaay. Not sure how, but I'll take it."

She promised to call him later and zipped back to get her truck as her feathered friends declared war over what was left of her breakfast.

CJ went to see her uncle after she left Sal's and then spent the day in her office. They planned to move Harry to a standard hospital room between three and four that afternoon, so she returned to MUSC at two thirty.

Bethany had been Harry's nurse this morning, but CJ understood Nurse Annie would replace her and work until eight, and Nurse Cara would relieve her for the overnight shift. She hoped there'd be an overlap and the young nurses would be there simultaneously. It was the only way her plan would work.

She rounded the corner and almost bumped into a young woman. "Hello, Annie," she said. "It's great to see you. How was your evening?"

Her brown eyes flashed. "It was fun. I wasn't out too late since I had to work today."

CJ spent a few minutes chitchatting with her and then pushed the door open to her uncle's room. He was wide awake, watching a fishing show. She kissed him on the cheek, dropped into the brown recliner, and he narrated for her. A young man stood on the boat's bow, casting a bright yellow lure into the lilies to catch bass.

She leaned forward. Nurse Cara's voice was right outside the door. Seconds later, the young nurse with hazel eyes peered into the room and smiled at Harry. "Today's the big day. We're gonna take you for a ride." Her eyes never left him.

"Hey, Cara," CJ said.

"Oh. Sorry. I didn't notice you."

CJ asked about her night and received the same response—fun, but not late. The young woman's bloodshot eyes told a different story. "When are you moving Harry?"

Cara twisted her mouth. "I'm not sure, but I think in fifteen minutes. I checked, and his new spot is ready."

"That's great. Listen, before we leave here, I'd like to celebrate Harry's accomplishment and all the help you and Annie have given him."

"Sure. That'd be wonderful."

Cara finished her tasks and told her she'd round up her partner. A few minutes later, the two entered. CJ stood and pulled out a soft-sided cooler she'd brought with her. She removed a bottle of champagne and four crystal flutes. She made a show of popping the cork and pouring the bubbly liquid.

"First, I'd like to congratulate my dear uncle for graduating from the ICU." Everyone laughed. She turned to the two young women. "Second, I want to tell both of you how much you've meant to us and to thank you for your hard work."

CJ handed everyone a glass and held hers up. "Unc, here's to you leaving the hospital as soon as possible."

He peered into his flute. "Wait! Mine barely has anything in it."

"That's because you only get a taste," CJ said. "You're sick, remember?"

"Spoilsport."

She chuckled. "Let's try this again. Here's to Harry!"

"Here, here," both nurses said in unison. Everyone took a swig, and she collected the empties and set them on the side table.

"I'll go wash those for you," Nurse Annie said.

"That's okay," CJ replied, holding up a palm. "I'll wash them later. Let's get this old man moved."

She carefully placed the glassware back in the cooler. CJ had two flute types, one with gold trim and the other silver, and had made sure the nurses used different ones.

She stood theirs upright in the cooler while she laid hers and Harry's on their sides.

"Okay. One last item," CJ said. "Can you ladies stand by Harry so I can get a photo?"

The two joined him, one on each side, and offered enthusiastic smiles. She clicked several shots and thanked them. An orderly arrived, and the nurses helped prepare the bed.

She waited until the nurses rolled her uncle out the door, then she quickly put their glasses in paper bags and scribbled names on the outside. After putting them back in the cooler, she left the room and caught up with the group.

At nine o'clock, CJ said her goodbyes to Harry and Nurse Cara and headed for her truck. As soon as she exited the door and stepped onto the sidewalk, she called Eddie. She asked if he would call his cousin and see if there was any way she could get a fast turnaround on DNA analysis.

She was sitting in her truck waiting when he returned her call. Unfortunately, he told her it would take at least two weeks for SLED to run the tests. She called her captain but had no luck obtaining permission to use a private lab. Funds weren't available. *I can't wait for two weeks.*

Her heart rate elevated as she thought about the nurses being around Harry for several more days. She didn't believe they'd hurt him, but she couldn't be sure. It was a risk she wasn't willing to take. Then she remembered something Thomas had told her, and her fingers punched his number.

"Sorry to bother you so late, but I need guidance."

"No worries. What do you need?"

She explained the situation, and he agreed that waiting on the results wasn't an option. However, he might have a solution.

"I have a friend and colleague who started a private lab about ten years ago," he said. "He does DNA testing, among other things, and is considered an expert. Law enforcement agencies across the state use him, and he's tremendous on the stand."

"Can you ask how much two samples would cost?" she asked. "I need a rush and am willing to pay for it myself. I can't have Harry at risk."

"I'll call him. A saliva sample for a single person should be the cheapest, and you only have two." He chuckled. "He owes me a favor, anyway. Sit tight."

A woman in her eighties ambled by using her walker. Despite the pleasant evening, she was bundled up in a winter coat. The older woman's lips curved into a smile when she saw her watching. Within seconds, a young man joined the woman and helped her into a car, and they drove off.

CJ jumped when her cell phone buzzed and sucked in a deep breath as she answered. "Any luck?"

"I'll text you the address for the lab. A man named Bob Benning will meet you and take the samples. He'll have your results within forty-eight hours."

"Thank God. How much do I owe him?"

"Nothing. As I said before, he owed me one. By the way, do you have a chain of custody form?"

"Yes. I keep some in my truck along with my sample collection equipment. Eddie made me a full kit and trained me to use it."

"Smart. If you find any useful evidence, you don't want to have it thrown out of court."

She thanked him, and as soon as her cell phone chimed with the address, she took off for West Ashley.

FORTY-SIX

Wednesday, May 11
Downtown Charleston

Scarlett stared at the two men as they slowly made their way down the corridor. She followed them, staying well back. She'd love to hear their conversation, but it didn't matter.

Her lips curled into a smile when they got to the elevator. Instead of turning back, the man who'd recently had double bypass heart surgery hit the *down* button. *What a naughty boy.*

She waited until they entered and the door closed, then raced to the stairwell. If she was right, she knew where they'd exit. She opened the first-floor door, stopped short, and ducked into a hallway. The two men left the metal box and turned for the outside door.

Scarlett trailed them as they strolled into the trees inside the horseshoe drive area. Traffic was heavy along Ashley Avenue, but the vegetation muffled most of the noise. She stood behind the trunk of a tall oak tree, where she had a view of their path. She squeezed her eyes shut.

Never forget, Scarlett. Men are worthless, and you should never get attached. Instead, always keep control, get your money, and use them to give you your baby girl when the time is right.

She'd been around both men enough to know they would suit her needs. She had one in mind and was confident her charms would work. She knew how to handle men and make them do whatever she wanted. As they turned to go back inside, she smiled and hustled to beat them back.

CJ had only been to a strip club twice in her life. Both times, she'd been working cases in Boston that required it. She wanted to arrive early enough to avoid the drunken mass of men, but late enough so that most of the dancers would be working.

Her plans had included bringing Janet. However, the girls would be more open if it was just her, and she didn't expect trouble, anyway. She turned right on Pittsburg Avenue and into the parking lot lit by flashing neon lights—Ricky's

Cabaret. She stared at the door for several minutes before climbing out and heading to the front double glass doors.

As she approached, a burly Black man well over six feet tall opened the door for her. He'd clearly spent a lot of time in the gym. His arms were as big as her legs, and his T-shirt was painted on. He offered her a friendly smile. "Welcome to Ricky's. Ladies don't pay a cover and get half price on mixers."

The thumping of the music from inside was deafening. She leaned in close, motioned, and he bent down. "Listen. I'm a detective with the Charleston PD. I'm not here to hassle anyone, just looking for some information on one of your dancers."

He stood to his full height and twisted his lips. "What kind of information?"

"Who she hung around with … that sort of thing."

"Who?" he asked as he closed the distance again.

She leaned to his ear. "Rebecca Jennings."

He rubbed his face. "Aw, man. It was terrible what happened to her. Poor girl had her issues, but she was a sweet person."

"Do you know any of her friends?"

He shook his head. "No. I knew her from her comings and goings here, but that's it."

"Is it okay if I ask around?"

"Yeah. I can't tell you no, but I'd like to tell the manager, so he approves it, not me. You packing?"

She waited until six young men entered and lifted her jacket.

"Nice Glock," he said, "although the manager's not a fan of having guns in the place." He shrugged. "But you being a detective and all, we'll live with it. Follow me." The giant of a man led her into the fog of cheap perfume and to a wooden door. He banged on the door and a wiry man several inches shorter than she and the exact opposite of her escort appeared.

"This young lady wants to talk to you for a minute," the burly man said.

"Come on in," the manager said, leering at CJ. "We're always looking for hot ladies, but you'd show better with less on." He closed the door behind them, which hardly softened the thumping bass of the music.

She gave him her best dazzling smile. "You think I could work here?"

"Oh, yeah. Based on what I see, you'd do well. How 'bout you remove your jacket and let me get a better looksee?"

She shrugged and slipped off her jacket.

His eyes started from top to bottom, but stopped and went wide at her waist.

"You like my gun and gold badge?"

"Uh ... look. I didn't mean to be disrespectful, and you never told me you're a cop."

"You never asked, but relax. As I told your doorman, I'm not here to cause any issues. I assume all your lovely ladies are eighteen or older, and no one has any illegal drugs."

He shook his head. "Absolutely not. We don't hire underage girls or allow any drugs in the place."

"See, we're all good then," she said, smiling even though she knew he was lying. She put her jacket back on. "I'll ask a few questions and be on my way." As she turned to go, she couldn't resist patting her butt. "You think men would like my ass?"

He wiped his forehead. "Oh, yeah. You'd be a hit."

She winked at him and walked out. There appeared to be twice as many people in the cavernous room as when she arrived. She tipped her head at the doorman and he returned a nod.

"Would you like a table?" a young woman with platinum-blond hair and more makeup than clothes asked.

"Something out of the way, please."

The young woman led her to a two-seater near the wall adjacent to the raised stage. CJ told her she didn't need a drink, but would appreciate it if she could send over a dancer. The woman smiled and nodded.

"Oh, wait! How many dancers do you have working?"

The woman glanced at the clock over the bar. "It's nine, so we have a full slate of twelve tonight."

CJ thanked her, and off she went. A few minutes later, a scantily clad young woman approached. What clothes she wore were neon yellow.

"You wanna dance?" the girl asked.

She motioned to the empty chair. "No. But can we talk?" She laid a twenty on the table.

"Sure. That'll cover two songs," the young woman said as she dropped into the chair.

"Well, I'll get to it since I don't have much time. Do you know Rebecca Jennings? She probably goes by Sunshine when she's working."

She pursed her ruby-red lips. "No. I remember her being here a time or two, but I don't really know her."

"Fair enough. Tell you what. If you send another girl over, there's another twenty in it for you."

Neon yellow grabbed the twenty, grinned, and took off.

The process continued. CJ went through seven dancers and two hundred and eighty dollars before she found the person she was searching for—a young lady called Star, who was probably pushing the bar on no girls under eighteen years old.

"So you know her?" CJ asked.

Star shrugged. "I knew her. She's dead. Stupid bitch jumped off her balcony and killed herself." She sniffed. "It's a shame. She was a nice person and always watched out for me." She leaned in closer. "Sometimes the men get a little too aggressive, and Sunshine knew how to calm them down without disrupting the flow."

CJ's brow furrowed. "Disrupting the flow?"

"The cash from their pocket into yours. That's what this is about. Extracting money with the least amount of effort possible." She produced a tube of lip gloss—CJ could not see where there was room to store it on her scant dress—and spread it across her lips. "I mean, some girls enjoy bumping and grinding on the men, but most of us just want our dollars and move on."

"Did you ever meet anyone who was friends with Sunshine? Someone who didn't work here."

The young woman stared into space for a minute, then said, "One girl came in a few weeks ago. She was dressed to the nines. Asked for Sunshine, and they went to the back."

"What's the back?"

"The VIP rooms. I was curious since this chick was drop-dead gorgeous, and I'm a lesbian. Sunshine told me all they did was talk, and the other woman wasn't interested in women." She twisted her lips. "Funny thing though, Sunshine also told me the girl hated men."

"Did she mention anything else?"

Star shook her head. "Not much. Sunshine left not long after that to do the girl a favor."

"Do you remember what night that was by chance?" CJ asked.

The young girl thought for a moment. "Let's see. I only saw her once after that. It was … three Fridays ago."

April 15. The night Charles Ralston was poisoned.

"Do you think you'd recognize a photo of this woman?"

The girl dropped her eyes to the twenty lying on the table and raised her eyebrows. CJ dropped another twenty down. "There's another in addition to that one."

She nodded. "Sure. I could."

CJ thumbed through her cell phone photos and showed her one.

Without hesitation, Star pointed. "That's her right there."

"You're certain?"

"Positive. Damn bitch was smoking-hot."

Another twenty dropped on the table and CJ stood. As she turned for the door, a drunk twenty-something asked her, "Shit, baby. How much for a lap dance?" Several of his buddies standing beside him burst out laughing.

She leaned in close, almost nose-to-nose. "You and your buddies don't have nearly enough cash to afford me." She scanned them from top to bottom and added, "Even if you did, none of you could handle it." She pushed her way through them and headed for the door as they whooped and hollered. Her burly friend held the door open for her.

She sat in her truck and stared at the photo of the smiling faces of the two nurses. *I would have bet on the other one.*

FORTY-SEVEN

Thursday, May 12
Downtown Charleston

Dawn was absent as CJ sat in her office and stared at the photo on her cell phone. Raindrops drummed against the window and trickled down the pane. The weather matched her mood.

Her instincts had told her Annie was most likely the woman with Ralston, but she was wrong. Instead, it was Cara, based on what Star had told her. But the fact that the young woman knew Jennings and had asked her for a favor was only circumstantial. It didn't prove she was at the Duncan House. CJ needed more evidence.

I need the DNA results.

She picked up her cell phone and called Uncle Craig. She asked if he'd go to the hospital and stay with Harry, and she'd come later. He never questioned why. Instead, he said, "No problem."

At 8:30 a.m., there was still no Sam. Janet was out on a case, but where was her sidekick? Rubbing her eyes, she roamed to the window. The sky had lightened, but the sun was still fighting to break through the heavy, dark clouds.

Fifteen minutes later, the door rattled open and Sam entered. "Sorry I didn't call. I had to pick up some information a friend found for me." She dropped her bag on her desk. "Give me a minute, and I'll show you something interesting."

CJ slid into her chair at the table and the younger woman joined her. "Here is the file for Scarlett Rutherford. It's been updated with what I just obtained."

"Scarlett?" CJ asked as her brow furrowed.

"That's her real first name. Cara is her nickname."

CJ opened the manilla folder and scanned it. "This says her mother is Susanna Davis, who lives in Beaufort, and she has a sibling. Oh, shit! Her half-sister is Ava Ralston."

"Ava is another nickname," Sam said. "Her real name is Savannah. One of the problems I've had is finding older information. It wasn't in the system, which is unusual. It's almost as if it's been hidden."

CJ stood and went to the board and started writing. Five minutes later, she stepped back and stared at the bullets.

- *Susanna Davis had Savannah ("Ava") Gibbs in 1976, thirty-five years ago*
- *Susanna Davis had Scarlett ("Cara") Rutherford in 1986, ten years later*

"Here's what's throwing me off," she said. "Was Davis married to these men at the time? If she wasn't, how did her daughters wind up with these last names?"

Sam smiled. "I had the same question." She explained that in South Carolina, paternity is determined in one of four ways—the couple is married, recently divorced, or a voluntary paternity acknowledgment is filed. The last way was through a court order.

Staring at the board, CJ said, "We have a Eugene Gibbs who was poisoned. Was he Savannah's father?" She dropped back into her chair and asked Sam to do more digging into the background of the mother. "Also, search for what you can find on Sophie Ralston, since Charles wasn't her real father. My bet is her father is our second victim, Thurmond Wilkins."

"I found the little girl's birth certificate, and her last name was Gibbs, the same as her mother. Unfortunately, the space for the father's name was blank." Sam went to her desk. "I'll go back and dig. I may as well search into Scarlett's father, Carlton Rutherford."

CJ picked up her notebook and headed for the door. "I'm going to talk to Stan and get a warrant to get a DNA sample for Ava ... I mean Savannah."

"Cap, you got a minute?"

Captain Stan Meyers spun his chair around and waved CJ into the chair across from his desk. For the next fifteen minutes, she wove through the twisted story. Finally, she summarized what she suspected. Scarlett Rutherford had slept with her half-sister's husband and poisoned him. Savannah Ralston had slept with Thurmond Wilkins and done the same.

He leaned back and exhaled. "Holy shit! The key is, can you prove any of this in a court of law?"

"I'm waiting on DNA for Scarlett, and if it matches what we found at the scene, would that be enough?" she asked.

Pursing his lips, he shook his head. "She can argue she slept with him but didn't kill him. The info from the stripper helps, but it doesn't tip the scale. The solicitor won't push a case without concrete evidence."

She rubbed her face. "So I need more?"

"Yep. You need more."

"Okay, for Savannah, I need a DNA sample. We have the DNA from the Wilkins scene, but nothing to compare it to. Can we obtain a warrant?"

He folded his fingers into a tent. "I'd support it, but we need a judge to agree. They may balk since you don't have information tying her to Wilkins. Do you have something?"

Shifting in her chair, she said, "Nothing solid."

Exhaling, he turned to a card file. "Let me take a crack at a judge who's our best shot. I'll take the angle the woman may be responsible for murdering her husband. That's easier to explain than we have a hunch she may have murdered a man ten years ago."

CJ stared at him as he made a call. His back was to her, but she could tell it wasn't going well.

Finally, he hung up and spun around. "Judge needs something to support a warrant—a witness, fingerprint, or DNA."

"I can't obtain DNA without a warrant."

Grunting, he said, "The chicken and egg dilemma."

A heavy sigh escaped her, and she stood. "I'll work on getting more on Scarlett in anticipation of her DNA returning as a match."

"Any ideas on where you can find more evidence?"

"Yes, let's hope I'm right."

FORTY-EIGHT

Thursday, May 12
The Boroughs

CJ pulled into the visitor parking space in front of the Duncan House. The rain had slowed to a mist, but she slipped on her raincoat, anyway. She climbed out and scampered to the door. Cynthia Marks, who had staffed the desk the last time CJ visited, peered up at her and frowned.

"What do you want this time?" she asked.

CJ smiled brightly. "I need to speak to Larry again."

"He's not here."

"Are you sure?" she asked with narrowed eyes.

"Positive."

She nodded. "Funny. It sure looked like him through his office window." She started for the door to the back. "I'll double-check. It'll only take a sec."

Cynthia jumped up to block her, but she was too late.

"Hello, Mr. Simpson," she said as she stood in his open doorway. "I have a bone to pick with you. You lied to me."

His eyebrows shot up and he stuttered, "Uh—uh, I never lied to you. You need to leave. My attorney told me to only speak to you in his presence."

She stood her ground as he sagged into his chair and hung his head. "Do you think Ricardson has your best interests in mind, or is he covering his own ass?"

His jaw dropped, and his eyes blinked wildly. He opened his mouth, but nothing came out.

"Here's the deal. I've got information that won't look good for you, but if you come clean, I'll put in a good word with the solicitor." She shrugged. "It may help shorten your prison sentence."

He rocked back and forth in his chair and fidgeted with his hands. "You're lying." Then, jumping up, he gave her his best macho impersonation. "Off my property, now!"

"Well, that's unfortunate, Larry," she said, shaking her head. "I like you, and hate for you to take the fall for your buddy." She turned to go.

"Uh—what do you have?" he asked.

Bingo. Smiling, she turned back and said, "As I'm sure you're aware, I can't share evidence with you." She approached him and put her hand on his arm. "You seem like a decent guy, and I despise it when people like you are taken advantage of."

Nibbling his bottom lip so hard she expected blood, he finally broke. "If I help you, you'll tell the solicitor I cooperated?"

"I promise."

"One other thing. Can you keep it to yourself where the information came from? They'll kill me if you don't." His hand swiped at his eyes.

"Sure. But be aware, if this goes to trial, I can't promise you won't have to testify. I'll arrange protection for you if it comes to that."

He slowly nodded. "What do you need?"

She told him one thing that bothered her about the Ralston crime scene was the door was locked when he went to check on him. "Whoever poisoned him may have taken his belongings and missing linen, but Charles was alive for several hours before the poison took effect. So I believe someone went into the room after the vic was dead and took those things." She leaned in close. "It was you, wasn't it?"

The waterworks erupted, and Larry's shoulders shook. "Yes." He wiped the snot from his nose with his hand as he stood and motioned to her. "Come with me."

She followed him to a locked closet in his first-floor suite, where he pulled out a cardboard box. He closed the door and locked it. "Here," he said, pushing the package to her.

After she'd slipped on a pair of surgical gloves, she used scissors to cut the duct tape along the lid and lifted the flaps. Gently, she pulled out a brown paper bag. Inside were the missing bath linens from The Ashley bathroom, but what piqued her interest was a small bottle.

Holding up the glassware, she asked, "What was in here?"

Larry shrugged. "I'm not sure. I found it on the floor under the sofa in the sitting room." He stared at the ground. "I was told to take the stuff out of the bathroom and anything else that didn't belong."

"By who?"

Rubbing his face, he said, "Ricardson."

"What about the belongings and his Range Rover?"

"I was told to give them to Sunshine. She met me and took them." He sniffed and pinched his nose. "It was to set her up in case anyone got suspicious."

"In case no one bought the heart attack?"

He nodded and slid a dresser drawer open. "There's one more thing," he said as he held out a yellow manilla envelope. "I may as well give you everything."

Her eyes scanned the sheet of paper she pulled out of it. *Damn.* She returned everything to the box, picked it up, and started for the door. Before she left Larry in his chair with his head hanging morosely, she told him she'd do her best to help him.

"By the way, I'm leaving through the back door. And Marks isn't your friend either."

CJ called Eddie from her truck and explained what she needed to get to him. He agreed to meet her in the Ashley-Rutledge garage at MUSC and examine the evidence. "I'm positive we have prints on the jar. Now all we need are some to compare them to."

FORTY-NINE

Thursday, May 12
Beaufort, South Carolina

Susanna Davis peeped through the gap in the curtains and studied the silver Mercedes as it came down the driveway. The car stopped in front of the house, and the driver with graying black hair and an overly pointed beak stepped out. "Why in the hell is he here?" she murmured.

She strolled to the gold sofa in the sitting room and her fingers tightened on her brightly colored robe. She'd slept late after entertaining most of the night, and her head pounded. The last thing she needed was to talk to this fool.

The maid, who reminded her of a penguin, waddled to answer the knock. The woman barely had the door open when Percy Ricardson burst into the foyer.

"I need to speak to Miss Davis. Where is she?" he demanded.

"Mrs. Anna is busy at the moment. You'll need to come back later, and I suggest you call first."

She tried to block him, but he pushed past her and called, "Anna?! I need to speak with you." Again the woman tried to keep him from going any further. He jabbed his finger in her face. "Get the fuck out of my way!"

"Let him in, Candace," Susanna called out.

"Yes, ma'am."

He rounded the corner, and his eyes scanned her sitting on the sofa, her arms spread across the cushions on each side. "Are you sick? I've never seen you not dressed."

"No. I'm a bit exhausted from a late night."

"Oh."

"Since you've barged in, you might as well sit your ass down." She pointed to a dark brown leather chair to her left in front of a fireplace, and he did as he was told.

"Why are you here?"

He rubbed his face with both hands. "I'm getting worried. We have a detective digging into Charles Ralston's murder and—"

"Oh, my!" She offered him her best fake smile. "You murdered someone?"

"You know damn well what I'm talking about! I had nothing to do with it."

"Calm down, Percy. Don't be so dramatic." She pulled her arms down and leaned forward. "Why are you so upset?

It's not the first time someone in law enforcement has stuck their nose where it doesn't belong."

He shook his head. "This is different. This bitch is a real problem."

She raised her eyebrows and said, "Ahh ... you're terrified of a woman."

He jumped to his feet. "Not just a woman, a detective, for Christ's sake. She's not like the others. She doesn't give a—"

"Sit back down! God, you're weak." She glared at him. "You're not half the man your father was. He's gotta be rolling over in his grave at what a piece of shit his son has become." She stood and drifted to the bar along the side wall. "What you need is a drink."

"I don't need a drink," he said. "I need you to listen to me."

She wheeled around. "Don't you ever tell me what I need to do!" Then, continuing to the mahogany cabinet, she mumbled, "Let's see, you like bourbon with water, if I remember correctly. Of course, no one should ruin a top-shelf Wild Turkey with water, but I'd expect nothing less of you."

"Damn, you're a hateful shrew."

She smirked. "Now, now. Don't be nasty." Her fingers tugged on the bow and her robe fell open, exposing her naked body. "I can remember several times when you've enjoyed my company."

She focused back on his drink and peeked over her shoulder. Percy had buried his face in his hands as he slumped. Her hand pushed the bottle back, and she grabbed a bottle of Cabernet from a bottom shelf. She poured the dark red liquid into a Bordeaux glass.

"You don't get it," he said. "This is bad."

"I'm out of bourbon, but I have something better." She handed him his glass and slid onto the footstool in front of his chair, never bothering to cover herself.

"What's this?" he asked.

"It's a three-hundred-dollar bottle of Cab. Shut up and drink it."

He took a sip. "This is too sweet. You didn't get your money's worth on this crap."

Her hand pushed the bottom of the glass back to his mouth. "There ya go—drink it down. It'll calm your nerves."

"Yeah. You're probably right." He finished it. After wiping his mouth, he said, "I'm telling you, this is trouble."

"Why don't you explain why you're about to wet yourself?"

For the next several minutes, he told her he was afraid CJ O'Hara would uncover his pipeline from the Palmetto Men's Society to the underground prostitution ring centered around her house. To make matters worse, O'Hara had information on the deaths of Thurmond Wilkins and Charles Ralston.

As he droned on, Susanna returned to the bar and made herself a drink—top-shelf Kentucky bourbon, no water. She kept her back to him while he moaned about going to jail. When he finally stopped to breathe, she faced him. "Feel better now that you've gotten that off your chest?"

"Hell, no!"

"That's because you're a sad little man with no balls," she said.

"You best not get comfortable either. If O'Hara gets me, she'll get you."

Her hazel eyes flashed. "So now you're threatening me?"

He squirmed. "No. It only makes sense."

She gazed out the window. "Your father was a real man. Worthless as hell, but he had his uses."

"Yeah. Dad screwed you, and you had your little bitch of a daughter, but that doesn't make—"

She hurled her tumbler at the fireplace and barely missed hitting him. "Don't you get snotty with me! I'm not a weak little piece of ass. Unlike you, I can handle my business. So what are you doing to handle yours?"

"I—uh—I've been having her followed."

She wiggled her fingers. "Ooh, that'll scare her off." She burst out laughing. "Let me help you. Put a bullet in her head if you can't pay her off."

His eyes bulged. "I'm no saint, but I've never killed anyone. Are you crazy?"

She closed the gap between them, leaned down, and whispered in his ear, "It sure took you a long time to figure that out." Her slap landed hard on his cheek, nearly knocking him to the floor. "Now, get out of my fucking house!"

His wobbly legs carried him out the door and her eyes followed his car as he slowly left the way he'd come. She shook her head. *Men are so worthless.*

Percy Ricardson never made it back to Charleston. His car was found in the parking lot of an Exxon gas station on Savannah Highway, less than a mile from the Ashley River Memorial Bridge. The responding officer called it in as an apparent heart attack.

CHAPTER

FIFTY

Thursday, May 12
Downtown Charleston

CJ found Craig laughing with Harry when she entered the hospital room—something about a recent fishing debacle. She smiled. "You must be feeling better, Uncle Harry?"

"I am. In fact, I'm ready to go home."

Nurse Cara entered, squeezed past her, and went to his bedside. "Not yet, darling. The doctor says you have three more days with me."

The smile disappeared from CJ's face and her pulse quickened. She had to hide what she knew about the young woman. "Uh—hey, Cara."

The nurse's hazel eyes twinkled as she glanced over her shoulder and smiled. Then, without a word, she returned to multitasking—tending to her patient and flirting with Craig.

"I'm totally fine now. I'd be better off at my own house. Do you think we could talk—"

"Nope. No sweet-talking the doctor," Cara said. "It might work on me, but not him." Once she'd finished her tasks, she gazed at Craig. "I'm ready for my lunch break. Are we still on?"

"Absolutely."

"I don't have much time, so you can escort me downstairs." She extended her hand. "We can grab a bite there."

The two of them left the room.

"She's such a sweet girl," Harry said, breaking CJ's trance. "She's been trying to convince me all morning that she should stay with me after I go home. Cara has a few days—"

"Not gonna happen," she said. "I'll be the one staying with you."

He exhaled. "I didn't agree, but maybe it would be a good idea since she's a registered nurse and you have your cases."

She moved to the side of his bed and took his hand. "It's not up for discussion. I'm staying with you. Besides, you hardly know her."

They spent the next forty-five minutes talking about her cases. She was careful not to disclose some of what she knew or suspected about his nurse. The last thing she wanted was to put stress on him. When Craig and Cara entered the room, she quickly changed the subject.

Her eyes were glued to what the young nurse had in her hand—a Dr. Pepper can. She took the last sip and tossed the empty into the trash behind Harry when her name was called over the intercom.

"Gotta go. I'm supposed to work in the ICU for the rest of my shift. Bethany will take over for me here."

Craig offered to walk her out as he was leaving for a couple of hours to grab some stuff for his brother.

"How young is too young?" Harry asked once it was only the two of them.

CJ's head snapped to him as her stomach lurched. "What?"

He shrugged. "I'm sixty-one. What age woman is too young for me to date?"

"Oh. Uh—I—I'm not sure. Are you thinking of asking someone out? Look, if it's Ca—"

"Bethany," he said. "She's single, forty-six, and I thought maybe I'd see if she wanted to go to dinner."

Relieved, she grinned. "Really. Well, it never hurts to ask. Of course, if she's smart, she'll say yes. You're quite the catch, Mr. O'Hara."

"Oh, yeah. Every woman wants a man with a bad ticker." He poked her in the side. "Of course, if she says no, I can always ask Annie or Cara."

She leaned down, kissed his cheek, and whispered, "If you ask out a twenty-five-year-old, remember, I have good aim." Her eyes caught the can in the trash as she stood. She wanted it, but how could she take it without him knowing?

"What's in the bag?" she asked, pointing to a brown paper bag on the tray beside his bed.

"Craig brought me some stuff from the store."

She opened it and laid the contents on a shelf by the sink. "Did he get everything you needed?"

He nodded and stretched. "Yeah, as long as I go home on Sunday."

Her hands gripped the bag. "Hey, how 'bout you find the fishing show we watched the other day?"

She quickly slipped the can into the bag as he flipped through the channels and wrapped it in her rain jacket. She learned more about fishing in the Keys for the next two hours. When Craig returned, she told them she'd be back later.

───

CJ punched Eddie's number into her cell phone and told him she was on her way to the Forensics Services Lab when he answered. He said he had some information on the glass bottle from the Duncan House.

"Does this mean you found usable prints?" she asked.

"It does. I'll be ready to discuss my findings when you get here. By the way, I found two different prints."

She parked, hustled through the lab door, and found Eddie leaning over a microscope. She exhaled. "Okay, let's hear it."

"I found three fingerprints of the same person and one print of a second individual." He motioned her over and pulled photos up on his computer screen. "Both sets are the second-most common type, the whorls pattern."

She leaned in close, staring at the images. "Okay, how do you know they're from different people?"

"The Galton's details vary." He added a second image on the screen and pointed to variations in the ridges. "These are from two different people. I only have one print from the second individual, and it's not as clear as the other, but enough to make a determination."

She pursed her lips. "The one on the right is smaller."

He nodded. "Yeah. It's either due to a lower pressure from the fingertip or a smaller individual. It's hard to tell."

"Now for the most important question ..."

"Neither is in our state system or AFIS," he said, referring to the federal Automated Fingerprint Identification System. "I'm sorry. By the way, there was some residue in the bottle. I've sent it off for analysis. I'm not sure what—"

"Deadly nightshade," she said. "Have the lab test for that."

He slowly nodded, picked up his phone, and called the analyst. "He's gonna run the analysis next."

She held up the paper bag she had clutched in her hand. "I may be able to help with the prints. I think I have what we can use to identify who touched the bottle."

Furrowing his brow, he said, "Okay, how 'bout you fill out the paperwork to log it in while I examine what we have?" He used his gloved hand to remove the can from the bag. "Dr. Pepper," he mumbled.

She stared at him while he worked—examining the can under a light, taking photographs, dusting, and lifting. Minutes seemed like days until he stood, stretched, and told her there were usable prints. "Like the ones from the Duncan House, these are the whorls pattern. I'll double-check them, but I think they match."

"So the ones on the bottle are the same as those on the can?"

He nodded. "Yep. Whose are they?"

"Scarlett Rutherford. She goes by the name Cara. And she's Harry's nurse at MUSC."

———

CJ left Eddie and returned to her truck, excited and terrified at the same time. She now had a valuable piece of evidence on who murdered Charles Ralston, but the person was the one caring for her uncle. When her cell phone buzzed she jumped, and her heart went to her throat when she recognized the number.

"Hello, Dr. Benning."

"Hello, Detective. I have the information you requested."

She scrambled to grab her notebook off the passenger seat and pulled out her pen. "I'm ready when you are."

"I ran a DNA analysis on the two saliva samples you delivered and was able to complete profiles for each. Unfortunately, neither are in CODIS, but one matches the DNA profile provided by SLED."

The Combined DNA Index System, or CODIS, was a nationwide database that contained DNA profiles for a wide range of criminal offenders, evidence from crime scenes, and information about missing persons. She had used it many times.

Paper rustled on the end of the line. "Sorry. Here it is. The one that matches is for Cara Rutherford."

"Thank you so much, Dr. Benning. Please email me your report, and I'll be happy to pay you."

"No," he said. "Like I told you, Thomas and I go way back, and I owe him. Do you need anything else?"

She chewed the inside of her cheek. "Uh—I may have another sample soon. I know you're busy and—"

"Whenever you're ready, bring it over and I'll get it done." He chuckled. "My tab with Thomas is long."

She thanked him, hung up, and stared at the night sky—the rain had gone and the yellowish half-moon stared back.

FIFTY-ONE

Friday, May 13
Downtown Charleston

CJ downed the last drops of her third cup of coffee and headed over to grab a fourth. It was 6:00 a.m. and she was already back in her office, even though she'd only left at two o'clock that morning. She was preparing for today's arrest of Scarlett "Cara" Rutherford. She wanted her ducks in a row before she briefed the captain.

She scanned the board and nodded as she tasted the hot, black liquid. Her summary was ready. A low growl rumbled in her stomach, reminding her she hadn't eaten since ... well, she couldn't remember. She could go forage in the bullpen or call Sam. Before she could decide, a knock took her to the door.

Ben stood with an ear-to-ear grin on his face. "Parrish delivery service. Can I speak to the lady of the manor?" He held up a dish covered in aluminum foil. "If you've eaten, I can give this to the guys down the hall."

She pressed her lips to his without thinking and dragged him into the room. "You read my mind. I'm starved." She cut her eyes to his. "Assuming, of course, what you have is edible."

He placed the dish on the table and pulled the cover off. "Homemade biscuits with your choice of sausage patties or bacon and cheese."

"Wow! Who made these?" She winked. "Did you get these from Sam?"

"No. I made them with my own two hands." He shrugged. "I dropped one on the floor, and Jake inhaled it. He's still kicking, so they're safe."

She grabbed some paper plates and napkins, and they sat at the table. Ben was right. The food was delicious. After gobbling down one of each type, she told him about today's planned activities, namely arresting Scarlett and rattling Savannah Ralston's chain.

"Have you told Harry you're about to arrest one of his favorite nurses?" he asked before he shoved a bite in his mouth.

"Oh, shit! No. I do need to tell him." Her heart rate picked up. "He's gonna be devastated. I've been so damn busy solving this and protecting him ..."

"He'll be fine. Disappointed, sure, but it's not you who poisoned a man."

They sat quietly, and her mind raced. She'd need to tell her uncle before she put handcuffs on her murderess.

"What's your plan?" Ben asked.

She explained she would ask Scarlett to meet her outside a side entrance. The young nurse started her shift at nine, and CJ wanted to avoid a scene inside the hospital. She would give the administrator a heads-up.

Glancing at the clock, she told him she was briefing Stan and Assistant Solicitor Tim Drummond in twenty minutes. He took the cue, kissed her, and headed out the door.

Not long after Ben left, CJ briefed Stan and Drummond on the evidence she had for the suspect. Everyone agreed she had what was needed to make an arrest and for prosecution.

Once she got to the MUSC, she spoke to Harry. His eyes stayed wide while she told him about Scarlett.

Ultimately, he said, "You never know what some people are capable of and can hide from others."

With the formalities completed, she found a spot under a massive oak tree and waited. Finally, at 8:40 a.m., Scarlett pushed out the door, smiled, and headed her way. If she suspected anything, she never showed it.

After CJ introduced her to Janet, who had joined her, she said, "Scarlett Rutherford, you're under arrest for the murder of Charles Ralston." Then, she read the young woman her rights as Janet applied the handcuffs.

"I see you know my real name," Scarlett smirked. "I'm not sure what I've supposedly done wrong, but I'll play along." Her hazel eyes flashed as her face went dark. "You're not gonna like how this turns out."

In silence, the three women made the short ride back to the LEC, where Scarlett was placed in an interrogation room. She sat with her hands folded as CJ left the room and found Janet.

"What do you think?" Janet asked.

"I'm not sure. She's as calm as any I've ever arrested. Either she's in denial or—"

"Nuts."

"How 'bout you wait in the viewing room while I go get the captain, then I'll talk to her? I want the two of you to hear what she has to say."

———

CJ opened the door to the windowless box, slid into a metal chair, and opened her notebook. Scarlett sat there casually, staring at her nails. Her soft, kind veneer from when CJ interacted with her in the hospital was gone.

CJ asked her if she wanted an attorney present, to which the young woman declined since she'd done nothing wrong. CJ nodded and started her questioning.

Scarlett denied knowing Charles Ralston, being at the bed-and-breakfast, or anything about the deadly nightshade.

"How did your DNA get on his body and the bedsheet under him?"

"No clue. Maybe the lab fucked up."

"What was in the bottle with your fingerprints on the outside?"

"Another screw-up by the lab."

"Was the favor you asked Rebecca 'Sunshine' Jennings for—to help you get rid of Ralston's Range Rover and giving her his belongings—a setup?"

"Never heard of her."

"How come a witness puts you at the Duncan House on the night Ralston was murdered?"

"They're lying."

CJ laid down her pen and stared at her. This was a waste of time. The woman had decided denial was her defense. She closed her notebook and stood. "Let me ask you one more thing. Why did your sister, Ava, tell me you did it?"

The woman's face went red and her eyes squinted. "She's my half-sister and a fucking liar. That bitch wanted him dead and probably did it herself."

CJ leaned down and put her palms on the table. "So, you do know her and admit she's your sister?"

"Half-sister!" Scarlett's face twisted into a menacing glare. "Men are womanizers and man-whores. Yeah, I screwed my half-sister's husband, but your beloved Charles couldn't even get me pregnant. The world is better off without him." She slammed her fists on the table. "I want a lawyer."

"That's your right. We can have one appointed if—"

"I don't need a government handout! I have plenty of money."

CJ nodded. "Okay. I'll arrange for you to make a call. Who's your attorney?"

A sadistic gleam filled her eyes. "Percy Winston Ricardson III. He'll straighten you and this whole damn department out."

"You better think of someone else." She closed the gap between them. "Ricardson is on a cold metal table in the morgue."

The sadistic gleam on Scarlett's face slipped into a look of panic.

FIFTY-TWO

Friday, May 13
Downtown Charleston

"Thanks for coming in, Ava." CJ offered the wife of the late Charles Ralston a gentle smile as she placed a bottle of water in front of her. "I wanted to update you on the case involving your husband's murder."

Ava Ralston peered at her and slowly nodded. Her lips opened, but no words came out.

CJ cleared her throat. "I'm pleased to tell you we caught the person responsible for his murder. She's in custody."

"She?" Ava said as her eyes narrowed.

"Yes. We've arrested a nurse who worked at MUSC. A twenty-five-year-old woman named Scarlett Rutherford."

The woman's honey-brown eyes gazed at the door and then downward at the table. "Uh—that's terrible."

"This is her," CJ said as she held up a photo. "Have you ever seen her?"

Ava glanced at the image for less than two seconds. "No. I've never seen her before." Her breathing kicked up a notch.

"I hate to ask, but were you aware your husband was seeing her? According to our suspect, they had an intimate relationship."

The woman wiped at her eyes even though they weren't wet. "I did not. As I've explained, my husband and I were madly in love, and there's no way he'd cheat on me. This sorry bitch is lying."

CJ shrugged. "This woman, Scarlett, claimed she was pregnant or something to that effect."

"Is she?" Ava asked as she leaned forward.

"Pregnant? No, I don't think so." CJ moved closer and said in a low voice, "I'm not sure this young woman has all her marbles, between you and me." She held the photo up again. "But you're sure you don't know her or have ever seen her around? She goes by the name Cara, if that helps."

Ava shook her head aggressively. "No. Never."

"I'm sure this is difficult for you. I'm so sorry. Do you have any brothers or sisters to help you through this?"

"Uh—no. Like I've told you, I'm an only child, but have close friends to support me."

"Okay. Well, I wanted you to be confident justice will be served for Charles. And if you don't know this woman, I guess that's all I have."

"I can go?" she asked.

"Yes. Thank you again for coming in."

The woman was nearly out the door before CJ finished speaking. Janet joined her, and the two agreed the grieving wife was hyperventilating in her BMW about now.

"Too bad she didn't drink her water."

CJ stood and said, "Yeah, it was worth a shot. I've got one other card to play, though."

CJ parked several doors down from Richie Pickett's King Street law offices. She didn't want to risk he'd race out the back door if he saw her pull up. As she neared his offices, she picked up her pace and swung the glass door open to face the same blonde-haired young woman she'd seen before.

"Mr. Pickett's in a meet—"

"I'll show myself in, thanks." CJ yanked the door to his office open and glided in.

Richie had his back to the door and fumbled to click his computer monitor off and spin around. He jumped to his feet.

"I sure hope the porn you're drooling over isn't of underage girls, Mr. Pickett," CJ said.

His face went bright red. "I wasn't watching porn! I'm reviewing videos for an important case. Why are you here?"

She suppressed her laugh. This guy was as disgusting as they came, and she loved making him squirm. But since he was already shaken up from being caught with naked young women on his desktop, she might as well seize the opportunity to rattle him more. "I'm here because you keep telling me lies and omitting key facts."

He stuttered and stammered, claiming he didn't know what she was talking about. His recital of how what he'd told her was true was comical. She let him prattle on for several minutes before she raised her hand and he shut his mouth.

"Here's the deal, Richie. You've been covering for your client to the point where we're losing the plot. For example, you said she's an only child, and she had nothing to do with her husband's death. It also took me forever to unravel your lies about where she was on the Friday night in question. I understand the need to protect your client, but you're pissing me off." She knew if Pickett was smart, he'd throw her out, but he wasn't; plus, he was panicking. It was a perfect combination for her.

He rubbed his face and blew out a long breath. "Look, Detective. I'm not sure what you want from me. It's my job—"

"Are you an accomplice in all this?" She narrowed her eyes. "You admitted the two of you have been having an affair. Perhaps you decided to—"

"Stop! Enough. Let me think." He fell hard into his chair, almost tipping over. She began to think she'd pushed him too far and he may keel over on her, but he managed to compose himself and held up his palms. "I'm not part of this, and I'm unaware of anything she's done to her husband. There! Are you happy? I've betrayed my client."

"Not really. You haven't provided me with anything."

He leaped up and yelled, "Then tell me what you want!"

"Oh. That's easy. I need a DNA sample to rule her out for murdering her husband."

He had no way of knowing she'd arrested the person who had killed Charles only hours ago unless Ava had told him. She read his confused face and knew they hadn't spoken. He'd demand she obtain a warrant or subpoena if he was worth half as much as he charged his clients. But, lucky for her, he wasn't.

He picked up his phone. "Okay. I'll tell you what. I'll call and ask my client to—"

"She won't agree. So here we go again, round and round." She rotated her head in a circular motion.

He hung up the phone and plopped down again.

Her eyes stayed peeled on him as he rubbed his chin. *What's he up to?*

"What if I give you a sample?" he asked.

Her brow furrowed. "Why do I need your DNA? Unless you had—"

"Not mine. Hers."

CJ squinted. "I'm not following you."

He scratched at his beet-red nose and wobbled to his feet. Her eyes followed him as he slogged to his cadenza, pulled open a drawer, and grabbed a plastic bag. He stared at it, stepped over to her, and held it out. "This is hers."

She reached out, took the bag, and held it up. "Is this what I think it is? If so, how the hell do you have them?"

His shoulders slumped and in a low voice he said, "It's a pair of Ava's panties. The last time we had sex, I stole them."

FIFTY-THREE

Sunday, May 15
Wando, South Carolina

CJ helped Harry put the groceries away she'd picked up for him at the Piggly Wiggly. He had done his best to convince her he was fine to shop for himself, but ultimately, he gave up and agreed to stay home.

"Okay. So here's the deal. Craig or I will stay here for the next week or so." She wagged her finger at him. "And you'd best not be trying to sneak out. In fact, where are the keys to your Jeep?"

"Aw, come on. You can't take an old man's keys away. What if there's an emergency and I need to—"

"Your brother or loving niece will take you wherever you need to go." She hugged him and gave him a peck on the cheek. "You're the most stubborn person on the planet."

He chuckled. "Takes one to know one."

She handed him a calendar where she'd listed names. She peered at him as he scanned it and twisted his lips. "I've indicated who will be responsible for the daily meals and who's staying overnight."

"Jeez, this is worse than the hospital," he said. "Uh—I do see one change needed."

Her eyes followed to where he'd pointed to Thursday night. She scowled at him. "What? You don't want Ben and me to grill salmon for you?"

His fingers ran through his salt-and-pepper hair. "It's not ..."

"What?"

"I have plans. Before you start screeching about me leaving the house, I'm not going anywhere. It's—well, Bethany wants to come cook dinner for me. She's off that day and asked—"

"So you have a date? You're saying a woman is coming over, and you have a date." She burst out laughing. "Damn, that was quick."

He shrugged. "She asked, so what was I supposed to say?"

She took the sheet, marked through her name, and added Bethany's. She held it to him, and he nodded. "There. Salmon will be moved to Friday night."

Once he settled in his chair on the back deck, she busied herself, ensuring his clothes were clean and laid out for the week. She'd agreed with Craig she'd handle the apparel side of things as he despised doing laundry.

She joined Harry, and the two sat and enjoyed the late afternoon sunshine. He asked her for a beer, which earned him another scolding. He grumbled but agreed he'd leave off the alcohol until the doctor approved it.

"Look," she whispered as she pointed to the marsh. "There's my pelican. I've missed my funny-looking friend." The bird with his enormous bill had his wings spread, drying himself. "Tell you what," she said as she stood. "I'm gonna bake the chicken and feed you an early dinner. You need to get to bed soon."

He rolled his eyes. "It's still daylight."

She leaned down and kissed his forehead. "I'll let you stay up until the sun goes down, and if you're a good boy, you can watch TV for a while." He grumbled as she headed to the kitchen.

At six o'clock, they sat and ate on the deck. Harry tried to convince her he wouldn't get a chill, and she agreed if he'd wrap a blanket around himself. He bitched about sweating to death, but she laughed at him and informed him it was the only way he could stay outside.

Two hours later, she tucked him in and handed him the remote for one hour of TV. "At least they let me watch my shows anytime I wanted at the hospital," he griped.

"Yeah, well, no nurse is waiting to poison you here. I'll be around the corner in the den, so yell if you need anything." She closed his door and hustled to the couch and her files.

Thirty minutes later, her cell phone buzzed. She exhaled when she saw the number. *Dr. Benning.* This could be the results of the DNA sample she'd dropped off Friday evening after leaving Pickett's office.

She answered it and carefully listened as he confirmed he had extracted and analyzed a suitable sample. He had obtained a solid profile and compared it to the one provided by SLED for the Wilkins case. Savannah "Ava" Ralston's DNA was a match. CJ had her second murderess.

He advised he'd email the report over. She thanked him, hung up, and called her captain. They agreed it would be best to arrest their suspect sooner rather than later, as there was a chance she'd run. Unfortunately, there was no way to know if Pickett had felt remorseful and tipped Ava off.

She pushed the bedroom door open. "Uncle Harry, Sam's coming to stay with you. I need to go arrest Savannah Ralston for murder."

His mouth dropped open. "Wait! Isn't she Cara's sister?"

"Half-sister, so yes, they're siblings."

"What the hell is wrong with that family?" he asked as he shook his head. "I'll be fine. There's no need for Sam to drive all—"

"She's already on her way and knows it's lights out at nine."

"Well, I bet she'll let me have a bedtime snack. She makes the best cookies."

Crossing the room, CJ leaned down and grinned at him. "She also knows there are no sweets allowed."

After her replacement arrived, CJ sped to the LEC. On the way, she briefed Solicitor Drummond, and he agreed she had enough to proceed with Ava's arrest. However, with no witnesses or fingerprints, her case wasn't as strong as the one for Scarlett, so she hoped for a confession to drive the nail in the coffin.

Officer Johnny Jones and a younger female officer who appeared to be no more than twenty answered her call request for a patrol with two uniformed officers. Johnny introduced her as his trainee, and the young woman's damp hand shook hers. It would be her first time arresting someone, and she was visibly nervous.

The officers followed her to Dunes West. CJ prayed their target would be home when they arrived. Her prayer was answered when she pulled into the long driveway and the lights inside broke the darkness. Before approaching the house, she shined her Maglite into the window of the detached garage and saw Savannah's jet-black BMW parked inside.

"Is there a chance she'll try to run?" Johnny asked as he joined her.

"I highly doubt it," she said. "I'm not sure where she'd run to. Your cruiser is blocking her garage, and there's no way she can outrun us on foot."

"Any weapons?"

She exhaled. "A possibility. Records show her husband owned several guns, so let's put on our vests, just in case." *Maybe I should have called SWAT.*

The three prepared themselves, and Johnny decided to station his trainee near the back door.

It never hurts to be ready for any scenario, CJ thought. She climbed the steps and rang the doorbell. Moments later, she noticed movement in the door's sidelights. The door lock clicked and Savannah Ralston appeared in the doorway, a glass of white wine in her hand.

"Why are you here in the middle of the damn night?" she demanded, slurring her words. "I have a good mind to sue—" She froze as Johnny stepped to CJ's side, her eyes blinking wildly.

"Savannah Ralston, you're under arrest for the murder of Thurmond Wilkins," said CJ as she took her wineglass.

Johnny stepped forward, cuffed the stunned woman, and recited her rights. Then he radioed for his trainee to join them.

"Mommy!" The mini version of Savannah stood barefoot inside the doorway in pajamas with seashells on them, her eyes watering. She focused on CJ and screamed, "Why are you taking my mommy?!"

CJ bent down. "I'm sorry, sweetie, but we need to talk to your mom at our station. Is anyone else here?"

Tears streamed down the little girl's face, and she shook her head. CJ's heart sank, and she inwardly chastised herself for not having a better plan for handling the daughter. "How 'bout you ride with me, and you can go with us?"

Her little mouth twitched, and she nodded her head. "Can you help me pick out an outfit?"

"Uh—sure." She told the two officers to take Savannah to the station and book her, and she'd follow as soon as she dressed the little girl.

FIFTY-FOUR

Sunday, May 15
Downtown Charleston

It was nearing midnight when CJ turned the knob and opened the door to the cramped interrogation room. Someone must have used the room to eat—a mixed odor of fish, ginger, and garlic tickled her nose. The elevated temperature and lack of windows only added to the uncomfortableness in there.

The metal chair scraped the floor as she pulled it out and sat across from her second murderess, Savannah "Ava" Ralston. The woman rested her forehead on her folded hands and made no movement when she entered.

"Savannah, how 'bout we talk?"

Her head lifted slowly, and she eyed CJ warily. Like her sibling, her wide eyes indicated she'd noticed she had been called by her real name. "Why am I here, and where is my daughter?"

Clearing her throat, CJ said, "We told you why you were here when we arrested you. As for Sophie, she's safe and sound with one of our officers down the hall. We fed her a snack, and she's asleep on a couch. I'll arrange a foster family for her first thing in the morning."

As CJ started her questioning, her conversation with Scarlett replayed itself. Her older half-sister denied she knew the victim, had never been to the Duncan House, and any evidence saying otherwise was an obvious mistake.

"We found one other interesting item," CJ said. "We don't have your daughter's DNA yet, but based on our expert, I bet she's Wilkins's child. He's the person who impregnated you, isn't he?"

The woman's honey-brown eyes flashed and narrowed as her face went tight. "You've got a lot of nerve—"

"I'll have a warrant shortly, and we'll collect a DNA sample from Sophie and confirm I'm correct."

"Don't you fucking dare touch my baby!" The restraints on her wrists kept her from lunging across the table.

CJ continued with her theory that after Savannah became pregnant, she had poisoned Wilkins with deadly nightshade. The woman's DNA on the bed where his lifeless body was found was sufficient to convict her. "Plus, we have someone who puts you at the Duncan House on the night in question."

Savannah's face twisted, and she snorted. "Ricardson would never ..." She stopped when she realized what she'd said.

"You're correct. He's dead, but his manager of the Duncan House at the time would."

"That worthless piece of shit, Simpson!" she said, sneering.

CJ noticed the woman had shown no surprise at the news of the attorney's death. "Yes. He'd be the one." She knew she was bending the truth, but Savannah confirmed what she suspected. The little weasel of a man had helped cover up her crime. CJ would force Simpson to give her the information. "Look. We can go on like this all night, or you can tell me why you poisoned the father of your child."

Icy eyes glared at her.

"By the way, my researcher found this." CJ slid a sheet of paper across the table and the woman glanced at it. "It's you, or your body double, in the ad. I'm sure you're aware that even though Craigslist doesn't operate an Erotic Services section any longer, the old stuff on the internet never goes away."

Finally, after two minutes of silence, CJ flipped her notebook closed. "Since you're making no effort to help yourself, I must inform you the solicitor will seek the maximum sentence." She leaned forward. "This means your daughter will grow up without her birth mother." CJ stood and went to the door. Before walking out, she said, "I'll ensure the little girl has a happy home and a mother who loves her. Not for you, but for her." She was closing the door when Savannah called her back.

For the next fifteen minutes, Savannah told her the sordid tale of being forced into prostitution when she was only sixteen. She provided her services to men in the Palmetto Men's Society, most of them at least three times her age. Finally, at twenty-five, it was her time to get pregnant and have a daughter.

After she'd had Sophie, she tried to turn her life around and married Charles Ralston, but the craving for men's attention had been too much, and she'd secretly returned to her old ways. However, she couldn't use the same group of men as before without Charles finding out, so she'd created the Craigslist listing.

CJ stared at her notes. "Who forced you to prostitute yourself?"

"I'd rather not say. It'll only cause me more trouble."

"It appears to me that heading to prison for the rest of your life is trouble enough."

The woman's eyes went wet, but she held her tongue.

"All right. What's magical about having a child at twenty-five?"

"That's how we do it in our family," she said. "You have to be pregnant before your twenty-sixth birthday."

CJ slammed her hand down on the table. "Who in the hell made up these asinine rules that you and your half-sister followed?"

Again, two minutes of silence passed as the two sat quietly. Savannah stared at her hands while CJ stared at her.

"Okay. If you don't tell me, I have nothing to offer to help you."

"If I talk, will it keep me out of jail?"

"No, you're going to prison, but it may reduce the sentence. Judges always look kindly on those who help us find those who have committed crimes." She leaned across the table and lifted Savannah's chin with her pointer finger. "You were sixteen, for heaven's sake. If you tell me who started you on the downward spiral, it has to be worth something."

"My mother," she whispered. Then she roared, "It was my fucking mother! She forced Scarlett and me onto our backs as soon as we turned sixteen. While others got a new car on their birthday, we got paraded into a sitting room, taken upstairs, and screwed." Her fists rattled the table. "I hate that bitch, and she feels the same about me."

"Why would she hate you?"

"Because I left and wasn't under her thumb anymore. I tried to change my ways, but the real reason is, I married one of them."

"One of them?"

"A man. She hates men and taught us to do the same. I broke her golden rule."

CJ waited for the woman's rage to subside and her breathing to slow. "Did your mother do the same?"

"Same what?"

"Did she get pregnant at twenty-five and then poison the man who gave her what she wanted? Perhaps Eugene Gibbs, your father?"

No words were spoken, but there was a curt nod.

"What I don't understand is Scarlett. Your mother had her well after she turned twenty-five. How can—"

"She fucked up, and it was an accident. She almost had an abortion, but when she found out it was a girl, she didn't." Her mouth twisted. "Another one of her rules for us girls was no male babies. Those were to be disposed of like all men once they were no longer useful." Savannah laid her head down on her fists. Then, without lifting her head, she asked, "Can you do me a favor?"

"It depends what it is."

Tears ran down her face as she peered up and sniffed. "Make sure Sophie is well taken care of for me. I've put three million dollars into a trust, so money's not an issue."

"That I can promise. I'll speak to Pickett and—"

"I fired his ass." She provided another attorney's name, and CJ jotted it down.

"One more thing. Don't let my wicked mother have her."

"I'll do what I can, but she's the next of kin, so it'll be up to a judge."

"What if I ensure it can't happen?"

"How so?" CJ asked.

"Go to my house and let yourself in. There's a hide-a-key under the pot of flowers on the right side of my back porch. You look in the top left-hand drawer of my dresser in my bedroom. There's a brush with hair on it in a white paper bag hidden under my panties. You take it to your DNA expert."

CJ's brow furrowed. "Whose brush and hair is it?"

"It's my bitch of a mother's."

FIFTY-FIVE

Wednesday, May 18
Beaufort

CJ sat at a four-seater wrought-iron table on Harry's back deck, enjoying her coffee as she examined the report Dr. Benning had emailed her the prior evening. Based on his analysis, the DNA from the hairbrush and Gibbs samples matched. Susanna Davis was her third murderess.

She rubbed her eyes and gazed across the marsh as the sun peeked over the horizon. As soon as Craig arrived to stay with Harry, she'd head to the LEC and organize her team for the two-hour drive to Beaufort. She'd coordinated with the Beaufort PD and arranged for two officers to meet her.

"Sweetheart, you can leave. I'm fine to stay alone, and my brother will be here any minute." Harry joined her at the table with steam flowing from his oversized *I Love to Fish* mug. "I love this view this time of the morning, the salty odors, and the noise of the birds waking up."

He asked her about her plans, and she spent a few minutes describing the day. "I'm sure the chief is pleased with your work," he said. "You've only been a lieutenant a few weeks and have solved three murders. I know I'm damn proud of you."

"Thanks. The thing is, these cases have bothered me more than most. There are so many more victims than the three men who were killed." She stretched her arms. "I can't wrap my head around a mother who would force her daughters to have sex with men at any age, much less sixteen."

"The world can be ugly at times," he said. "It's important you don't let it drag you down with it." He pointed to a flock of redwing blackbirds. "Those guys have been coming around a lot here lately."

"Uh-huh."

"How're things between you and Ben?"

She smiled. "I'm afraid I'm falling for him, which terrifies me."

"You don't need advice from a lifelong bachelor, but you're gonna get it, anyway. Ben's one of the good ones, and he loves you."

She cut her eyes to him. "You into matchmaking now?"

"No, but the deal with my heart has made me rethink many things." He sighed. "I missed out on my chance. Don't you miss out too."

Was it because you had to raise me? She was about to ask him to clarify when Craig bounded up the steps.

"Never fear, the day shift is here!" He grabbed a coffee and swapped spots with her at the table.

She pressed her lips on each of their foreheads and hustled to her truck.

———

CJ reviewed where and why they were headed to Beaufort with her team in the LEC's parking lot. She was pleased Johnny was going along with his trainee, and the young woman didn't appear as nervous as she had been on their first arrest mission. Janet hopped in her truck, and Johnny followed in his cruiser. She didn't expect trouble from a sixty-year-old woman, but a small army would ensure the event went smoothly.

Traffic was light, and their flashing lights made the drive faster. They reached the city limits within an hour and a half. As agreed, two Beaufort PD officers met them about a mile from their destination—a sprawling estate on the edge of town.

Flashers off, the three vehicles wound their way through the oaks and magnolias to the front of an impressive three-story structure reminiscent of a plantation house. Janet whistled and mumbled, "*Gone with the Wind.*" CJ parked, and the two women climbed out. She told Johnny to come with her, and the other officers to stand at the ready by their cars.

As CJ approached the front door, she caught a glimpse of a woman about her age peeking from behind the curtains before she disappeared. She told Janet to wait at the foot of the steps. As Johnny followed her up and she reached out to knock, the woman who had seen them coming opened the door. On instinct, both CJ's and Johnny's hands went to their Glocks.

"I'm sorry, ma'am. I didn't mean to startle you," her greeter said. "Miss Anna is expecting you. Please come in, and I'll escort you to her."

What the hell? CJ thought.

As they rounded the corner, an older woman sat on a gold sofa as if posed. She was immaculately dressed in a flowing white dress. Her brunette hair was in a bun, and her diamond necklace sparkled.

"Please have a seat," she said. "I understand you've come for me." Something between a smile and a smirk crossed her face. "Assuming, of course, you've come for Susanna Davis."

CJ stepped forward and dropped into an armchair across from her. Johnny remained standing near the door. "You're correct. We're here for you."

"Well, I suppose I knew this day would come," she said as she winked. "All good things must come to an end. Can I get you and your handsome partner anything to drink?"

"No, thank you."

The older woman nodded, then leaned forward. "He's a lotta man," she whispered. "You two ever—"

"Miss Davis. Let's focus on why I'm here," said CJ.

Waving her hands, Susanna said, "I know why you're here. You think I did something bad, but you're mistaken."

CJ raised her eyebrows. "How do you figure poisoning a man with deadly nightshade isn't bad?"

"It's all a point of view, young lady. I do have to say, you're gorgeous. I'm sure men fall over themselves for you." She picked up her teacup and sipped. "Men are like that, ya know? They only think with their little head. Men always think they hold all the power, but in reality, we women have control. Shake your ass, bat the eyes, use a little charm, and you can lead a man around like a puppy. I always told my girls—"

"Let's get back to the man you murdered, Eugene Gibbs. Remember him? He's Savannah's father."

Susanna shook her head and sighed. "That one is an enormous disappointment for me. An ungrateful little bitch. I understand you have her and my Scarlett locked up. How did you catch my sweet Scarlett?"

"We have several pieces of evidence, but to be honest, her perfume triggered her capture."

Susanna's lips curled. "Ah, yes. It's a lovely scent, isn't it?" She intertwined her fingers. "Do you know why it's so unique?"

CJ shook her head. "Why?"

"It's homemade—comes from right here on this property. Nothing else like it in the world."

"Let's get back to Mr. Gibbs."

"Oh, yes. Sorry. Eugene was a piece of shit. A damn good lay, but not worth keeping around in the end. I should get a medal for dispensing with him."

"So you admit you murdered him?"

"Yes, but it wasn't my fault. Percy Ricardson insisted I do it. Not the shitty weak one; his father. God rest his soul."

"He insisted?"

"Oh, yes. I'm a proper lady and would have never done such a heinous thing if I wasn't forced. He was mad when he learned Savannah was Eugene's daughter, not his."

CJ stood. "The courts can sort out your reasons, but all I know is you killed a man." She motioned for Johnny. "Susanna Davis, you're under arrest for the murder of Eugene Gibbs."

Johnny applied the handcuffs and read the older woman her rights, and they walked her to the door.

"I do have one request," Susanna said.

"What's that?"

"I'd like to ride with this strapping young man, if that's okay."

"Suit yourself."

As they led her down the steps, she asked for a minute to talk to her housekeeper. CJ nodded, and she leaned over to whisper something in the woman's ear.

"Yes, ma'am. I'll tell her," the housekeeper said.

FIFTY-SIX

Wednesday, May 18
Downtown Charleston

CJ slid into a metal chair across from Susanna Davis in the stuffy interrogation room. The sixty-year-old woman sat with folded hands and a charming smile. Opening her notebook, CJ peered at the older woman. "Here's what I don't understand. How did all this start?"

"Well, dear. I suppose it all started when I was in my early twenties. I met Eugene at a party, and he asked me out. I hadn't dated much, so I was excited. We went out a few times, slept together, and I was soon with child."

"But why did you kill him?"

"Oh, that's easy," she answered, flipping her hand. "Eugene lied to me and told me he wasn't married—he was, so he had to pay."

"So, it wasn't because Percy Ricardson Junior told you to do it?"

Susanna leaned forward. "No man could ever tell me what to do."

CJ stared at the older woman's guilt-free face. "But what about the prostitution? How did it start?"

Susanna sighed and cocked her head. "I decided all men are scum, and I'd use their weaknesses against them from that point forward. So I created a group of like-minded young women, and we proceeded to take our share of power and money."

CJ continued to ask questions, and the older woman openly answered them. She explained how she'd trained her daughters, and when they turned sixteen, they'd joined the "family business." The woman had no remorse or regret. In fact, she bragged about how talented her daughters were with men.

"Both my girls used the tricks I taught them—how to show just enough skin, charm, flirt, and touch to drive a man insane with desire." She winked. "Once you get a man in the right state of mind, you're in control. Don't tell Savannah, but Scarlett is my favorite. She was talented at an early age."

"But they were only sixteen."

"They were already grown women and irresistible to men." She leaned forward, eyebrows raised. "Can I leave now?"

"No. You're not going anywhere." CJ stood. "If I have anything to do with it, you'll never set foot outside a jail cell again."

Susanna chuckled. "We'll see about that, dear."

CJ shut the door behind her and motioned to an officer that the prisoner could return to her holding cell. She shook her head, exhaled, and entered the viewing room. A man in his mid-sixties peered up at her through wire-rimmed glasses too small for his face. His salt-and-pepper hair was thinner than when she'd seen him last.

"Well, Doctor Greedsy, what do you think?" she asked.

He glanced down at his notes, and his chocolate-brown eyes scanned. "Based on the information you've provided and the interviews, all three women are misandrists, in my opinion."

Her eyebrows pinched together. "I've read about that. It's the female version of misogyny—women who hate men."

He shrugged and smiled. "A simple definition, I suppose. Misandrists are micro-aggressive toward men. They crave being the center of attention, use their sexuality to manipulate others, have a twisted sense of boundaries, lack empathy, take a sadistic pleasure in fooling others, and consider others, even children, as an extension of themselves."

He removed his glasses and wiped them with a handkerchief. "There are other characteristics, but these apply to these women. For example, Susanna turned her underage daughters into prostitutes. Savannah married but returned to her old ways. And Scarlett slept with her half-sister's husband."

"Why wouldn't men steer clear of these women?" she asked.

"Well, it's not like misandrists wear a sign. Men find them exciting, flirtatious, and charming, and they use this to lure their target in. Of course, all these women are gorgeous, adding to the attraction."

She nodded as her mind recalled Ralph Randolph's man-haters comment. "How does someone become a misandrist?"

He shrugged. "I'm no expert on the subject, but I'd say it's taught at an early age. Unfortunately, too many parents and adults pass on terrible traits to their children, whether intentionally or not. There's no doubt in my mind the mother knew what she was doing."

"If that's the case, how did Susanna learn?"

His brow furrowed. "I don't have an answer for her. But perhaps the experience with Gibbs triggered it, like she said. Although I'm not sure I believe that."

He said he'd email her his report. Her eyes followed him as he wandered down the hall, and then she hustled to her office to check the files to hand over to the solicitor for prosecution—one for each of the three women, and Larry Simpson.

Ricardson had a file, but someone had already seen to his punishment—death from ingesting deadly nightshade.

The man had paid the ultimate price for wielding power and control over the Palmetto Men's Society, the dollars he received for funneling men to Susanna Davis, and free sex. He had been instrumental in covering up the deaths of Wilkins and Ralston.

I wonder if he realized he was Susanna's pawn.

Simpson had helped cover up the murders, but his real crime was trying to fit in with a group of men who were using him. Sam had found documents showing that the purchase of the Duncan House wasn't legitimate. Yet again, Ricardson had played Simpson. At least he was smart enough now to cooperate and would receive a plea deal for a reduced sentence. While he couldn't provide a list of Palmetto Men's Society members, he turned over seventeen names of men who'd frequented the Duncan House and used escorts. The SVU would investigate them.

One question stuck in her thoughts. *Who taught Susanna Davis to hate men?*

FIFTY-SEVEN

Thursday, May 19
Downtown Charleston

CJ sipped her coffee as she sat across from Sam at the table in her office. Her cell phone chimed, and her eyes scanned the text.

"Chief wants to see me," she said. "I'll be back as soon as I can." She grabbed her notebook and hustled down the hallway to the boss's office, where she smiled at the middle-aged woman with curly black hair staffing the desk. "I've been summoned," CJ said.

The woman motioned for her to go right in.

"Hello, sir. Did you need to speak with me?" CJ asked once inside the office.

The towering chief of police stood by his desk, smiled, and pointed to a woman who sat on his brown leather sofa. "I'd like you to meet Miss Stella Davis."

CJ approached her and offered her hand to shake.

The woman, who had to be in her eighties, wore a canary-yellow dress with a white sweater. She was frail, but her hazel eyes were sharp under her gray hair. "I'm honored to meet you, young lady. I've followed your work, and you're quite impressive." She patted the cushion. "Please sit here with me."

CJ dropped beside her. "Is there something I can do for you, Miss Davis?" she asked.

"First, please call me Stella," she said as she warmly smiled before her face took on a pained expression. "Second, I drove from Beaufort to apologize to Walter and you personally."

Her brow furrowed. "Uh, I'm sorry ... for what?"

The woman's boney fingers dug through her white purse, pulled out a tissue, and she dabbed her eyes. "For my daughter and granddaughters. I'm embarrassed and horrified at what they've done and truly sorry you had to deal with it. I'm so ashamed of them."

"Oh, I see."

"I told Walter they've committed heinous acts, and while I beg for mercy, they have to be punished for their sins." Tears ran down her cheeks, and she reached over and squeezed CJ's hand. "I obviously failed as a mother."

Stella told her the only thing she knew was what was printed in the newspaper, and she'd appreciate knowing the details. CJ glanced at the chief and he nodded. Then, as delicately as possible, she explained the charges they faced. Throughout, the older woman whimpered, rocked, and mumbled prayers.

"How did they kill these poor men?"

CJ cleared her throat. "They used poison."

Her hand flew to her mouth. "That's awful. It would be such a painful way to die. What kind of poison?"

"A toxic plant called deadly nightshade."

"I've never heard of … where in the world would they get such a dreadful thing?" Her face turned angry. "I'm tempted to go give them a piece of my mind. I raised them better." Then she broke down in tears again. "At least, I thought I had."

The woman asked a few more questions, dug into her purse, and pulled a folded sheet of paper out of a white envelope. "The other reason I came to Charleston is I understand my great-granddaughter is here. The poor little thing is probably terrified." She held the paper out to her. "I want to take her home with me."

CJ's eyes scanned the document. It was a court order to assume custody of Sophie. She stood, handed it to the chief, who reviewed it and said, "Based on this, you have the right to take her with you."

"Wait," CJ said. "Are you sure you will be able to care for her? She's only ten and—"

"Oh, yes. I'm eighty-five and limited in what I can do, but I have four full-time staff who will cook, clean, and handle anything needed."

"But—"

The chief's eyes shot CJ a stern look. "Well … if you're sure, it makes sense. You are the only relative who can take her. Do you live at the estate with your daughter?"

"No. I did many years ago, but moved to a smaller place." She wiped her nose. "If only I'd have stayed, I could have kept an eye on things and none of this would have happened. Can we go get my angel now?"

CJ told her a foster family was caring for Sophie, and she'd call them to arrange a time to pick her up. She stepped out of the office into the hall and returned within a few minutes. "I was able to reach them. They took Sophie to the Charleston Zoo but said they'd be home by 2:00 p.m. Is that okay?"

Stella Davis stood and warmly smiled. "Yes, two o'clock is fine. My driver will take me to lunch, and we'll meet you in the lobby at one thirty." She hugged her, shook the chief's hand, and strolled out the door.

CJ waited until Stella was out of hearing range and turned to the chief. "I'm not a fan of this, sir. Something doesn't—"

"She has a legal document signed by a judge, so we have no choice. Besides, she's the little girl's kin."

"I know. But—"

"No buts. Take her to pick up the girl."

"Yes, sir." She marched out the door. *Something's not right about this.*

At 1:25 p.m., CJ met Stella Davis and her driver in the LEC lobby. She told them the foster family didn't live far away, and if they followed her, she'd have them there within fifteen minutes. She waited in her truck until a new black Cadillac Escalade emerged behind her.

The Carter family home was in the South of Broad district. The two-story structure was painted a robin's egg blue with white shutters and trim, and the area in front of the house was petite, not a yard, but a narrow patch of bushes and flowers.

As CJ climbed out of her truck, Jolene came running out the door, down the three steps, and hugged her. Sophie trailed behind her, all smiles. Each of them had a stuffed giraffe under their arm.

"Hey, girls. I see you brought part of the zoo home with you," CJ said.

Rachel Carter stepped out onto the porch and waved. "My husband is going to be disappointed he missed you, Detective. Unfortunately, we never had a chance to properly thank you for all you did for us at the hearing."

"Meemaw!" Sophie squealed as she ran to her great-grandmother, who carefully approached them using her cane to avoid falling. The little girl wrapped her arms around her as Stella squeezed her tight, then the two joined CJ.

"Rachel, this is Stella Davis. She's Sophie's great-grandmother. As I indicated on the phone, she's come to pick her up and take her back to Beaufort."

"I'm pleased to meet you, ma'am. Of course, we'll hate to see our little guest leave us, but I'm happy she has someone who loves her and will give her a home."

"It's my pleasure to meet you too," Stella said. "I can't thank you enough for caring for my angel until I could get here." She motioned to the driver, and he handed her a white purse. "Can I pay you for your trouble?"

Rachel put her palms up. "Heavens no. It was only one night, and we loved having her here. She and Jolene had the best time."

Stella nodded. "Sophie, please say your goodbyes and go get your belongings. We have a long drive home and want to be on time for dinner."

"Yes, ma'am." Sophie turned and headed up the steps and through the front door with Jolene in tow.

While they waited, the three women talked about how pretty the flowers were, what lovely houses were in the area, and how much Sophie loved cookies. CJ was relieved when the little girl returned, wheeling a soft-sided pink suitcase. Five minutes later, she waved as the black SUV pulled away.

"If you don't mind me saying, you don't seem all that happy about this," Rachel noted.

CJ shrugged. "I am. It was a surprise, I guess. I didn't realize the little girl had anyone besides her mother and grandmother."

"Listen, I know you're busy, but could you stop by later today, say five thirty? Brian will be home from work. Of course, we'd love for you to have dinner with us, but if not, he'd have a chance to thank you in person."

"You could see my new room," Jolene said.

"I'll tell you what, I'll take a rain check on dinner, but I'll come by." She nudged the little girl. "I gotta see your room."

Rachel clapped her hands. "Wonderful! We'll see you later."

CJ trudged back to her truck and headed back to the LEC for a three thirty meeting with the captain. The weather was warm, but chills ran through her, and her fingers were frozen. *This meeting's gonna suck.*

FIFTY-EIGHT

Thursday, May 19
Downtown Charleston

"Come in, Detective Jackson," Stan said. He pointed to a man sitting on his left. "This is Investigator Jeff Cody from the Office of Internal Affairs."

Vincent Jackson's eyes darted from person to person—Stan, the man from OIA, and CJ sitting in the corner. "What's this about?"

"Have a seat," Stan said, motioning to the chair in front of his desk.

Doing as he was told, Vincent sat. His breathing picked up, and he fidgeted. "I'm busy with my cases, so I hope—"

"We've discovered something that has us concerned," Stan said as he slid a sheet of paper under the detective's nose. "You've taken money to suppress evidence on at least two occasions we've found so far. Care to explain?"

"Uh—I don't know what you're—"

"That's a bank statement of deposits into your account," Cody said, tapping the paper. "They match the information a witness provided us."

Vincent rocked back and forth, and moisture glistened on his forehead. "I think I need to talk to my rep."

"Effective immediately, you're suspended without pay," Stan said as he stood. "You can go with Investigator Cody. He'll walk you through the process."

The shocked detective sat there, staring at the floor.

"Go on. Get the hell out of here."

Vincent struggled to his feet and his eyes caught CJ's. "You did this, you bitch. You were threatened by me and—"

"No. You did this to yourself," she said. "And what pisses me off is it's a black eye for all of us."

CJ returned to the Carter home at 5:40 p.m. The appreciative parents gave her a house tour and showed her the little girl's freshly painted light pink room with white furniture—there were bright colors everywhere.

After the tour, everyone settled on a floral couch and side chairs in the den. They discussed Jolene's schooling, activities they'd involved her in, and a vacation to Hawaii they had planned for the summer. It was six thirty when CJ stood to leave.

"Wait, Miss CJ," Jolene said. "I gotta go get something." Within minutes, she returned and held out a tattered brown leather book. "Sophie forgot her special book. Can you give it to her when you see her, please?"

"Sure. I'll make sure she gets it."

Jolene motioned, and she bent down. The little girl whispered, "You're not supposed to look in it. Sophie said it's top secret."

CJ hopped in her truck, waved goodbye, and headed to her apartment. Her eyes dropped to the book in the passenger seat at a stoplight. *What's so secretive?* She reached over, picked it up, and opened the cover to see a name. Then she thumbed through it. Her eyes went wide, and her jaw dropped. *Oh. My. God.*

FIFTY-NINE

Friday, May 20
Beaufort

CJ hadn't slept. She had been consumed by the words in the tattered brown leather book Sophie had left at the Carter's house. She had to arrest another person—someone behind the sordid ring of secrets, deceit, and murder.

She picked up Janet at the LEC at seven thirty and they headed south to the Davis estate in Beaufort, where they had arrested Susanna. CJ had called the local PD and arranged to have two officers provide support.

As she drove, she briefed Stan, and he agreed to give the chief a heads-up. She smiled when he told her the judge had denied bail for Susanna, so all three women were stuck in a cell until their trial.

An hour and forty-five minutes later, she steered onto the long driveway to the sprawling property. CJ parked and hopped out of her truck, staring at the magnificent white structure before her. The bright sunshine and clear blue sky offered a perfect spring morning. The birds sang, and the landscaping was pristine, with deep green grass and multi-colored blooms. She climbed the steps and knocked on the door. After several minutes, she tried again, but there was still no response. *Where the hell is everyone?*

She retraced her steps and joined Janet, who stood by the truck. "I find it hard to believe no one is here," CJ said. "And where are the Beaufort PD officers?"

Janet shrugged. "Can we obtain a search warrant?"

"Probably, but it'll take time." She stared back at the house, and a thought popped into her head. "Perhaps she knew we were coming."

"How?"

"She realized Sophie left the book and took off," CJ answered as she pointed to the far end of the driveway. "There's our backup." A Beaufort PD cruiser pulled in behind her truck, and two young men joined them.

"Sorry we're late," the taller officer said. "We got hung up on a wreck. Where do you need us?"

She rubbed her chin. "I've knocked a couple times, and no one answered. Without a warrant, we can't force our way in." She pointed to the left side of the house. "Janet, how 'bout you go that way, and I'll go the other? Maybe we'll find someone working who can help us." She told the two officers to remain out front.

CJ rounded the house, peering in windows as she went. There was no sign of anyone or lights on inside. She stared at a garden area and a massive greenhouse at the back of the yard. Her eyebrows pinched together as she shielded her eyes from the sun—she swore she saw movement. Drawing her Glock, she cautiously moved forward.

Making her way along the paths through bushes and flowers and finding nothing, she stopped and stared at the glass structure. Unfortunately, numerous plants blocked her view inside, so she proceeded around the side to the door. Twisting the knob, she entered and her mouth dropped open when she saw darkish green plants as tall as her along one of the walls.

She holstered her weapon and pulled her notebook from her beltline at the back of her jeans. Her fingers fumbled with the pages until she found the copy of the photo of the deadly nightshade plant Thomas had given her. She held it up and whispered, "Atropa belladonna."

"Very good, Detective."

CJ's head snapped up to find Stella Davis at the end of the row, aiming a Derringer pistol at her.

"Most people can't recognize it until they see the bell-shaped purple flowers and ripe, shiny black berries." She smiled. "My favorite plant has many names—deadly nightshade is the most popular, but some call it devil's berries, naughty man's cherries, devil's herb, or the one I prefer … beautiful death."

Unlike the frail person CJ had witnessed yesterday, this woman appeared strong, steady on her feet, and …

dangerous. "Miss Davis, put down the gun. There's no way you're getting out of here. There are three other officers here with me."

The woman's lips twisted into an evil grin. "I know, but they're not here now, dear." She sighed. "Sadly, my stupid little angel left my book, so I knew you'd come after reading it and finding I don't have another home. I'd hoped the book might be lost, but ..."

"I read it cover to cover," CJ said. "My biggest question is, why?"

Stella's eyes flashed. "Well, since you're about to die, I'll tell you."

She said she'd been a proper Southern belle when she met Delmont Davis at eighteen. He had made a fortune in shipping, and she was thrilled when he asked her out. After a year of dating, where he was a perfect gentleman, they were married on the grounds of the estate in a lovely ceremony. After the reception, he'd whisked her away to Savannah for their honeymoon. She was a virgin and nervous about the wedding night, but he'd promised to be patient and gentle.

"That was a damn lie," Stella said, her teeth clenched. "When he was unhappy with my performance, he forced me to do horrible things. Once he was snoring, I slipped into the bathroom, curled up in the corner, and cried all night."

"Why didn't you leave him?"

The older woman laughed. "You don't leave a man like Delmont Davis. I was terrified of him, and he was clear he'd kill me if I said a peep. So I sucked it up and made the best of it." Her eyes turned glossy, and she continued her story.

She wasn't allowed to leave the premises unless accompanied by her husband, who also had to approve any visitors. That's when she got into gardening. First, she'd designed the garden with its winding paths. Winter was an issue, so she'd convinced her husband to construct the greenhouse.

"I'd always liked exotic plants. That's how I came across my beautiful death. It's exquisite, although highly toxic, so I had to grow it with care. After practice, I became an expert at raising it." She gazed at her creation and then returned to her story.

She'd tried to get pregnant for several years, hoping to make Delmont happy. When she wasn't able, they saw a doctor and found out the reason wasn't her; it was him. He was sterile, but he blamed her for not being better in bed.

"That's when the incident occurred that started it all," she said.

Her husband began bringing his friends from the Palmetto Men's Society to the house for parties. She was expected to be charming and serve them. One night, when they were drunk, her husband and two other men dragged her upstairs, and soon after, she found herself pregnant.

"That's when I decided men were pieces of shit and sometimes no longer useful. So, I told my loving husband I had enjoyed my time with his buddies, and he should invite them over again." Her face twisted. "After they'd had several glasses of wine, I served them my special drink—juice from nightshade berries mixed with Cabernet. They'd had a lot to drink and never noticed the difference."

She exhaled. "The worst part was that until the poison took over, I had to lie underneath one of my husband's sweaty friends, but it was worth it. I got to watch him die a horrible death. My husband and the other man were dead when I went downstairs."

CJ shook her head. "How did you cover up their deaths?"

Stella said when the detective came to ask her if she'd seen the men, she acted distraught, told him they'd gone fishing with her husband, and must be lost at sea. To seal the lie, she begged him to stay and console her. Then she slept with him.

"But you had to do something with the bodies."

Stella pointed to the tall plants. "Turns out my babies love human remains. Four bodies are resting there, and you'll be the fifth."

"Four?"

"Yes, Susanna added Carlton Rutherford," she answered as her brow furrowed. "Where was I? Oh, yes. After I'd dispensed with the men, I rounded up some young women and started providing services to others in the society. Ricardson funneled men to me, and I ensured they left satisfied."

"Percy Ricardson?"

"Yes. But not the shitty little weak one. His father."

"Who killed Ricardson III?"

"I had Susanna do it."

"Wait. Susanna told me she had started everything. She never men—"

"She lied. My girls will always protect me at any cost." She glanced around. "Well, dear. I've humored you with my little tale, but I'm tired of talking, so it's your time to die."

CJ's eyes caught movement as Janet appeared at the glass door behind Stella. As the knob twisted and the door eased open, she stalled. "Wait, Stella! Before you kill me, at least tell me why you told your daughter and granddaughters they had to get pregnant when they were twenty-five."

Janet crept slowly on her tiptoes until she was within ten feet of the older woman.

"It's the same age I was when I got pregnant." Stella raised the pistol she'd lowered slightly and grinned. "Well, enough chitchat. It's time for—"

Janet lunged and hit Stella from behind as she grabbed her wrist and yanked her arm sideways. The pistol went off and shattered the glass wall. Stella cursed at them as they cuffed her and pulled her to her feet, and the two officers burst through the door.

"How 'bout you guys load Miss Davis in your car and follow me back to Charleston?" CJ asked. "I can have one of our cruisers meet us, so you won't need to make the entire trip."

"No!" Sophie screamed as she raced toward them as they crossed the yard.

CJ intercepted her, dropped to her knees, and wrapped her arms around her. "Don't you hurt my Meemaw!"

CJ held the little girl tight as the officers led her great-grandmother away. "It'll be okay, sweetie," she said as Sophie's tears dripped on her shoulder. "Shhh ... it'll be okay."

Once Stella was loaded into the cruiser, CJ asked Janet to ride with the officers. She didn't want the woman out of their sight. "By the way, thank you for saving my life."

Her partner smiled at her and dropped into the back-seat of the cruiser.

"Come on, Sophie. You can ride with me." She helped the little girl into the passenger seat and buckled her seat belt.

SIXTY

Friday, May 20
Downtown Charleston

CJ crossed the Ashley River Memorial Bridge and dropped into Charleston when Sophie noticed the leather book between the seat and the console. "Oh, you found my book," she said as she picked it up.

"Yes. Jolene told me you left … wait, you mean your great-grandmother's book, right?"

She shook her head. "It was hers, but she gave it to me." Her eyes peered out the window. "I'm s'posed to study it, so I can learn."

CJ swallowed hard and glanced at her as Sophie flipped through the pages. "I'm not sure I understand."

"I have to know our family traditions, silly." Her lips curled into a smile. "Auntie Scarlett said I did a good job."

"What job, sweetheart?"

"Meemaw helped me make it, but Mommy took me to Auntie's and let me put the berry juice in the wine … it was time to get rid of my stepdaddy."

Saturday, June 18
Downtown Charleston

CJ stared at Ben as he made his best man speech for his brother, Will. She had to admit he was incredibly handsome in his traditional black tux. The crowd laughed at his jokes, and eyes went moist when he choked up, saying how much he loved his brother. His eyes cut to her when he said, "Love is hard to find, but worth the journey."

The ballroom at the Regency Charleston Waterfront was as spectacular as planned. Sheer white curtains from the ceiling swayed from the fans strategically positioned in the corners, and the candles flickered in the dim lighting. Once the dinner and speeches were complete, everyone filled the dance floor.

"May I have this dance?" Ben asked, his amber eyes sparkling at her.

She stood and took his hand. "I'm not much of a dancer, but Sam will kill me if I don't try." She ran her hands down her pale blush bridesmaid dress and pushed a stray lock of hair back into place.

"I've already told you, but you are breathtaking," he said as they moved through the crowd. "Hands down, the best-looking woman here."

She leaned back and grinned at him. "Watch out, the bride will hear you."

He nodded and pressed his lips to hers.

For the next two hours, the mass of people twisted, stepped in unison, and swayed. She danced with Mason Ravenel, Sam's father, and Bill Parrish, Ben's father, and took a turn with Harry, although he was restricted from dancing too much. He'd brought Bethany, who kept a close eye on him. CJ wasn't sure if it was because she was a nurse or if she liked him, but they were cute together.

Stan approached her while Ben grabbed their drinks. "This is a wonderful party, Lieutenant, and you look beautiful."

"Thank you, sir," she said.

"We're not going to discuss any work tonight, but I want to congratulate you again on solving the Davis cases. Drummond told me they'll spend the rest of their lives in prison."

She thanked him and peered at Ben, who was whispering to Harry. Ben laughed and headed toward her. Stan patted him on the shoulder when he appeared and headed to the dance floor.

"Who knew the captain could move like that?" Ben asked.

"Yeah, I was worried about reporting to him, but he's been a great boss."

The music lowered, and the young woman CJ had met when she had first toured the room announced it was time to gather for the married couple's departure. Everyone moved outside, lined the stone path, and Sam and Will made their way through the sparklers and into a white limo.

"Wanna take a little stroll and enjoy the fresh air?" Ben asked.

CJ nodded, and he took her hand and led her out onto the porch. Two nights past full, the moon shone on the Ashley River, and stars twinkled against the dark sky. He wrapped his arm around her and they strolled down the walkway onto a small wooden pier.

She leaned on the railing, gazing across the sparkling water. "Sam had a perfect wedding, didn't she?" He didn't respond, so she turned. He was down on one knee, and his eyes glistened under the moonlight. She covered her mouth with her hand.

"CJ, I loved you the first time you walked into the lobby." He sniffed. "It took me a while to admit it, but I can't stand to think about not having you in my life. It's only been a little over a year, but ..." He flipped open a tiny, red box. "Cassandra Jane O'Hara, will you marry me?"

Tears ran down her cheeks, and her shoulders shook. She nodded, and when he lifted her off the ground, she whispered, "Yes, absolutely, yes."

He placed her down and slipped a princess-cut diamond ring on her finger. "I hope you like this. It was my mom's, but if you don't—"

"I love it," she said as she pressed her lips to his and then whispered, "Do you think Sam's gonna be pissed? Most women aren't too fond of anything to take the spotlight off their day. I—"

"Don't worry about that. Sam's gone, and ... I covered all the bases," he said, pointing toward the hotel. "Both your uncles gave me their blessing."

Applause erupted from the porch, and she hid her bright red face against Ben's chest. Craig and Bill cheered while Harry cried.

Ben took her hand and led her back up the walkway. "I was thinking maybe you and I can take a trip together," he said.

"I'd like that. Where?"

"I don't know. Where would you like to go?"

"Well ... I have a brochure for a place I'd love to go. It's in the middle of nowhere and looks beautiful—fishing, whales, eagles, otters, and other wildlife."

"Where is it?"

"Alaska."

———

Scarlett zipped up her orange jumpsuit and watched the guard slip away down the dark hall. She dropped onto her cot, pulled the plastic stick from under her mattress, and the corners of her mouth curled upward. She stared at the small glass jar her stripper friend, Star, had smuggled into the jail and then tossed it into the trash. Who cared if the guards found deadly nightshade residue in it? She was in prison for life.

My baby girl is coming—too bad her father won't be alive to meet her.

THE END

ACKNOWLEDGMENTS

Above all else, I'd like to thank my readers. I'm honored so many have joined me on this journey. I wrote this book for you, and I hope you enjoyed it. I would be grateful if you could write a review. Reviews are a way of introducing others to a book that intrigued you and perhaps made you read with the lights on. I'd love to hear what you think.

You can reach me on my website, Facebook page, Instagram, Twitter, or Goodreads.

———

This book would not have been possible without the inspiration from the people and places that make up the Lowcountry. Most of the locations, streets, and restaurants are authentic.

I'm incredibly grateful to those restaurants that allowed me to include them in my novels: Poogan's Porch, the Boathouse at Breach Inlet, Vickery's, The Wreck of the Richard and Charlene, Coconut Joe's, Henry's on the Market, and Dunleavy's Pub. If you make it to Charleston, I highly recommend you visit them.

It takes a village to publish a book, and I owe a giant thank you to all those who helped with beta reading, editing, and designing: James Osborne, Joanne Lane, Lee Ann Wolff, and Danna Mathias Steel.

Finally, I thank my wife, Lisa, for her continued support.

ABOUT THE AUTHOR

 John grew up near Nashville, Tennessee, and now lives in the California Bay Area. His love for the South Carolina Lowcountry stems from the time he spent living in a beach house outside Charleston. This portion of his life inspires his writing and many of his characters. Besides books, he loves spending time with his family, especially his two grandkids, and going to the mountains, the beach, and fishing in Alaska.

Discover more about John Deal on his website.

www.johndealbks.com

Connect with John online.

www.facebook.com/JohnDealBooks

www.instagram.com/johndealbks

www.twitter.com/JohnDealBks

Made in United States
Troutdale, OR
05/06/2024

19690874R00236